AFTERNOON DELIGHT

When the kiss had gone on far too long for either of us to pretend we didn't want it to go on, he pulled back.

"I'm sorry," he said, and he was trying to look serious.

But he didn't look sorry or serious. He was smiling, and I had goose bumps again, but not the creeped out kind.

"I'm not," I told him, and he gave me this big, open grin and laughed out loud.

Without asking me if it was okay, but it was, he drove us out of the Colony and turned left up the coast highway, away from LA.

He pulled into a parking lot near Sycamore Cove that had a view of the rock-studded beach and wind-whipped trees and drove to the far end of the lot where there were no other cars or RVs, and then he pulled me against him and kissed me again.

"I don't usually—" he said.

"Me either," I breathed.

We kissed and kissed until my lips felt swollen. We necked and nuzzled, and he slipped the straps of my dress down my shoulders and buried his face in my skin. I leaned back in the warm sunlight and felt absolutely delicious as his kisses moved lower and lower, and the sun, or something, made me feel so warm all over I was practically melting.

He looked up at me. "Do you have any plans this afternoon?"

"Not anymore," I admitted.

Genie Davis

The Model Man

ZEBRA BOOKS
KENSINGTON PUBLISHING CORP.
www.kensingtonbooks.com

ZEBRA BOOKS are published by

Kensington Publishing Corp.
850 Third Avenue
New York, NY 10022

All Kensington titles, imprints, and distributed lines are available at special quantity discounts for bulk purchases for sales promotion, premiums, fund-raising, educational, or institutional use.

Special book excerpts or customized printings can also be created to fit specific needs. For details, write or phone the office of the Kensington Special Sales Manager: Attn. Special Sales Department. Kensington Publishing Corp., 850 Third Avenue, New York, NY 10022. Phone: 1-800-221-2647.

Zebra and the Z logo Reg. U.S. Pat. & TM Off.

ISBN 0-8217-7977-X

First Printing: January 2006
10   9   8   7   6   5   4   3   2   1

Printed in the United States of America

For my amazing children.

Chapter One

They plucked him like a prize fish from the Southwest swell off the jetty, two men in linen suits and pastel tee shirts like they'd just walked out of an episode of *Miami Vice*. He was sixteen, tall and big boned, with tanned good looks that kept his mother from entirely despairing of what she called his "dearth of brains."

Even the other kids trolling for surf didn't think much of him. "Outta the way, dude," they'd shout and slam their boards down the face of some perfect ride, pushing him out of the lineup.

Girls who should've liked him because he was cute didn't because they said he was "stuck on himself." Well, maybe he was; he liked looking at himself in a mirror, practicing different ways of combing his hair.

It was a habit that served him well for a while, once the linen suit guys showed up. They gave him and his mom papers to sign and themselves power of attorney, and they sent him off without having to finish high school, which he was gonna flunk

out of anyway, to jet set around Paris and Málaga
and New York, showing off swim trunks and underwear and hats and a funky purple-checked suit and
Hawaiian shirts and good electric razors. They took
pictures of him showing off, and he appeared inside
some of the hottest magazines around the world,
as well as on billboards and bus sides. He was a success.

Now everybody thought it was a good thing when
he stood around and checked his hair—they said
he was dedicated to his craft. Other guys never really
took to him, but oh man, the girls started liking him
now. Other benefits were the booze and the pills
and the parties and the people who'd take pictures
of you doing all kinds of things, not just posing in
pretty clothes with shiny products and smiling a
knowingly vacant smile.

But he didn't stay sixteen forever, and he didn't
even stay twenty-one; he was twenty-two when he
came back to the beach, broke, and latched onto
the first scheme of many that shaped, and apparently took, his life twenty years later.

I read about Richard J. "Ricky" Littlejohn in one
of the alternative weekly papers that specializes in
noirish yet politically correct exposés about crooks
and politicians and the latest sex fad.

I wouldn't have picked up the paper and read
about him at all, except I was stuck waiting for a
mark who was late but who kept calling me on her
cell phone.

"I'm just a teeny bit late, and with traffic—it
would mean so much if you'd wait for me, Christina."

Usually, it wasn't a good thing when somebody

you had set up kept you waiting; it meant they were wise to the con you were running or they were getting cold feet. Still this one, Mrs. Leroy Jenkins, had a nice desperate quality in her voice, and I had this kind of desperate thing myself about paying my rent, so I stayed put in the one room storefront I worked out of from time to time, one alley away from the Venice Beach pier.

I twiddled my thumbs and thought about how much money I might be able to get out of Mrs. Jenkins and wondered if I'd get enough to put something in my cupboard besides the bag of potato chips and the marshmallow snowmen from last Christmas that were still there. We were already into the "ten more shopping days 'til" countdown for this year.

Surely, in light of this festive season, I deserved something like a rosemary roasted chicken with little new potatoes and asparagus, already prepared from an upscale market, so I could just plop it on the table in front of me, light a jasmine-scented candle or two, open a bottle of cheap Sauvignon Blanc, and tell myself, Christy, just settle back and enjoy yourself; you've worked hard.

Well, maybe work wasn't exactly how I'd describe what I did, even to myself, but sometimes it was hard and it took a lot of effort, and if I came up with the cash, I deserved to enjoy myself just as much as your average banker, lawyer, or Enron executive, didn't I?

I wasn't sure I liked the direction of my own thoughts, so to distract myself I picked up that newspaper, yellow and wrinkled, folded beneath the base of a potted plant on the window sill.

Ricky Littlejohn's sordid life was even more

distractingly wretched than mine, and I was quite absorbed when Mrs. Jenkins showed up, but not so absorbed that I didn't immediately toss the paper in the trash can and greet her with open arms.

I probably should've kept the paper and had it framed, considering the big effect reading that article was about to have on my life.

But at the time, I was focusing only on Mrs. Jenkins. The thing you always have to do when you're going to hit somebody up for something is to stay locked on them. That person has to be the most important being in the world to you. He or she has to feel that you feel that way. If the person does, he or she will do anything you want because it's a natural thing, people wanting to be the most important thing in the world.

Mrs. J. was a sixtyish woman in a fur coat that looked like coyote, despite the seventy-five degree LA winter outside. We'd met as I often meet people, through an Internet chat room devoted to the quasimetaphysical, and she was after reassurance that her late husband had truly loved her, even though when alive, he had paid her little attention. All the more reason for her to devour mine.

"His idea of love was silence. Silence and handing me diamond tennis bracelets and platinum charge cards at all the best stores. Money cannot buy you happiness," she told me.

It depends where you shop, I thought. But aloud I said soothingly, "Of course not. All the same, the aura I'm getting from you is of someone beloved."

She was teary eyed with happiness as I reassured her that her husband was speaking to us through my crystal ball and the cards I had spread across my velvet-draped table.

"Yes, he loved you more than anything—he could not express his spiritual side to you, his emotions. He realizes now that he used objects as pledges of his devotion—"

"Oh," Mrs. Jenkins breathed happily. "This is wonderful."

I was teary eyed myself. "Sometimes we're just unable to show someone how much we care—words are hard to say—but now, now your husband wants . . . he truly wants—"

I stopped, looked around me, bewildered.

"What, what does he want?" she asked, leaning forward across the table.

I sighed. "Even now, it seems, he's finding it difficult to tell you. I'm losing the connection."

I stared into the crystal ball, she stared at me, and we sat like that in silent concentration for a good minute and a half before I leaned back, closed my eyes, and sighed.

"I've lost it. It's a shame too; there seems to be something he's absolutely yearning to say."

"Why did you lose him?" she asked, reaching for my hand.

I took hers in my own and patted it gently.

"I'm not sure," I said, trying for perplexed yet enlightened. "Really, what it comes down to sometimes is that the spirits need more encouragement."

"Encouragement?"

"Like anyone else, residents of the spirit world need a helping hand from time to time. They feel shy or inhibited, afraid that their overtures to us on this mortal plain will be rejected or ill received."

"Oh, I see," Mrs. Jenkins clucked.

"A séance often provides them with more confidence. A spiritual support group, you know? I can arrange one very easily."

"Oh, I don't know," she said, and she licked her lips.

I shrugged. "It's your decision, of course. But it does seem as if there's some urgency at work here. As if whatever your husband has to tell you could really make a difference in your life."

She eyed me for a moment, which I didn't really like. I smiled. She smiled back.

"How much will it cost?" she asked.

It was always the really rich ones who worried about how much something like communication with the dead would cost. As if you could put a dollar value on something like that.

"Five hundred," I told her.

"Can I pay with a credit card?" she asked doubtfully.

I shook my head sorrowfully. "The reason I always request cash is very simple. You have to keep money pure. Anything that feels too much like . . . like commerce . . . interferes in the process, disrupts the spiritual connection with the departed."

"Oh," Mrs. Jenkins said.

'Oh' was apparently her favorite word. It bought her time to consider her options for free.

"I think we should attempt to regain contact quickly. Sometimes our dear ones spiral away from us, disappointed that we're not more persistent in our efforts to gain contact. If we could finalize our plans today, we could convene again tomorrow afternoon."

"He really loved me . . ." she mused, more to herself than to me.

And this is where my profession becomes more

of a service business than a sales operation. "He certainly did. I can feel the vibrations of his love all around us in this little room. Can't you feel it? And whether he's able to complete his conversation with you or not, I'm sure he's happy that just for a few moments, he was able to share with you."

"Oh," she said again, this time moistly, and she was pulling out her Christian Dior wallet.

I got seventy for the day's reading and the five hundred for a séance the next afternoon at five.

"Dusk is an excellent time to reach the spirits," I assured her.

I let her out graciously and watched her drive away before I packed up my velvet and cards and crystal ball, readying the room for its telesales operation in the morning. I left a twenty and a note for the office manager that I'd need the room again for a few hours tomorrow afternoon and locked up.

I wasn't lying when I said dusk was a good time to reach spirits. This particular twilight found me rapidly approaching two cases of fifty dollar a pop—excuse the pun—champagne and that was mine for the taking.

I was cruising my favorite studio lot, which was awash in the magical blue last light that colors many a Los Angeles winter, just before the splash of tangerine sunset fades behind the darker blue of the Hollywood Hills. It was just like something out of the movies that were filmed there.

Buoyed by my success with Mrs. Jenkins, I'd hurried to my apartment, which was half of a narrow duplex behind a little stucco house dwarfed by an enormous date palm. I slipped a large chunk of my

take into an envelope, labeled it "rent," and stuck
it under my landlady's door. Mrs. Marinak lived in
the stucco house, her tiny front yard gooey with
fallen dates.

She was Czech-Russian, and the little English
she spoke was laced with scowls and invectives, so I
rang the bell only once and scampered away again,
my heels squishing the dates on her sidewalk, while
her poodle was still barking.

Breathing a sigh of relief, I beat a hasty retreat
to my place. I unlatched my multiple door locks,
relatched them, and clicked on the lights.

I keep things pretty simple—a utilitarian dinette
set and a sofa and end tables from one of those
furniture stores on Western Avenue with the signs
in Korean as well as English. It was cheap and modern, and when it all fell apart, it wouldn't be particularly missed.

I also have an antique roll top desk that I res-
cued from a Hancock Park estate sale and a brass
bed left by a previous tenant, who, judging by the
red flocked wallpaper she'd applied in the bed,
bath, and closet, may have fancied herself running,
or maybe did indeed run, a bordello.

Since Mrs. Marinak's rear duplex apartments
were jerry-rigged out of a garage and storage space
and hidden from the street down a long gravel
drive, it was the type of place bound to attract
those not interested in attracting too much attention or long rental applications. It also had character, I thought, of a somewhat seedy sort, with a slim
view of the Hollywood sign and a lacing of palm
fronds out the windows. It perched on the border
between West Hollywood and Hollywood, much
closer to the fast food and Pay Day Advance check

cashing boutiques clogging the main Hollywood arteries to the east than to the designer clothing shops and tapas cafes crowding the western end of town

I ignored the dishes in the sink and the messages on the answering machine, changed from the gauze granny dress and rose quartz jewelry that clients expect their psychics to wear into a sleek, little black spandex number.

I might've hit thirty, but I hadn't hit it that hard, I still look pretty good in spandex. I threw on some good quality, drippy faux diamond earrings and a pair of black pumps with impossibly tall heels.

And I was off to a party at the biggest studio lot in greater Hollywood tonight, an action movie premiere. Elaborate circus-like tents were set up on the lower lot, beneath which were elegant flower-laden tables. Christmas trees covered with little white lights and miniature replicas of the titanium explosive devices featured in the movie bordered the lush buffet line.

Food spilled out of silver serving dishes, open bars flowed, magicians and costumed characters resembling the futuristic alien empaths in the actual film roamed, while photos were snapped and TV cameras rolled recording this cavalcade of celebrity and near celebrity.

And behind the tents, the catering trucks were bustling hives of activity as workers transported food and drink. Among the drinks provided were cases and cases of champagne, not to mention excellent single malt scotch, the finest Kentucky bourbon, the best Russian vodka.

My friend Louie, who lives in the other half of Mrs. Marinak's duplex and dresses like a cowboy but likes hip hop, works the trucks when he can. He gets half of whatever profit I make from whatever beverages I can get away with confiscating and reselling on his cue.

The beauty of this is that nobody ever reports stolen party liquor, probably because nobody even notices that it gets stolen. It certainly was no surprise how much alcohol the famous, their hangers on, or the underpaid press could consume, so surely a few extra cases here or there were meaningless. And, naturally, budgets for Hollywood parties, while not running as high as the budgets for the actual movies they were designed to celebrate, were lavish enough that those few extra cases never pinched a pocket.

Talk about a victimless crime—it was a profit item for the caterer whether the stuff was stolen or consumed; either way the cases that came in did not come back out again, and no one counted the empties. In case they did, Louie usually kept a few cases of empty bottles purloined from other parties on hand.

Louie couldn't take the booze himself—too many coworkers watching; no time to make good an escape and still keep his job, which of course he wanted to keep, both for the paycheck and so we could perpetrate future pilfering.

On the other hand, I couldn't just walk in and take the stuff, of course. I had to get into the party and look like I belonged there, which meant an invitation and a parking pass.

I'd secured both weeks ago, as soon as Louie clued me into the party date, thanks to my buy one day, get a year free pass to my favorite film studio and theme park.

I take the tram tour so often, I could give the tour myself. One sound stage has a ghost in it. No sound stage bears the number thirteen because it might be bad luck. That duck pond serves as an ocean, that giant drive-in movie screen as a sky, those Western town windows are made with break-away candy glass that shatters without hurting anyone. Like many things in LA, really, moviemaking is a kind of scam, an illusion.

Yes, I could give those tram tours. But instead I just ride the last one of the day out, right back to the side of the disembarkment platform where they park the cars for the night, the same side that leads into the lot again.

I take photos with my disposable camera, a prop out of film, until I'm sure the tram driver and tour leader aren't watching me, and then I scamper behind oleanders and lose the Hawaiian outfit, or brand name tee shirt or whatever it is I'm wearing to play tourist, and I just walk down the hill, past the real, working fire station that was once a set for *Emergency 911*, looking impatient, like I'm a publicist who's lost her way. And when someone asks— and sometimes they do ask—can they help me?, I look more impatient still and name the production company office I've lost my way to and get myself accompanied, actually accompanied, to my destination.

It's like having a police escort to a bank robbery, except it's nowhere near that dangerous, but of course, it's not quite that lucrative either. All I'm after is a party invitation.

People leave them lying around—pinned to cork boards, on their desks, on their secretaries' desks. Like the liquor I take, nobody really notices if the invitation disappears. If they do, they berate their assistants for a while, and then the assistant calls up whoever is in charge of issuing such invitations and asks for another one.

Some people might say there are easier ways to make a living, but I haven't found one yet. I came to LA to be an actress when I was sixteen; I was a good actress even then, and I'm a better one now, although nobody has ever appreciated my skills enough to want to put me on camera without suggesting I take off my clothes first. So I've used my skills in a different way.

My transition from wannabe screen artist to scam artist was gradual and only minimally tainted with the bitterness of sour grapes. Waitressing was exhausting and paid little. Headshots, the *de rigeur* photographs for actors to present to agents, managers, talent scouts, casting directors, and directors, in order for them to reject you more easily, were expensive, as was the postage required to mail them and the gasoline required to go on auditions, where they can reject you in person.

Of course, the headshots weren't quite as expensive as applying for credit cards and using the cash advances one could get at loan shark rates to create a "short subject" film as a calling card.

By the time it was legal for me not only to vote but also to drink, it was becoming very clear that although I couldn't make a living from acting, acting would take anything I could have otherwise lived on from *me*.

I met Louie around then. At the time, he was writing screenplays and working as the assistant to a Beverly Hills "hairdresser to the stars." He was doing pretty good at the hairdressing gig at least, until he spent a little too much time working on a steamy love scene for the script he was sure was going to be "it" and make him, as his agent always told him he already was but the world just hadn't realized it yet, "an A-list writer."

His preoccupation led to a teeny weenie accident with China White—the hair dye, not heroin—which caused temporary baldness and an exorbitant, hair dryer smashing hissy fit by one of the celeb clients.

Anyway, Louie did my hair cheap after hours for cash; he continued to sneak me into the salon for a weave even after he was canned; thus a true friendship was born.

We were both broke, and we both liked dressing up in costumes, so although his did lean toward cowboy drag queen, we decided to turn our talents to kids' birthday parties.

We printed up a flyer, ran an ad in *LA Parents Magazine,* and conjured up character parties from fairy princess—yes, I was the fairy princess—to Power Rangers, Pokémon, Pooh Bear, you name it. It wasn't a bad idea, and we might've made money on it, except for the annoying habit of doting parents who lived in five to twenty-five million dollar homes chronically bouncing checks.

It seemed as if the bigger and more elaborate the party and the more money we put into it for costume rentals and the like, the more likely the check was to bounce.

It was ironic, but true—big shots bounced checks while parents who gave parties in the East Valley at little parkettes may not have gone for the biggest potential profit party package, but they usually paid in cash. Unfortunately, they didn't pay enough cash to keep the business going.

The night we gave up on the business, we were pleasantly drunk on a half case of beer. That night, we printed up another flyer and went sneaking around Beverly Hills giggling as we left it in the mail boxes of the rich and fatuous.

"Does your child long to write hundreds of rejected spec screenplays only to be told 'It's brilliant but rewrite it for free, make the lead a monkey, and we'll option it for a $1?' Go to thousands of auditions only to be told he or she isn't 'quite what we're looking for?' Direct his or her own feature film and get hundreds of thousands of dollars into credit card hell only to be told that 'it's too mainstream to be an indie and too indie to be a studio release?' Well wow, let 'em start now! With our very own DISCOURAGE YOUR CHILD FROM A FRUITLESS AND POINTLESS CAREER IN THE ENTERTAINMENT INDUSTRY BIRTHDAY PARTY—make sure your child KNOWS the only good degree is in engineering, law, or premed and that selling aluminum windows sure beats any creative work ever! Run by entertainment industry pros who've been there and done that! We'll bring REAL sleazy agents, fawning casting associates, maniacal producers, & wannabe producers who work out of their garages straight into your home!"

We actually got a few phone calls, but not enough to keep on with the business while we waited for small claims judgments against our past clients, some of whom denied ever giving a birthday party and ever even having children, much less racking up four thousand dollar debts to entertain them. It amazed me then how easy it was for people to lie. Lying was easier than telling the truth.

Louie got into catering, and I took a job in the

wonderful, growing industry of telemarketing, selling magazine subscriptions that don't arrive in the mail; then overpriced printer cartridges, which were really used refills; then the highest quality home security systems that didn't work. I did pretty well at it, practicing what I'd learned from watching rich former clients take on small claims court. Lying really was easier than telling the truth, at least if you wanted to make any money.

And then I started thinking, *wait a second, I'm the one with the convincing sweetheart voice and the honest blue eyes, and I'm only getting ten percent of the pie? I'm the one taking the smell out of the scam, and you're making me sit in an airless room and keep your hours? I don't think so.*

So I went out on my own.

Of course, the downside to any sort of self-employment, whether it's strictly above board or somewhere below it, is that sometimes, it's a long time between jobs, as it had been this past, miserable November.

But what goes down eventually has to come up, which is also the punch line to a bawdy joke Louie tells. Now, badabing badaboom, I'd worked the psychic bit I hadn't pulled off in months for my rent money, and I had this party to hit, all in one gloriously hazy southern California day.

The party was in full swing—local news and *Entertainment Tonight* jockeying for interviews; lower level cast and crew snagging prime rib and grilled lobster like they'd never seen such food before; Vicodin rendering big talent comatose; Cialis rendering small talent large in the back seats of rented limos; agents and publicists and producers, yes, even the producer whose invitation I'd snagged to get in the door, circling table to table like sheep waiting for the sheep dog to lead them in the right direction.

Nobody ever mistook me for an actress, which made me a little sad, but then, the part I was playing now was "I belong here," and if I was an actress and nobody knew who I was, then I wouldn't belong there.

So instead, I was an agent or publicist or producer's assistant groomed for power. I affected a businesslike air, returned nods of greeting to people who figured they *should* know who I was, and milled around purposefully until I found Louie, wearing his trademark cowboy boots and pouring liberal drinks at one of the bar stations.

I sidled up to him and waited until there was a gap in the steady stream of people dying of thirst.

"You better let me do you soon," he sniffed. "Your hair looks horrible."

"The booze?" I smiled.

"Inside the left rear exit door of sound stage thirty-one just behind us. On a dolly. Two cases Dom Perignon, couldn't get the Smirnoff."

I shrugged, took a glass of that Dom, and looked longingly at the buffet. I grabbed one deviled egg and let it go at that. It was never a good idea to spend too much time at the scene of a crime, even if the food did look tasty.

A salsa band was playing, the dance floor was heating up, and security was watching a minimally clad MTV act get ready to take the stage in silver bullet-shaped bras.

I snuck out of the tent and around the sound stage, cracked the exit door, and slipped inside. I waited for my eyes to adjust to the gloom, pulled off my earrings, donned a white catering blouse thoughtfully left for me by Louie, and pushed the dolly of champagne out to the parking lot.

My heart always pounded just a little when I was committing an obvious theft, or maybe it was just the fact that champagne cases were heavy so it was hard work hoisting them into the trunk of my car.

Whatever the cause, my heart rate didn't even out until I was off the lot and driving down Cahuenga. I was still hungry; one deviled egg doesn't cut it after a day as adventurous as mine, so I swung into the Pavilions market on Sunset and hit the deli.

I had to wait so long behind a guy in red leather pants who was trying to pick up the tattooed and lip-pierced goth checkout girl that I ate one of the two sweet King's Hawaiian rolls that came with the roast chicken. But at last, red pants gave up, and I paid for my chicken dinner and went home.

Mrs. Marinak's TV was on, and her poodle was barking, but I didn't have to worry about her confronting me tonight. No worrisome eviction notices on the door. Back rent paid, groceries in my hand, and twenty-four hundred dollars' worth of champagne in the trunk of my Corolla, for which Louie and I would get a thousand.

Not much could be better, I thought.

I turned on the lights, kicked off my shoes, and flipped around my pirated black box digital HBO channels. They were running *Excess Baggage* again, which I'd only seen twenty-three times, admiring the zestful craziness Benecio Del Toro turned on sometimes turned me on, but still twenty-three times was enough. There was the Def Comedy Jam, and a really bad basketball comedy about a guy who dressed up as a woman in order to be told he "got game," *Sex in the City* reruns, which annoyed me because (a) I was having very little sex these days and (b) even if I had the money, I would never spend seven hundred dollars on shoes or wear dresses covered with little baby bottle pins—although when I thought about it, selling really ugly knockoffs of really ugly expensive shoes might be another way to make some money.

There was a horrible documentary about homelessness that came too close to my recent lack of rent money for comfort; something in Swedish about a hermaphrodite; a teen comedy about astronauts in high school; a Steven Segal movie; and a miniseries about carnival workers, the devil, and the dust bowl that was roiling with angst and made less sense than anything Louie had ever written while applying hair bleach. Benecio it was.

While I was watching him overcompensate for his weak lines, I ate my chicken, licked my fingers, and called a few people—Jack James, my liquor buyer, to let him know I had a delivery ready; Louie to let him know I'd made it safe and sound but wouldn't be awake when he got in; two former fellow thespians I used for my séance gigs with tomorrow's time and place and a promise of forty bucks each. It was all answering machine and I finished up fast.

I checked my own messages—pay your phone bill soon, Louie in the afternoon reminding me about the party, a recorded message that wasn't a sales call but involved a department store credit card and was very important.

I sighed. It had been a successful day all told. I was, or would soon be, flush for me, with no taxes to pay on my take. I'd consumed a good and necessary amount of protein. I'd paid my rent. I had digital cable, even if there was nothing much on it.

Still, it would be nice if on top of all that, there was someone who called me or who I could call, who really truly cared about me.

I walked my chicken bones down to the dumpster in the alley behind Mrs. Marinak's and stared up at what I always thought of as a Hollywood moon. Big and bright and so pretty it was almost fake as well as absolutely indifferent to anyone who stood bathed in its glow.

Chapter Two

Jack James, bargain liquor store owner, was antsy on the phone.

"No, don't come by," he hissed. I could hear his fingers drumming and him exhale from a cigarette. "State board of equalization. Looking at books. I'll come to you this time."

I could almost see his loose underlip quivering, the perspiration on his flushed brow, the undulation of his pale blond eyebrows.

"Address. Come on, address."

I hesitated. I didn't give out my address lightly. In fact, I didn't give out *my* address at all. I'd been doing business with this man going on two years, and it was with reluctance that I gave him the address of the storefront in Venice. I suggested a meeting time that was after the telemarketers had bailed but an hour before my scheduled séance. I also stated that he had to be on time or I would be taking my bubbly elsewhere. Not that there was any place else to take it.

"Cross street," he said, more drumming, more exhaling.

I gave it to him, repeated my warning about timeliness and hung up.

I didn't even want Jack seeing me transform into Madame Christina, so I brought my gauze and my crystals with me and stayed in jeans and a tee shirt. Jack had somehow transferred his antsyness to me, so I was early. I took a walk to kill some time.

Venice was bustling with the usual weekend crowd on roller blades, unicycles, and scooters, young hardeyed guys in baggy shorts dragging pit bulls and oblivious yuppies pushing SUSs—sports utility strollers—big enough to match Mommy's Hummer, Expedition, or Cadillac Escalade and give the pit bulls and roller-bladers a run for their money.

Jody Maroni's Sausage Stand spiced the air, a band played salsa and another one played reggae, a guy swallowed phallic-looking swords, and another guy had trained a cat to play a piano. Not very well.

Right by the pier, there was Christmas music in the air, and candy canes were being handed out along with the usual religious tracts by Mr. Greg. He was a Venice mainstay who played "children's Christmas Christian music" year round and took donations to support his ministry, which was supposedly—any day now—moving to Haiti to save the children there or to allow easier access to his off-shore bank accounts.

I splurged on a raspberry lime Jamba Juice and walked out along the pier, far enough to lose Mr. Greg's raspy off-key enthusiasm. I watched the waves hit the shore. I watched a good looking guy muscle a wave out of a lousy little break. I imagined him looking up; seeing me; and boom, falling in love or at least falling down with me on the sand.

Then I imagined that he was probably as dumb as that ex-model I'd read about, Ricky Littlejohn, and some of the pleasure went out of the fantasy. People were always telling me I was too smart for my own good, and I had to agree just then.

As soon as I could be reasonably sure that the telemarketers had decamped for the weekend, I brought my psychic accoutrements into the storefront and waited for Jack.

Apparently, I didn't have to wait long because I had no sooner started burning incense to rid the phone room of the unséancelike odor of cigarettes and cheap pizza, than there was a knock on the door.

"Good, you're early—" I began, but got no further because I'd never seen this guy before in my life, although honestly, truthfully, I wished I'd seen a lot of him before.

He was in his early thirties, and he had big brown eyes; thick, wavy dark hair; a wide, generous mouth; and great cheek bones. He was built, as Louie would've said, like a Greek chorus. He was wearing a nice sport jacket over a polo shirt, and his chinos hung pressed, but not too crisply, over a pair of interestingly funky snakeskin cowboy boots. As Louie was such a connoisseur of cowboy boots, I was immediately impressed. These didn't come from Payless.

"Early for what?" he asked, and his voice had this charming drawl in it, while his eyes were moving over me appreciatively.

Without anything more being said between us, there was this surge of almost electric current moving from him to me and back again. I passed my hand over my head just to be sure that all my hair wasn't standing on end.

"I'm expecting someone," I said curtly to take a little of his charm away.

"I hope they have an easier time finding you than I did. You are Christina, right?"

Well, I was either Christina the seer or Cee Cee the bootleg liquor saleswoman, or I was Christy, me—I wasn't sure which role I was supposed to be playing for this guy yet. So I didn't say yes or no; I just looked at him, which wasn't altogether hard on the eyes, and let that current thing run through me, making me all pleasantly tingly.

He moved a step closer, and almost like we were magnets or something now, I moved closer too. But I didn't say anything.

He made an effort to stop the staring and the moving and explain himself.

"You gave a family friend quite a reading about six months back. But she didn't have a phone number on you, no e-mail, nothing. Just this address, and most of the times I've come by, you haven't been here; just a bunch of guys talking on the phone. Couple days ago, one of them said I might catch you this weekend."

Someone had a big mouth, I thought.

"I don't usually make a habit of seeking out psychic advice. But you were so highly spoken of—" he shrugged and flashed a brilliant smile, and I couldn't help it—he made a great deal of my wariness slip away like an old coat, discarded in the sun.

"She met you in some chat room, I guess. Said you were the real thing, not like one of those phonies who advertises in the Yellow Pages."

I glanced at my watch. If Jack was on time, I couldn't possibly fit a reading in now. And yet I wanted to. I at least wanted the excuse to take his hands in mine and run my fingers over his palms. I licked my lips.

"If you could come back later this evening, I'll give you a reading. Or tomorrow, just about any time—"

"I don't want a reading myself. At least, not exactly."

And from the depths of his jacket, he pulled out a wallet, and from the depths of that wallet, he flashed a badge.

I took a step backward. So this was how the end of the world began. With an incredibly cute guy I was undeniably attracted to using some kind of Southern accent to say politely I was under arrest.

But he didn't say that. My dismay registered with him, and he tucked the badge and the wallet away hastily.

In his haste, I saw the flash of a gun in a holster beneath his jacket. I felt the world spin around me, and for a moment, I was dizzy with regret for my entire life up until now.

"Are you all right?" he asked solicitously.

"What do you want?" I croaked.

I was at this guy's mercy, and I didn't like it. Suddenly, I was pissed off. I had done nothing that bad. Stolen stuff that nobody missed; made promises of hope to the hopeless, kind of like my last agent; impersonated a producer, which just about everybody in Los Angeles does at one time or another.

"I want your help," he said simply.

He took my hand, but apparently not to cuff it.

His hand was warm and dry, and it felt far too good in mine. I didn't like that either.

"Joe Richter," he continued, "Homicide."

"Homicide?" I dropped his hand abruptly.

He was smiling again, and I was just standing there, not running, like the deer in the proverbial headlights, watching the light coming closer and closer—o-o-oh, I'm floating high above the earth.

He had way too nice a smile to be a cop.

"You don't smile like LAPD," I said bluntly.

"And you're not wearing a turban or staring into a crystal ball," he threw out.

Well, I would've been if I'd already dressed for the séance.

"You don't sound like LAPD either."

"The 'don't sound like' is Texas. Mayville, Texas, near the Gulf. My old home may be long ago and far away now, but this I have always remembered—in Texas, we usually smile when we ask for a favor."

"In LA, most people smile when they're trying to run a number on you."

"I don't like running numbers on people. The alphabet's a much easier hustle."

It was a slim joke, but we both laughed like it was a much better one, and I relaxed just a little. Enough so that I stopped clenching my fists at my sides, which I hadn't even realized I was doing. I hoped he hadn't realized I was doing it either.

"I'm working on a very difficult case. I'd really appreciate any help you could give me on it."

My mouth dropped. "You want my help on a case?"

He nodded.

"I don't do that type of thing." I shook my head vigorously. "Negative vibes. I help loved ones communicate with deceased loved ones. I don't solve crimes. I—" I stopped before I could say something really stupid like, I perpetrate petty ones.

"You talk to the dead, right? That's what my mother told me."

"Your mother?"

My wariness came back—if he was from Texas, his mother was from Texas, and I would've remembered a Texas accent.

"Yes. I told her how stuck I was on this case. And she told me what happened to a friend of hers who lives out here. You talked to her friend—and the friend's deceased sister. She passed away in a car accident? You were apparently very impressive. I scoffed at first, but that was weeks ago, and I'm ready to try just about anything now."

A sister. A car wreck. Okay, there was a lady back in July, who had a deceased accident victim sister. She had a flower name that I was trying to remember when the detective flashed some of his own psychic perception.

"My mom's friend's name is Rose. Rose Holloman."

That was it, Rose. Rose something with an H. It wasn't like I kept records. If it was the same Rose, there were lots of tears. There was a reconciliation with the deceased over a collector's edition Barbie. We had four or five sessions before I figured I'd ridden that pony as far as it would go.

"The bedroom slippers," I said. "Our last meeting, she gave me a pair of hand knitted, pale blue bedroom slippers."

Joe shrugged, "Sounds like something she'd do. Sweet old lady. But look, I'm not going to give you slippers. And I'm not asking for charity. I'll pay you for your time," he said.

"I don't think—" I began, but the word pay was always of interest, and I let him interrupt me.

"This won't be a big deal. No trips to the station or anything like that. I want to keep this low key. If anybody else working the case here in LA found out I went to see a psychic, I wouldn't be the rube from Texas, I'd be the fool from Texas."

He laughed agreeably, and I found myself laughing along with him. His eyes were merry and easy, and he was still with pleasure, taking me in. And I still, with pleasure, felt the little snapping electricity between us. Why did the guy have to be a cop?

"It's funny, I pictured you as being about sixty-five with Don King hair," he said.

"That was before the botox," I replied, acutely aware of Louie telling me my hair was not at its finest.

"My mom's friend said seventy an hour? I could make it a hundred. I wouldn't need more than, say, four hours of your time. I'd like to take you to the scene and just see what you come up with."

Four hours. A hundred per hour. Tempting. Guy with a great smile and open, interested eyes. And talk about hair. His was just unruly enough you wanted to touch it, smooth it down. And maybe he'd reach up and touch my hand touching his hair and then who knew where our hands would touch next.

Four hundred dollars to spend time with him. Him who was a cop.

Once again, I shook my head vigorously.

"I'm sorry."

"Oh, come on. I finally break down and try to find you; I look for weeks; I swing by one last time on this fine Saturday afternoon and actually find you, and now you're going to turn me down?"

"I'm afraid so."

If only he wasn't so cute, I could've kept the regret out of my voice. If only his eyes weren't so locked on mine, I could've looked away. But the regret was there, and the looking too.

"You want to help. I know you do. I'm not going to leave until you say yes. That's how I get the most hardened of criminals to confess their crimes. I just won't leave. I stick to them like glue. They have to give in eventually, just to get rid of me."

I didn't even particularly want to get rid of him, but he was a cop, and them's the breaks. The breaks I never seemed to be given.

I sighed. "I might want to help, but I can't. It's not something I'm good at, plugging into murder scenes."

"All you have to do is try."

His eyes appealed; his smile pleaded. He held his hand out to me, and I thought if he touched me again, there was no way in the world I was going to be able to say no.

But just then, Jack James walked in through the door Detective Richter had left slightly ajar and cleared his throat.

"Cee Cee?" he asked. "You got company?"

He was appalled, and fresh sweat broke out on his already oily Neanderthal forehead. "Maybe another day—?"

One of my unwritten rules was never hang on to stolen goods longer than absolutely necessary, and it directly followed the one about getting paid for whatever you could get paid for immediately before somebody changed their mind about paying you.

"No!" I barked at Jack, "today's just fine."

And I gave in to the charming detective just like that. Even without him touching me again. "Alright, sure, yes, I'll help you."

"Should I wait—?" Detective Richter was eyeing the melting blob that was Jack with distaste.

"No!" I shouted again, this time at the detective. "My client needs my full concentration."

"What smells in here?" Jack asked, gagging on the incense. "A Hare Krishna die or what?"

I rubbed my hands together and turned to Joe. "Tomorrow. I'll meet you here. In the morning."

Even telemarketers took Sunday off.

"Nine?"

"Ten." I had to exercise a little control.

We shook hands on it. Oh man, what was it about taking his hand? Neither one of us wanted to let go. Jack had to clear his throat again.

Then Joe left, brushing past Jack, who was fanning himself with the alternative paper I'd left lying around the previous day.

"Need to take an antacid. Got any water?"

"Just champagne," I said. "I'll back my car next to yours. In the alley."

I looked around first to make sure the charming detective wasn't observing me from some rooftop or lurking inside the surfboard shop across the street, and then we moved our cars into the alley, parked rear bumper to rear bumper, and made our exchange.

Jack gulped antacids dry as he grunted the cases into the back of his cavernous old Cadillac. "Who was that guy anyway?"

I figured if I said it was a cop, even a cop from Texas, he'd have a heart attack right there.

"Just somebody who wants my help."

"Your other buyer? That your other buyer? I'll give you twelve hundred this time, okay? Can't beat that. Nobody can beat that. Don't meet him tomorrow. No other buyers, okay? State board's eating me alive. Don't grab a few bargains, you get chewed up and spit out and barbecued. Now you swear to it. Twelve hundred from now on and no other buyers."

We shook hands hard, but it wasn't his sweaty grip I was feeling—it was the dry, strong stroke of the detective's fingers on mine.

As soon as Jack left, I set out the candles and black velvet and slipped on a long, droopy silk shawl. I decided to can the turban. I shook off the feeling of Joe Richter's hand in mine; I pushed the image of those sleepy brown eyes away; I even managed to deep-six the idea that I was actually going to meet him again tomorrow. Christy's little crush had to be put aside now.

Madam Christina had to get ready for her next performance.

"I put on one of my best shows ever at that séance," I told Louie over chocolate shakes at Mel's Diner on Highland.

"I was energized. I really was. Mrs. Jenkins left a satisfied customer, believing love is truer from beyond the grave and planning to follow her husband's recommendation to adopt some cats. I'll give her a few weeks and then invite her back for an encore performance."

"You're a consummate actress," Louie said, happy with the six hundred bucks he had netted from Jack. "Born to take center stage. Who were your supporting players?"

"Violet Amberson . . ."

"The one with that smooth red hair that never frizzes. Starred in an Irish Spring commercial nine years ago and still gets residuals from Poland."

". . . Jerry Blaze . . ."

"Oily dark hair, booed off the stage at open mike night at the Improv. As I recall, he thought that was a good thing—it showed he was getting a reaction out of the crowd."

"He's mellowed."

"So he's the guy Jack James thought was another interested buyer?"

"Not exactly."

"What does that mean, not exactly?"

I frowned. A man on crutches, or rather a man who used the crutches as a prop to beg for money out on the Boulevard, was playing "Grandma Got Run Over By a Reindeer" again and again on the jukebox, and it was getting on my nerves.

"It was somebody else who just kinda showed up wanting my psychic assistance."

"Past client?"

"His mother's friend was."

I lowered my eyes, not really wanting to go any further.

"You like this guy," Louie said accusingly. "You think he's cute. Ha, you have a new mark, and you think he's cute."

"He's not a mark."

"No?"

"Well, I didn't pick him as one, anyway. He needs help with a problem, and I told him I couldn't help, but when Jack showed up, I agreed to meet the guy tomorrow. Just to get rid of him."

It was a lie, the just to get rid of him part, and for once, the lie didn't come easily.

"Sounds a little funky."

"I thought so at first, but—I don't know."

Maybe it still was. It was just that the guy was so good looking, and he had that voice, and he looked at me in a way that not a lot of cute guys had looked at me in a long time. And there was that weird electric thing going on between us; yes, I would swear under oath that it was between us, not just from my end. And then there was the fact that I just couldn't stop thinking about him.

"So if he's a little funky, tomorrow you'll get rid of him?" Louie asked.

"I don't know. If I can."

"Why couldn't you?"

"I wouldn't want him to get, you know, suspicious."

"You think he's cute!" Louie became accusatory and began shaking a spoon at me.

"I do not," I said, feeling my forehead flush.

"You aren't fooling me for an instant. The last guy you dated got a part as Oscar the slob in a dinner theater in Denver. And that was a year ago. You need somebody cute. But not a mark."

"He's not a mark," I blurted. "He's a . . . a detective."

Louie dropped the spoon he was shaking. "Please tell me you mean he detects stains in carpets or something."

I shook my head. "He's a cop. Investigating a homicide. Seeking psychic assistance—"

"From *you?*"

"His mother's friend liked me. He thinks I'm real. I don't want to announce, to a cop, that I'm a fake."

"So just don't show up tomorrow."

"That's an idea. But then I'll need to find a new rental for the psychic gig, and it's not all that easy to locate a spot that doesn't require first and last month's rent and identification and—"

"You *want* to see him again! You want to see a cop!"

I flushed again, partly pissed, partly embarrassed. "If he wasn't a cop . . ."

"But he is."

"He's from Texas."

"I don't care if he's from Mars. He's still a cop."

"He has really nice boots."

"So do I, and you don't want to date me."

"You're gay," I said.

"That's not the point."

"That is the point. We'd be married right now if we were interested in each other."

"Or at least living in an expensive New York loft like *Will and Grace*. How I detest that show! I detest the whole upper middle class thing. All gays are supposed to have money. They're all supposed to get manicures. I hate that."

Louie bit his nails.

"Maybe I should just meet him and tell him that I know I can't be of help and that I can't take his money."

"Oh, he's paying you for the pleasure too."

"Good money, a hundred an hour."

"Well," Louie said, calming down just a little. "You can use what he pays you to pay for the lawyer you're going to need after you date this, this . . . *detective.*"

The waitress brought us our check just as two punked up kids came in with a boom box blaring ancient Annie Lennox. At least it drowned out Grandma and the renegade reindeer.

The kids had safety pins in their ears and grabbed our waitress to ask her if the hot dogs were kosher. She said they were, but I doubted it.

Louie tapped me on the nose. "Hey, you even listening?"

I tapped him back, proving I was.

"It's not a date, and I don't really see why this is such a big problem," I said. "I'll admit straight out of the gate I can't help him, that I don't have any great insight. And really, why shouldn't I take his money? It happens all the time to real psychics, assuming any of them are real—they get brought in to find a kidnap victim or something, and they just can't 'see' anything. Everybody thanks them for their help, and they go away. Nobody scrutinizes them and tells them they must be phonies for taking a few bucks."

"It's not the taking I'm worried about," Louie said gloomily. "It's whatever you give in return."

"What I give . . . ?"

"Information. Maybe even without realizing it. Honey, there's a lot of cute guys in this town; you don't have to indulge in bedroom talk with a cop."

"Who said anything about a bedroom?" I protested.

I could feel the heat rise up in my cheeks and wash over my face like a wave.

Louie reached across the table again, and instead of tapping me on the nose, this time he fluffed up the ends of my hair critically.

"If you're going to date a cop, you might as well look nice for your mug shot," he sighed. "Come on back to my place, and we'll give you a trim."

*   *   *

Louie not only gave me a hair cut; he also gave me highlights and a ride to the beach in the morning, so I wouldn't have to pay to park my car in a lot for the day.

It wasn't just the cost of a parking lot; I didn't want to drive my own in case this detective thought to check the plate and pull the DMV and find an address I lived at several years ago and take it from there. I had assured Louie I'd be careful, and I would be.

I knew very well that I was vulnerable, that I should be avoiding this guy, not helping him. But I was curious. And I was also attracted, and it had been far too long since there had been anyone I was attracted to, and even longer really, since there was anybody who seemed to show a real attraction to me.

There's this sexism thing with cons. A guy can be a total scumbag, a lying cheating crook, but women just naturally think that when it comes to relationships, he deserves a fair shot. He probably is a perfectly nice guy; it's just the way he makes a living. But guys, even guys who are cons themselves, they find out a woman lies a little, hey, even about her taxes, they get all worried, like what else is she hiding or not being entirely truthful about? Maybe she's faking orgasms, has another guy tucked away on the side, or is stealing my credit card numbers. Whatever it is, she's probably not trustworthy.

Of course, I don't have to tell anybody who I am or what I do. And most times, I don't. But if you're going to actually do something about a little attraction, like act on it, eventually something comes out.

If I don't come clean about who I am, the whole

living a lie thing gets very tedious up close and personal. If I don't come clean and they find out I'm lying, I'm screwed. Yet if I come clean about who I am, I'm screwed that way too. Or rather, I never get screwed again.

Now today's situation was different. No danger whatsoever that I would ever come clean about the way I earn my rent to a cop. No possibility I would ever let him have a clue that I was not exactly who he thought I was. No concern about his opinion of me one way or another because he wasn't going to be allowed to form one.

This was a gig, not a date. I was just planning to actually enjoy this particular gig. I had nice hair, and I liked being looked at, and I liked it when he touched my hand. This was a little treat, a little flirtation, and another way to make a quick buck besides. And that was as far as it was going to go, ever.

If I was honest, at least with myself, it was probably as far as any attraction would ever go, the way my life was progressing. Just thinking about that hurt in some undefinable, deep down achy way, the kind of hurt I should've been immune to at this point, but instead, it left me feeling a little breathless, a little desperate. Wow, it really was easier to lie, even to myself.

Of course, it was possible that maybe, someday, I'd find a really big score or finally be discovered as the next slightly over the hill "it" girl. Not because of great, late discovered talent—I certainly wasn't that naive—but because I had made chit chat with the right producer at the right party. It was also possible that I would get out of the game once and for all and reinvent myself as anything I wanted, even a noncelibate Mother Theresa. Anything was, after all, possible, just not very probable.

Louie hadn't been long gone when Joe pulled up at the curb in a nice, but not too nice, classic Mustang convertible. Part of me wanted to just take off running. But then he smiled, and I didn't run.

"Detective," I said.

"Call me Joe," he said, flashing that smile again.

"This is a business relationship, not a personal one," I said, "Detective."

"But it would be very rude if you called me Detective, and I called you Christina. And I don't know your last name—"

My eyes flashed; I certainly wasn't going to volunteer it.

He went on, "If I call you *Madame* Christina and anyone sees me passing you money, we could attract the attention of the vice squad."

He pulled a crisp white envelope out of his pocket and handed it to me. I found myself taking and opening it to find the equally crisp hundred dollar bills.

"So please call me Joe," he said. "And that way I can call you Christina . . ."

"Christy," I amended.

I tucked the money away in my purse. There were only eight more shopping days until Christmas. What was the harm, really?

"I'll try my best to help you, even though it's not my thing, *Joe*. I just can't make any promises."

"I understand," he said. "This is a shot I have to take, that's all. Besides, with the hours I keep, I never usually get to spend a sunny afternoon driving up the coast with a pretty girl."

His drawl somehow made it sound less corny than it was. I got in the car. They always say you should fight every step of the way, that you should never go willingly. But I just got right in.

It wasn't just the lure of cold hard cash, or even his extemely warm smile, or my innate and sometimes troublesome curiosity. It was the feeling of illicit adventure, probably similar to the way the overprotected daughter of a small town minister might feel if an extremely good-looking mafioso asked for her advice on, say, organized religion.

I was doing a good deed, but it was a kind of a naughty, I know I shouldn't really be doing this kind of good deed.

"I got us coffee," he said. "I don't know about you, but I needed a little jump start this morning."

There were two cups of ordinary convenience store coffee in the cupholder, which I appreciated here in the land of the overpriced, addictively over-caffeinated latte. Like his car, it was nice, but not too nice.

He really could be the perfect guy, if he wasn't a cop.

I dumped a lot of sugar in my cup and sipped. I settled into the ride, enjoying the glimpses of blue ocean and palm-fringed expanses of sand. The convertible top was down; the sun was shining; we slipped through the Santa Monica traffic and past the brunch crowds in their gleaming Porsches, Mercedes, and massive four wheel drive vehicles that had never been four wheel driven anywhere more exotic than Gladstone's 4 Fish and Duke's of Hawaii, huge warehouse restaurants with ocean views, valet parking, and overpriced Bloody Marys. The front fenders of many of the shiny cars and the front doors of the restaurants were adorned with red ribbons and Christmas wreathes, and the valets were wearing Santa hats. In front of Duke's, there was a whole pile of artificial snow, with a plywood cutout of a surfing Santa in board shorts riding on it. There was nothing like the holidays in LA.

"Where are we going exactly?" I asked since I was pretty sure we weren't having brunch.

"A house up the coast. I don't want to tell you much of anything beyond that. I want you to feel the place, experience it. Come into it blank, and see what pops up for you."

"If there's anything at all that pops," I said, adjusting the skirt of my sundress.

He watched the adjustment out of the corner of his eye.

The skirt was short, and I knew I looked hot.

"I have a feeling about this," Joe said.

"I thought I was the one supposed to have 'feelings.' I thought the police worked with facts."

"I've been through the facts so many times they're worn out. Like some old quilt my grandma made. The squares are barely stitched together. Gotta find something new just to hold them."

"I'm not much of a seamstress."

"Look, maybe you just know something I don't. I'm a dogged pursuer, but I can't pursue somebody beyond the grave. Maybe you can."

The dogged pursuer part made me uneasy, made me wish that after all, despite the sunshine and the top being down and the coastal drive and the decent coffee, and the attractiveness of my companion, I'd taken Louie's advice and never shown up.

As if sensing my unease, Joe patted my arm. It was a nice pat that felt friendly without being intrusive. This was probably some cop trick he used.

"No matter what you come up with," Joe said, "I want to thank you for trying."

His hand lingered on my arm, and I felt that wonderful magnetic pull, but right at that moment, the magnetic thing made me uneasier yet.

Discreetly, I drew my arm away. He gave the faintest, smallest, almost unintelligible sigh.

That little sigh, what a nice touch that was. It was a near verbal expression of exactly how I was feeling myself. A kind of "I wish I could but I can't."

They sure raised them polite in Texas. Polite and good looking. He was totally charming and disarming. Of course, I didn't quite trust that. If he was obnoxious and couldn't give a crap about me, that I'd trust.

I eyed him from behind my dark glasses. He was clean shaven and tanned; he smelled like herbal soap and not some expensive men's cologne; he was neat, without looking like he'd spent too much time looking in a mirror. He was wearing a white shirt as crisp as that money envelope, nicely worn-out jeans, and those boots again.

He saw me looking at them.

"Got them in Mexico. Rattlesnake. Supposed to be good luck. I thought they were one of a kind, but you know, I've seen the same damn boots in the men's department at Neiman Marcus. Twenty times as expensive of course."

"What's a cop doing in Neiman?"

"Looking for clues in this very case," he said. "Definitely not buying."

The road opened up and showed us a full view of the blue sea and the ricotta, crumbling cliffs that were Malibu. We took a turn toward the coast, the turn for the Colony.

The Colony is a suburban enclave for the obscenely wealthy, the ridiculously famous, or those who wish they were one of those two things and who can afford to buy in. Some of the smaller houses are called bungalows. The larger ones look like palaces and don't have a cute name. I've been to parties there and overheard people talk about the place. There is a quaint feeling of being among your own kind if you live there, kind of like being in a white collar crime prison instead of, say, San Quentin if you're a check forger.

Joe inserted a key card into a slot in the gated entry. The tall wrought iron gate slid open, and we drove down a narrow, well maintained macadamized road lined with purple ice plants.

Many of the houses are sandwiched close together, and regardless of size, their backyards are all beach. Hence, the growing controversy about beach access by plebeian outsiders. As the argument goes, really, would you want some guy jogging through *your* backyard, or having his kid build castles in your sandbox? Of course, the so-called sandbox was actually *owned* by the plebeians who made up the public at large, at least below the ever shifting tide line.

We stopped in front of a house at the far end of the road that was separated from its nearest neighbor by what would soon be a faux Southwestern adobe now under construction on one side and a drop-off to the ocean on the other.

Joe made an effortless U-turn into the driveway like he'd been there many times and knew his way around. The house was a glass prism festooned with yellow police tape so sun faded that it looked like it had been there a good long while. It surprised me that the neighbors would put up with this sort of froufrou for long enough for the color to fade.

I stared at the house for a while, but its glass façade just reflected our car and the street and the sandy grass back at me and told me nothing.

We climbed out of the car, and Joe took a key from his pocket and unlocked a security gate, and then he took out another key and opened the front door. There was an alarm set, but he typed in the security code, and now we were free to wander about the place.

I wondered how common it was for cops to be provided with keys and security codes to the homes of homicide victims.

There was a tacky modern art nude hanging at eye level as you walked in and a neon beer sign.

"So, how do you want to start?"

"I'll walk through the house, see if I can feel anything. Then I'll work on connecting with the man who died."

"You know it's a guy," he said, easily impressed.

"The decor," I said and then wished I'd kept my mouth shut. That might be the most insight I'd be able to muster.

"Do you want me to come with you, or would you rather walk around the place on your own?"

"On my own," I said. "It'll be less distracting."

Maybe that way I could find out some more stuff by observation and not immediately expose myself as a fraud.

Joe nodded and sat down on the bottom step of a slender spiral staircase. He seemed tired all of a sudden, like he was glad to sit down.

I took off my sunglasses. I felt kind of done in myself, probably from the effort it took to maintain a businesslike distance from the guy. Despite knowing better than to even consider wanting it, much less knowing better than to want it, I nonetheless wanted nothing more than to sit down on the step beside him and let him hold my hand again.

"I'll start in the bedroom," I said, intensely aware of how just saying the word bedroom made me blush and of how, tired or not, he was glancing at my legs with quiet interest as I slipped up the stairs past him.

Chapter
Three

Upstairs, the house was all one big loft. It was the kind of large room about which some realtor might say, "It doesn't make the best use of all this space, but I know just the architect who could turn it into a master suite plus a nursery for the little ones . . ."

It was huge and high ceilinged and messy with discarded clothes. I kicked through them, nothing interesting, just dirty socks and balled up tee shirts. Probably, the cops had looked through the mess long before and taken anything that would've been interesting for their evidence room.

There was fake fur on the bed, and enormous pillows on the floor tossed among the clothes. The fake fur was zebra; the pillows were bright primary colors. It was like the leftover set from an old James Bond movie.

There was also a cathedral ceiling and a stunning ocean view. Detracting from the view were framed pictures of magazine covers and advertisements on every available space on the walls.

It was all pretty tacky for a rich guy.

I opened drawers: large size men's boxers; men's tee shirts, some of them sporting dim-witted sexual sayings like "Welcome to 'Ho-*lay*wood;" Hawaiian shirts; and a ridiculous collection of woolen beanie hats in all colors of the rainbow.

It was either a young guy, or a guy with no taste, or a guy with no taste who wished he was young.

I looked closer at the pictures on the walls. Every shot featured a young blond man with a chiseled profile, a cleft chin, and a blank facial expression, kind of like a mannequin that had come to life, except someone forgot to put in any personality.

It dawned on me slowly that the young chiseled man was the very same person in every ad and cover, although sometimes his hair was spiked and sometimes it was poufy and sometimes he was wearing a linen suit and sometimes bikini briefs. He looked vaguely familiar.

Okay, the guy that lived here was probably gay. *Queer Eye for the Straight Guy* aside, there were certainly gays who were slobs with lousy decorating instincts, just as there were gay guys like Louie who bit their nails and weren't particularly upwardly mobile.

The guy in the pictures was probably this guy's lover because the clothes in the drawers and all over the floor were about twelve times too large to fit the guy in the pictures.

In the bathroom, there was an empty champagne bottle, the good stuff Louie and I liked to steal, and a six pack's worth of beer cans.

The medicine cabinet was empty—most likely, the police had found items of interest there and cleared them out. It was unfortunate because I was hoping for a name on a prescription bottle at least.

I opened the glass doors of the walk-in shower, and I saw what must be blood stains. They were old and a little faded, but the sight got to me all the same.

I closed the doors again quickly, feeling a little sick, and went downstairs again. I infinitely preferred my crimes victimless.

"Getting anything?" Joe asked me.

I shook my head. Annoyed, I was getting annoyed. All I needed was somebody to start blasting "Grandma Got Run Over by a Reindeer," and my day would be complete.

"If the deceased passed away in the bathroom shower, maybe the killer was a fan of *Psycho*," I suggested.

"He didn't die in the shower," Joe said shortly. He looked at me a little sharply, not particularly amused.

"I see water around the victim though," I said. It was just a shot in the dark, but I thought it was worth taking.

He nodded noncommittally, but it was the kind of nod I'd learned to read as a yes, in my years of dead dialoguing, clearing chakras, and strolling through auric fields across all lifetimes.

"Drowned in the ocean?" I hazarded.

"Died in the hot tub."

"He went from the shower to the hot tub?"

"The shower has nothing to do with it," Joe said in a tone that brooked no further discussion on that particular topic.

He sure wasn't giving me much to work with. I let the subject drop and moved on around him into the living room. It was decorated in white and chrome, like a museum to the early '80s. It didn't look like anyone had ever spent any time in it. No magazines or books; the leather sofa looked like it had come right out of the factory; and there weren't any dirty clothes lying around on the floor.

I wandered into the big open kitchen, all flagstone and black onyx surfaces. I opened cupboards—lots of ramen noodles and soup cans and restaurant-sized vats of marinara sauce. Every cabinet I opened, there were more vats of marinara sauce, maybe a hundred jars of the stuff. This was a rich guy who was a slob, who never went in his living room, and who had no taste in food or clothes. He apparently poured tomato sauce down his gullet, maybe filled his hot tub with it.

There were big, shiny copper pots and pans hanging from hooks over the shiny industrial-sized stove. They didn't look used. On the wall, there were a series of sharp cleavers and knives with intricately carved Oriental patterns on the handles.

There was one knife missing. Maybe that was the murder weapon. Maybe the guy *was* stabbed in the shower; he just didn't die *in* the shower.

I was going to say something of the kind, but I held back. I shouldn't just take a wild guess this time; I should actually put it together if I was going to impress Joe.

But why did I want to impress him anyway?

What exactly was I doing here thinking about murder weapons and the crime scene? Who really cared? Just because Joe was a cop, and a cute one at that, he was just another mark.

He'd dropped right into my lap; I hadn't even had to coax him through a chat room conversation or spread out a deck of tarot cards in a bar and nurse a beer for hours waiting for somebody to ask me to read them.

Nope, Joe had come right to me, and I was tak-

ing his money and giving him a little hope in return, just like I had done for so many other clients
before him.

Hope was worth something; it was a very real
commodity. But just because I was giving Joe hope
that I could help him solve his case, it didn't mean
anything would ever actually come of that hope.
Of course, that was true of most things in life.

Joe stepped into the kitchen and flashed me an
encouraging, and undeniably sexy, smile.

"If there's anything I can do . . ." he began. He
let his voice trail off, and the smile turned self-
deprecating. "Like mutter an incantation or anything."

Man, he was cute. And the look he was giving
me—interested, watchful, attracted, all those things
mixed up and intense—was spilling over to me like
the rising tide outside this Malibu house. It really
would be sort of cool if I could help him, I thought.

"No, there's nothing you can do," I snapped.

I was annoyed—not only was there nothing he
could do, but there was also nothing I could do either, no matter how cute he was or how cool I had
suddenly decided it would be to help the guy out.
It's always a very bad sign when you start to run
your own scam on yourself.

I heated up all over just thinking about how stupid I was being or maybe from thinking about how
stupid I was being over him. To cool off, I opened
the fridge. Cartons of liquefying Chinese food and
a bottle of vodka. Nothing to say about that. The
best thing I could say so far was that there was a
missing knife and that maybe it meant something.
I kept that to myself for now, in case it was the best
thing I'd ever have to say.

I strolled into the dining room. It opened up

over a little bar area into a den. Both rooms were
as messy as the loft bedroom. But instead of clothes,
lying around downstairs were scattered stacks of
photo albums, newspapers, magazines, and file folders.

Idly, I flipped one of the folders open. It was a
tax return in the name of Richard James Littlejohn.
Ricky Littlejohn! I almost shrieked. What a gift this
was. I could actually impart information about this
dude. I'd just read about him in the newspaper.
But what had I read?

I racked my memory. I remembered picking up
the paper while waiting for Mrs. Jenkins. I remembered he'd been a surfer before he was anointed a
magazine stud; that he'd dealt drugs, worked as a
government informant, or at least said that he did;
that he had gotten fat . . .

Boy, he sure had gotten fat. The size of those
boxers! Unless he was doing plus size modeling
now, he hadn't had a magazine cover in a long
time.

I closed my eyes. I could hear Joe sitting back
down on the bottom step very quietly, so he wouldn't
disturb me. I could hear the ocean pounding outside on the beach. Then I heard a scream. I almost
screamed myself.

But it was only a gull right outside on the deck
lurking at the edge of the hot tub, having a fit
about something. Maybe the gull was communing
with the guy who died there. I laughed nervously.

"What's funny?" Joe asked, rising fast.

"The gull. It sounded like a human scream for a
minute there."

"Don't worry. You're safe with me," he said, and
he smiled and I actually felt like I was safe. But
then he looked at his watch a little impatiently.

I reached in my purse and pulled out a plastic bag containing one of my favorite props, a thick sprig of sage, and a cigarette lighter. I lit the sage and waved it around a few times. I liked the way it smelled, and it looked suitably eccentric.

"What are you doing?" Joe asked.

"Summoning the spirits."

Now was as good a time as any to call them up. I wouldn't remember any more of that newspaper article in, say, fifteen minutes. I let the sage waft for a while, and then I blew it out and laid it down in the kitchen sink.

Joe picked it up and wrapped it in a paper towel.

"Can't leave stuff lying around in here," he said.

I sat down at the dining room table, squinted my eyes, and did my séance thing.

"Ricky Littlejohn . . . can you hear me?" I raised my voice an octave and asked again.

Joe sucked in his breath, unduly impressed, and this time, I didn't blab that I'd just looked in a file folder and that that's how I'd come up with the name.

I waited a beat and then called out a third time. I felt like my timing was off. It was a lot easier when you worked this kind of scene with a couple of other semipros who could get into the moment and feed off each other and do a time-tested shtick. Monologues were always tougher than ensemble work.

"He's trying to catch a wave in," I said.

I sat for a while, cocking my head like a sparrow, as if I was listening for something or someone, other than the incessant gulls and the crashing of the surf outside Ricky's dining room windows.

"He hears me," I whispered.

Joe's warm brown eyes searched mine. "You really are good," he said softly, sincerely.

And maybe he was pretty good too, because suddenly, I believed him. I believed he was a really nice guy who just happened to be a cop who was looking for clues, whose mother told him to find this psychic who gave her friend great insight into her dead sister's soul. I believed that I could give in to whatever it was I was feeling and let him hold my hand and let whatever happened next happen.

Just because almost everything I did was a way to cover up something else that I was really doing, it didn't mean that everything everybody else did was to hide something, did it?

"Are you getting anything?" Joe asked a little anxiously.

I closed my eyes and hummed softly, thinking about what I wanted to say next.

Whether I was buying into my own scam or not, the bottom line was that I really wanted him to keep believing in me at least for a little while longer. Maybe long enough that I could feel his hand on mine again. I hummed a little louder.

Of course, Louie was right when he told me I shouldn't reveal too much to this guy. He didn't have to tell me; I never revealed anything at all to anybody, not even about my own feelings, not even to Louie most times. And I certainly wasn't intending now to tell Joe the story of my life. He wasn't that interested in me anyway, at least not yet. He was only interested in what I could tell him about Ricky Littlejohn's death. What was the harm in keeping him going a little while just to see if I wanted to keep him going a little while after that?

I opened my eyes and smiled my best beatific smile. "I'm getting something," I said.

Just like being an actress, so much of being a so-called psychic was simply going with what you knew, taking it one step further into conjecture, and making that conjecture into a kind of truth.

I stared just past Joe's head as if I was seeing someone else at the table. "Ricky always liked to look at himself in the mirror," I murmured, "that's what models do. But recently, he didn't like what he saw. He'd put on quite a bit of weight—"

"That's right," Joe said, his eyes lighting up.

Oh, he was cute when his eyes lit up.

"So he was thinking of getting liposuction," I continued.

It sounded like something a guy who had money who didn't like being fat who was once a model would do.

"Not just thinking!" Joe said excitedly. "He got it—"

I nodded my head as if I was listening to someone correcting me. I had Joe hooked now. It turned me on to be able to do this clever trick.

I might not have an audience of millions watching me up on a movie screen, but today at least, I had a good-looking, curly-haired guy with soft brown eyes watching me and admiring me, and what was really wrong with that? All the world, after all, was a stage.

"Ricky wasn't that happy with the results," I theorized.

Joe didn't stop me, so on I plunged.

"Ricky was in pain. Mental anguish. He says he saw his own mortality. And sure enough . . ."

I glanced at Joe. He was looking skeptical.

There was a moment of silence, I'd run out of steam. "He says it was tough on him, being in the body business," I said.

Joe lost the skeptical look and hunched forward across the table, hopeful and waiting once more. I'd hit on something.

"Go on," he said, "please. About the body business."

I closed my eyes. "He's leaving me," I said. "He doesn't want to be here."

That was the rule—go out on a positive connection. End things before you took another wrong turn. It was equally true of fake psychic readings and relationships.

Joe sat back and sighed. It was a very different kind of sigh from the one he'd used when I pulled my arm away in the car. This one was louder, harder, and most definitely tired.

"There's other places I'd rather be too. Like the Lakers–Oilers game at the Staples Center."

I folded my hands, and I let everything go silent except for the gulls and the ocean waves hitting the expensive shoreline and waited. If Joe wanted something more from me, he was just going to have to give me something else to work with.

"What about all the paperwork in the living room? Can you get anything from that—who was looking at it, maybe?" he asked.

What I got was that Joe thought the paperwork was important and that he didn't think it was just Ricky rummaging around for his high school yearbook.

I opened my eyes, made them wide with false insight. "Ricky wants you to know that even though he wasn't the most orderly man in the world . . . he wasn't the one looking through those papers."

"Right." Joe's voice was tight. Naturally, he already knew that. "Who then?"

I felt enormously put upon. I wanted to say, how

the hell would I know? Instead—"I told you . . . he's fading . . ."

"Was it one of the police investigators? One of his house guests?"

I remembered reading about the house guests in that news paper story. I cursed myself for not finishing it, for not being so great with names— what were the names of the guests, and were they men or women—?

"One of them was an ex-convict. He has a black aura . . ." I managed.

Joe nodded encouragement.

"He was in business with Ricky. I'm not sure what kind of business." Because I hadn't read that far.

"But whatever it was, they weren't getting along. They were fighting."

I had also seen a small black and white photo in the news article of the ex-con, whoever he was, holding a camera.

"He was a photographer, this partner. He used to take pictures of Ricky. Just not the kind in fashion magazines."

I didn't think this was anything new to Joe. Even if he wasn't the crack detective he made himself appear to be, he could've picked up *The LA Free Press* just like I did. Still, it was something to say.

"There was a woman too—Ricky was married to her once—Laura, her name was Laura . . ." I paused as if hearing the name spoken.

Joe was really into the Laura thing. His eyes had a real gleam to them now, like I'd finally gone where he wanted me to go. The problem was that where I'd gone was a dead end for me. I didn't know anything about her.

"She loved him. He didn't love her. He never really loved anyone except himself."

I paused. I paused for quite a while. Joe's eyes lost that gleam. There was a third guest; I knew there was a third.

"Go on . . ." escaped from Joe's lips.

"There was someone else here too, a young man . . . a musician . . . I can hear the music . . . I can't quite make out the words—a very steady beat though, very primal."

"Don't be too concerned with him."

"All I can really see is pain. There was pain all around Ricky in the end."

"Probably so since he was murdered," Joe said drily.

I scrunched up my nose. "I told you I wasn't going to be much help."

"You *are* being helpful," Joe assured me. "I just couldn't resist."

I tried to laugh, but I didn't feel like laughing. I rubbed my arms. I was surprised to find I had goose bumps. I realized that this house and those bloodstains in the upstairs bathroom, and the gulls screaming out on the beach were freaking me out. Or maybe it was the fact that I was actually trying to help Joe, or please Joe, or whatever I was doing still sitting here running the act past the place when the curtain should've come down on it. Maybe that was what was freaking me out.

"There's nothing else really. Nothing else that I'm seeing. A lot of blackness around him. Ricky is very difficult to reach."

"So you're getting nothing, nothing at all, about who might've been responsible for Ricky's death?"

In that news article, someone, some hanger-on or relative, had said that Ricky had a death wish.

"*He* was responsible. I think he wanted to die," I rephrased. "He's telling me he *wanted* to die."

"He didn't kill himself," Joe said sharply.

There was something about the sharpness with which he said it that made me think he'd considered the possibility though.

"I don't know who killed him," I said truthfully. "But there was death all around him."

"Fair enough," Joe drew in his breath. "What about Laura and Nelson?"

So that was the photographer's name, Nelson.

"For that matter, uh, Dennis, the musician. Are you seeing any of them?"

"They're not dead," I said, because it seemed to me they'd been interviewed for the newspaper article.

"You can't connect with anyone who's still alive?"

"It's not my gift," I said.

"Okay," said Joe. "Maybe it's not your gift, but maybe you can still get something on them."

He stood up and pulled me to my feet. "Why don't you take a look in their rooms? You might get a read on something there. Particularly Laura."

There was something in his voice that made me ask, "Why particularly her?"

"Woman to woman, whatever. I bet you could really tune into her if you tried."

"I doubt it," I said, although if their rooms held any personal items, I might be able to come up with something.

Still holding my arm, and with me letting him hold it, Joe led me back to the entrance. He smiled at me. It was nice having him hold my arm and smile at me.

He felt the goose bumps and rubbed my skin

with his nice warm, dry hand. I felt weak in the knees all of a sudden.

"Oh," I said before I could stop myself.

"Is this upsetting you?" he asked, and he sounded tender and concerned.

I felt ridiculously warm and fuzzy.

"I'm all right," I said curtly and removed my arm from his touch. I was okay as long as we had no physical contact. But as soon as he touched me, I just wanted him to keep on touching me. The thing was, there was this look on his face like he wanted to keep on touching me, too.

I don't know if there's such a thing as love at first sight, but at least, there is most definitely such a thing as lust at first sight, or at first touch anyway.

To quell any such feelings, I concentrated on where we were going. Opposite the main entrance, there were three steps down to a door that I had thought led to the garage but that instead led to a lower level that housed musty smelling bedrooms as plain as something in a Motel 6. Someone must not have told whoever built this house that it was a bad idea to build *down* at the beach.

In the hall, there were cheap framed reproductions of Mickey and Minnie Mouse doing nasty things on the walls. One thing you couldn't say about this Ricky was that he had any taste. I didn't imagine that pointing that out to Joe would be any revelation.

"Guest quarters," Joe said with a sweep of his arm.

The first bedroom was empty, the bed was stripped bare, and there were no personal belongings.

In the second, there was a sleeping bag as worn

out as any a panhandler would haul around South Central in a shopping cart. There were rolls and rolls of unexposed still camera film in McDonald's bags. There was also a weird lamp, the base of which was a pair of pink plastic woman's legs cut off right at the genitalia free crotch.

"The photographer's room," I guessed.

"Yeah," Joe said encouragingly. "Correct."

This psychic stuff was really pretty easy. Maybe this was how they all did it.

"Where's his suitcase?"

"Impounded as evidence. Photographs, video tapes. Nothing to do with the murder."

"Ricky wasn't one of the stars on the tapes?"

"It was all women. And farm animals."

"Ah."

"Are you getting anything?"

"Sick to my stomach," I said and moved on.

The next room was clearly the musician's. Guitar case, a stack of CDs, rolling papers.

"Dennis," I said, now pretty cocky.

"Actually, the ex-wife stayed here." Joe sounded pretty disappointed.

I made a big show of opening the closet, revealing miniskirts and macramé vests. I lifted the lid on the guitar case. It was really some kind of a makeup case, lined with faux leopard, containing little zipper pockets as well as a hair dryer.

"She was older than Ricky," I said. I wasn't sure if I'd read it or guessed it from the too young, 80s style clothes, but I had to redeem myself for the way I had just popped out with saying this was the musician's room.

"Yes," Joe said. A tentative note of interest had slipped into his voice, so I rode it.

"She was here to prove she still had it. Ricky rejected her. In fact, he made fun of her to his other friends. She was angry."

"Hm-m," Joe said.

"But there's anger everywhere in this house," I added, because even though any middle-aged woman who wore this kind retro attire was probably a cretin, that didn't necessarily justify me tagging her as the main suspect.

"She thought he owed her money," I said, because what divorced woman whose ex had a house in Malibu Colony wouldn't feel that way.

"See anything else about money?" Joe asked. His eyes were all agleam again, avid even.

Oh, so I'd struck a chord.

"He was hiding some from her, quite a bit." Again, what ex wouldn't.

"Do you know where?" Joe had an urgency in his voice now.

"Well, he didn't keep it in a safe under the stairs."

"Already looked there," Joe agreed.

Hey, at least there was a actually a safe, and it was under the stairs. That was pretty good guessing.

"Nothing else?" Joe prodded.

"The money, it's all shrouded in darkness," I said. "It's buried."

"Buried?" said Joe. "Do you know where?"

"It may not be literally buried. It could be hidden in someone else's name or stored in some underground account. Wherever it is, everything surrounding this money is . . . very dark."

"Yeah," said Joe grimly, "very damn dark."

I moved on down the hall, letting Joe follow me this time.

There was sheet music in the last room, but the closet was empty.

"The musician," I said by process of obvious elimination.

"He had already checked out before the police came. He's the only one of the three I'm not investigating."

"How come?"

"He had an alibi I completely believe."

Joe took my arm again, and I didn't stop him, even though he was kind of tugging at me as if he wanted me out of this room, as if he regretted letting me even see it.

"And the alibi checked out?"

"You don't need to spend time on this guy," he said curtly.

I stabbed in the dark. "There's something very secretive about the aura in this room. Different than the darkness around that money you were asking about. Something clouded though, obscure."

"Forget about him. He's not important," Joe said, and he was half dragging me into the hall.

I dug in my heels.

"He was a narc?" I asked. There was that stuff in the paper about Ricky being an informant or claiming to be.

Joe raised his eyebrows. "No, not a narc."

"He was some kind of undercover, right?"

"Nobody knows that," Joe said, eyeing me carefully.

"Who would I tell?" I asked.

"I'm not sure," he said evenly, maybe a little too evenly. "It doesn't really matter now."

It might not matter, but in a way it made me feel good having something on Joe without knowing why.

I was also unduly proud of having hit upon something true that at least seemed like something only a psychic could know, that at least had not been lifted whole from the pages of a weekly paper or based entirely upon commonsense conjectures.

Joe led me down the narrow hall past the bedrooms to a door that did lead to the actual garage.

The garage was carpeted with fake oriental rugs. Cheap industrial lighting hung from the ceiling. The garage was being utilized as an office. It contained file cabinets, three desks, wheeled chairs.

I opened a filing cabinet, but it was empty. Desk drawers, also empty. The only thing that wasn't empty were big wooden crates marked *Prima Marinara*. I counted twelve of the cases. The lids were all pried off, and inside were more enormous jars of the red stuff filling the kitchen shelves. The jars were all shrink-wrapped.

"He sure liked his pasta," I sighed.

"Doused in red sauce. Ate gallons of it."

I wasn't going to get anywhere on the marinara sauce. I turned back to the empty file cabinets.

"Somebody took all that paperwork in the den out of the cabinets here," I said.

"Apparently."

"Did they find whatever they were looking for?"

"Don't know." There was a small silence, and then Joe said, "I was kind of hoping you could tell me if there was really anything to find here."

I opened desk drawers. Pencils, time cards, an agreement for a cheap nationwide minutes phone plan.

A little more of that newspaper article snapped into focus. "He was telemarketing modeling lessons or diet plans. The ex-con was working with him."

Joe looked blank, maybe a little bored.

"Something to do with bodies," I said, remembering how Joe had perked right back up in the dining room when I talked about Ricky's lipo and the body business being tough. Maybe the guy did crappy plastic surgery right in his garage. That seemed pretty unlikely though.

Joe didn't say anything, didn't give me anything to work on, but he did look interested again. Bodies, that appeared to be the ticket here. Naked bodies maybe, there was always money in that, porn. The pictures Nelson had in his camera. I went with that.

"Ricky was shooting porn, and some of the girls had daddies or husbands or boyfriends who got mad. Maybe one of them killed him. Maybe one of them took his money."

Joe raised his eyebrows. "It wasn't porn."

Another slip on the psychic banana peel. I visibly deflated.

"I was right about the undercover guy though."

"Let that go," Joe said.

"Whatever they were doing back here, Ricky didn't come up with it on his own." I remembered reading that he was stupid. I closed my eyes like I was figuring something out. "It wasn't this . . . this Nelson's idea either. They were fronting for someone . . ."

"You're seeing this?"

He sounded so intent, so concerned. I just gave it up. I opened my eyes. I was honest. "I'm guessing. I don't think I can do more than that for you. I'll give you your money back," I added.

What kind of a sappy thing was that to say? I'd give him his money back?

But he shook his head. "You tried. I said there

was nothing else I wanted except for you to try. You're just one more angle I thought I'd work."

"Really? That's all?" I said. I was relieved, and I was teasing, but I was a little put out too. "And here I thought I might actually mean something to you."

We walked back down the hall. He hesitated outside Laura's room.

"I don't suppose there's anything else you could give me about Laura . . . maybe not even anything to do with Ricky's death. Just something that Laura might have done that could lead to—" he broke off.

"Lead to what?"

"To whatever."

I sighed. "Was it Laura's blood in the shower?" I asked.

Joe shook his head, his lips tight. "It was a guy Ricky had a fight with. But he isn't the murderer."

"You're sure?"

"I'm sure." He was very firm about it.

"Oh. The undercover guy. Ricky found out."

"He didn't find out. Somebody told him. You're close," he said, trying to smile, "but no cigar."

"You're close," Directors, casting assistants, and agents would say. "You made an interesting choice; What an interpretation, but it isn't quite what we're looking for."

Just once, just once, I wanted to hear "That's it; that's exactly what I wanted!" What role was I auditioning for now? Joe's love interest? Even if I did get it, long term, the part just wouldn't be right for me.

"So you really don't know anything more?" Joe asked me. "About Laura? Really and truly?"

"I don't know anything at all," I snapped.

Joe sighed. "I'm sorry," he said.

Although I wasn't sure what it was he had to be sorry for just then, I appreciated the apology all the same.

"Laura doesn't have a very firm presence in this house. She didn't really belong here."

"True," Joe agreed. He reset the alarm in the foyer, and we walked outside.

It was a relief to be out of the house; there really was some kind of trippy aura around the place—you didn't have to be a real psychic, or even a phony one, to scope that out.

Joe gave my shoulder a little squeeze as he unlocked his car. He opened the passenger door for me, and I climbed in.

Joe didn't start the car though; he just sat there, staring at the big, empty glass eyes of the house, at the yellow tape wavering like dancing snakes in the breeze.

"You know, it's funny. I guess I'm still just a small town boy at heart. Everybody wanted this guy dead. Who really cares who did the deed? The world's far better off with a guy like him gone. And yet, here I am trying to find out who offed him."

"You're trying to clear somebody," I said.

His eyes widened. I might not actually talk to the dead, but sometimes I'm dead right. He didn't admit it though.

Instead, he said "In a small town, you call it justice—a guy like this gets his, and you go on about your business; you don't try to find out who you should blame for meting out justice that was, in my opinion anyway, too long deferred."

"Maybe that's the problem you're having solving this case," I said. "Maybe you need to think more like a Angeleno."

He smiled at me. "I am. I brought in a psychic. What could be more LA than that?" He sighed. "But it's the damn truth. LA has never really been my scene."

"It's not mine either," I said. And that was also the damn truth, though maybe I'd spent the last fourteen years avoiding the realization.

And maybe because it was true, or maybe for some other reason, he leaned over impulsively and kissed me. And of course, I kissed him back.

It was like a lightning bolt came down and blasted me. It was all that electricity we'd been sending out to each other even while we had been working really hard to ignore the shock, plus something chemical and bittersweet with longing and all the loneliness and wanting two people could come up with. Or I guess you could call it just plain physical attraction. It was a little too special, though, to dismiss it like that.

Our kiss lasted a long time, went from lips to tongue and back again; lips and tongue moving along my neck, hands pulling me close; and then back to the lips we went. I could've kept kissing him like that for the entire afternoon. It felt very overwhelming and passionate and romantic, parked there in front of the house of a murder victim.

When it was far too long in going on for either of us to pretend we didn't want it to go on, he pulled back.

"I'm sorry," he said, and he was trying to look serious.

But he didn't look sorry or serious. He was smiling, and I had goose bumps again, but not the creeped out kind I'd had in the house.

"I'm not," I told him, and he gave me this big, open grin and laughed out loud.

"I was lying," he said.

Without asking me if it was okay, but it was, he drove us out of the Colony and turned left up the coast highway, away from LA.

He pulled into a parking lot near Sycamore Cove that had a view of the rock-studded beach and wind-whipped trees and drove to the far end of the lot where there were no other cars or RVs, and then he pulled me against him and kissed me again.

"I don't usually—" he said.

"Me either," I breathed.

We kissed and kissed until my lips felt swollen. We necked and nuzzled, and he slipped the straps of my dress down my shoulders and buried his face in my skin. I leaned back in the warm sunlight and felt absolutely delicious as his kisses moved lower and lower, and the sun, or something, made me feel so warm all over I was practically melting.

He looked up at me. "Do you have any plans this afternoon?"

"Not anymore," I admitted.

Which was how we ended up in a motel in Oxnard.

Chapter
Four

"Oh, my God," said Louie, appalled. "You're in Oxnard? Not Santa Barbara, not even Ventura or Carpinteria, but Oxnard?"

"Yeah, well," I said, being at my most articulate.

"Oh, my God," said Louie again, "he really is a cop."

The shower stopped running, and Joe stopped whistling.

"I have to go," I told Louie. "I'll see you tomorrow—give you a call, okay?"

Before he could answer, I hung up on him. And before he could call back, I shut off my cell phone. It was an afternoon of living dangerously.

Leaving Sycamore Cove, Joe slowed around the curve at Point Mugu for a kiss; I reached across the gear shift and stroked his leg. As we drove past the big rock, he slipped his hand down the back of my dress and unfastened my bra. This turned us both on so damn much he had to pull over by the giant sand dune. Kids usually toboggan down it, the LA version of a New England snow bank, but today nobody was around—maybe everyone was out Christmas shopping.

So he pushed my dress all the way off my shoulders and rubbed his fingers in circles over my breasts until my nipples were hard and my insides felt like jelly. He slipped my bra off my shoulders, over first one arm, and then down the other and tossed it into the back seat. His lips moved from my mouth to my neck and shoulders until he replaced the circles his fingers had made on my breasts with spirals from his tongue.

We were right, that's all—not just sexually right, but attuned to each other. And on top of that was the wonderful illicitness of just about doing it in broad daylight on a public thoroughfare, and on top of that, kind of like the crunchy peanuts on top of the whipped cream on top of the hot fudge, was the fact that he was the kind of guy I should avoid if I had any sense.

I guess I didn't have much sense because I sure wasn't trying to avoid him. I climbed onto his lap and unfastened his belt. He lifted my skirt, slipped his hands between my legs, and then his fingers moved up against my hips and started working my panties down. I moved against him, unbuttoning his shirt. Who knows what we would've done right there by the side of the road, the infrequent motorcycle racing by, if I hadn't arched back against the steering wheel and made the horn blast.

We sprang apart as the horn echoed out over the highway and dunes and waves; we laughed; and I got back into my seat, pulled down my skirt, and pulled up my shoulder straps.

"Don't put yourself too much together," he told me, his voice thick.

He drove one-handed the rest of the way, his

right hand stroking my thigh, his fingers slipping in and out of my panties.

I closed my eyes and just enjoyed it, half-drunk with the sensation of him stroking me by the time he pulled into the motel parking lot.

He got out and paid, and I just waited, the anticipation so strong I had to watch the second hand on my watch spin around just to catch my breath.

He sprinted back to the car—it was pretty obvious he could hardly wait either.

He left the car unlocked and the door hanging open, and we stumbled into the motel room and fell down on the bed. My dress and his jeans were off in a flash, our underwear stripped off like a mighty wind had taken hold of it. We didn't pull off the spread, and he didn't take off his shirt until round two, as we were giggling like a couple of kids.

"I wanted you so bad I could almost taste it," Joe admitted.

"No almost," I said from under the tent we'd made of the sheet.

Just as the sun went down, Joe pulled on his jeans, went outside, and retrieved my bra from his backseat. The sunset had left silky orange streaks in a deep gray sky, like a fire burning steady under ashes.

I still felt that fire inside of me, and if we hadn't been so hungry, I don't think we would've left the motel room at all. It took a lot of self-control to put our clothes back on, I'll say that much, at least on my part.

We couldn't seem to keep our hands off each

other even as we walked up the street for dinner. It was a little Mexican place, a storefront that the guy behind the motel desk had recommended.

We were the only people there who weren't Mexican and who weren't part of a huge family. There were mariachis playing "Feliz Navidad," and there was tripe on the menu, and they didn't serve margueritas, but they did sell tequila shots, and we had a few.

We were both giddy and loquacious.

"I like places like this," Joe said. "There were places like this in my hometown. Music, good tequila, nothing too fancy. Real."

"Real," I echoed while he stroked my hand and then, under the table, my leg. We kissed again.

"Everybody's running some kind of scam here. There's so much phony in LA," he said. "It's like peeling an onion. You get past one layer of BS, and there's another one strong enough to bring tears to your eyes."

I turned my attention toward my chicken mole. "You miss Texas," I said.

"I used to. Right now, I'm not missing a thing."

I laughed, feeling silly but pleased.

"There's places I wish I could take you to see back home. Wish I could just pack everything up and take you right now. Ranch land and big rivers. Red rock and blue sky. Places where you don't have to turn around and see anybody you don't want to see. All you see is yourself looking in the rearview mirror. And whoever's sitting in the passenger seat. And at night, you just settle back and watch the stars come out and the moon rise."

"Sounds nice," I said, and it did.

He drained his tequila and lifted my hand and kissed it. "You always live in LA?"

I shook my head. I flashed back to before I ran away from my grandmother's house to be famous.

"Spring Hill Lake, Pennsylvania. I bet I could give you a run for your money on the prettiest spot you've ever seen. Water's a perfect cerulean blue. Pine trees right down to the sand. It's a big lake, and on one side of it, you can get as far away from everybody else as you'd like. But on the other, you can rent paddleboats or a big old tire and float around. Buy soft serve ice cream at the dock. Or that's how it used to be. Now, I believe it's all condos. When I was a kid, I'd chase ducks around in the paddleboats. And when I got a little older, I'd chase the cute boys."

I wasn't sure I'd even told Louie that. I was raised by my grandmother after a second wife, and then an accident, took my father and illness took my mother, all before I was eight.

In spite of that, or perhaps because of it, it was like a dream, my growing up in Grandma's little town, in her small, neat cottage, the apple of the old woman's eye and the star of every school play. And every summer, as soon as the beach opened come Memorial Day, there were the long, hot, lazy days on or by the water.

"You ever catch one?"

"The boys or the ducks?"

"Either one."

"Sometimes. To both. They'd fly away."

I waved my hands and almost knocked over the candle. The flame went out. Enough tequila.

Joe straightened the candle and relit it.

"You miss that place, huh?"

I did, I actually did, although it had seemed far too tame and dull a place to stay much past puberty.

"I guess I do."

"You go back to visit?"

"No, no one to visit. My grandmother died before I moved here, and she was the last of my family. I am it," I said somewhat melodramatically.

"Why'd you come to LA?" he asked.

"To be an actress," I admitted. "But I didn't come close to chasing that one down."

Unlike fat, old, dead Ricky Littlejohn, nobody had ever discovered me at the beach. I felt tears start up in my eyes. Wow, definitely enough tequila.

"How about you? Why'd you come to the left coast?"

"I'm left-handed," he joked and then turned serious. "Big city, big plans, all that. Prove myself to the folks back home."

"Did you?"

"I'm still trying."

Something fell across his face, a shadow of regret. I knew he was going to change the subject before he changed it.

"Were you always psychic?" he asked.

"Psychic." I sighed. I'd forgotten about that. I'd forgotten that he was a cop. No more tequila ever.

"I suppose," I said. "I always had a sort of an insight."

If I really had third eye type knowledge, would I have ever moved here? Or would I have moved here and used that knowledge to succeed at the stock market and make my own movies off the proceeds? To hone in on exactly the right show business connection? To find the right place at the right time? Would I have given up on all that and just used my special gift like radar to find the man of my dreams? Had I in fact, in some twisted, crazy way, just found him?

Joe's lips moved along my neck and down to my shoulder. He was gearing up again. This man would certainly do for now. Better than do. He was much more than I'd been dreaming of, recently at least.

"What sort of an insight are you getting right this minute?" he asked.

"That maybe we should go back to the motel," I ventured, blinking those pesky tears away.

"Yes, you're psychic all right," he said.

We walked past the ninety-nine cent store, pausing to kiss in front of the window display of out-of-date nail polish, hot pink tube tops, lavender tinsel Christmas trees, and huge jugs of fruit punch. We walked past the hardware store and a closed Food 4 Less, still necking; we pressed together in the doorway against an old movie theater that was now a church, and beneath the mottled service bay of a gas station with the pumps pulled out, he backed me up against the wall and walked his lips down my neck and shoulders. Against the takeout window of a donut shop that also sold menudo, he hiked up my skirt, and I wrapped my legs around his hips. Yes, Oxnard was a very romantic town.

Back in the motel, we managed to douse the lights before falling down together on the bed, and while ranchero music streamed out of the radios of passing cars, we read each other's minds pretty well. Maybe he was a psychic too.

Joe was already up and dressed and watching the TV news at seven. He had the volume turned down really low on a CNN science report about a meteor shower astronomers were expecting to be visible that evening; the reporter was gushing about how wonderful it would be, quite a spectacular light show, and how many hundreds of years it would be until the meteors would fall again.

It was kind of the way I felt about Joe and me. We'd had quite a wonderful night, spectacular in its own way, and it would probably be hundreds of years before I had such a night again.

Joe and I smiled at each other, but we didn't touch, not even a good morning kiss. I think we both knew we had to be very careful about not touching if we wanted to leave the motel room.

Truthfully, I wasn't entirely sure I did want to leave, but he was clearly ready to go. So groggy or not, conflicted or not, I slipped into the bathroom. There was a low rumble that didn't come from the plumbing. I lifted the thick curtains that hung over the window.

It was foggy out, a milky white, the greater Los Angeles area's version of a winter blizzard whiteout back East. The sound was fog horns down at the harbor.

Some people used fog as an excuse to just hole up somewhere, like a motel in Oxnard, because it was dangerous to drive. I tried it out on Joe.

"You can hardly see the parking lot outside," I mentioned, toweling my hair.

"It'll burn off," he said, "by the time we finish breakfast."

So much for excuses to hang around.

The coffee shop was crowded, and it smelled like bacon, coffee, and politically incorrect cigarettes. Despite the damage to my lungs, I was relieved to see that Joe at least was not the sort of cop who busted people over unenforced smoking ordinances.

The buzz in the room precluded any intimate conversation, so we just ate. I got the feeling he was happier that way.

We had a huge breakfast—coffee and huevos rancheros and beans and salsa and bacon and tortillas. Then, still being careful about not touching each other—"After you," he said when I reached for the sugar—we got in his car and drove back down the coast toward LA.

The fog had thinned to the extent that you could see the road, although it hung in heavy strips over the ocean and the fog horns continued their mournful, goatlike bleating.

Forty-eight hours earlier, it had been sunny and warm, and we hadn't even known each other. I knew I looked hot in my little sundress, and I had used how I looked to get him to look at me and then to do a lot more than look.

And now all I was doing was looking down at my hands while I shivered in a white mist, coming off a bender of lovemaking and agave in Oxnard.

He was a cop and I was a con, and because of that, and doubtlessly a myriad of other things about our personalities, we were both shutting down, closing up, cutting each other off.

He didn't even know I wasn't who I pretended to be, and he was still cutting me off. Well, that was okay, really, wasn't it? He wasn't rejecting me; he was rejecting the unhelpful psychic who had offered herself up for a one night stand. Was it the psychic who had offered herself up, or was it me? I wasn't going to go there, not driving along swathed in damp fog both outside and inside my mind.

I thought regretfully of how I'd have to give up the storefront in Venice after all and that I'd stay off the chat room I'd found his mother's friend in, at least for a while, and that I'd never see him again more than likely.

I didn't think regretfully about our Sunday though; it was just that it was Monday, and it had to be over.

He broke the silence after a while, asking me if I was cold and pointing out a flock of pelicans huddled on a rock. A hard white light was breaking through the fog now, burning it away but not making the day any more cheerful somehow.

Joe pulled over and pointed out a lineup of surfers, looking, there in the breaking mist, in their black neoprene like the sea otters errant sharks sometimes mistook them for.

There was a moment when I thought he was going to reach for me or at least say some standard let down line, like he knew we weren't going to work out but that he'd sure had a nice time anyway.

Instead, he just sat like I wasn't even there, looking out at the water like it might tell him something. When he finally spoke, he was no more talking to me than he was to himself, really.

"Ricky used to surf up here at County Line," he said.

I stifled a sigh. He really was obsessed with this guy.

"He was wasted all the time; I don't know how he functioned, really. He said anything that came into his head. He forgot names and places, and he didn't keep appointments."

"Sounds pretty annoying," I said. But these habits probably didn't get him killed.

"Then he'd sober up for a while and turn on the charm; he knew how to give great smile apparently—he got the ladies with his 'you can be a star just like I was' crap; he got guys with his 'I know how it is to be down and out and I can help you' shtick, and it worked. It worked on people. When he did something really bad, people gave him the benefit of the doubt. Nobody believed he had the brains to do bad things. His stupidity worked for him! It amazes me how these cons get other people to believe they're on the up and up. I guess there's an art to that."

This hit a little close to home.

"I suppose," I said stiffly.

Something in my voice got to him enough that he actually turned and looked at me. His face, which had hardened into the dislike of his subject, shifted and softened. He smiled. Oh, that smile. He gave a pretty good smile himself.

He reached for my hand and held it before I could pull away. He stroked my fingers one by one.

Now, why did he do have to do that after all our careful rituals of not touching? The lack of contact was just beginning to work. I was starting to realize our little fling was over, completely over and done with, and then he had to touch me, and it wasn't really over at all.

"What's up with you?" I asked, and I sounded, even to my own ears, surprisingly pissed off.

"I'm sorry. I'm very sorry." His voice was soothing, and he kept rubbing my fingers with his own. "I know this isn't fair to you."

He dropped my hand and thumped the steering wheel in a way that made me jump. What *was* up with him anyway?

"This whole thing's a mess. That's what Ricky did—he made messes and left them for other people to clean up."

He looked so sincere and so troubled. A crazed maternal instinct rose up in me. I wanted to hold him in my arms and tell him it was all right, everything was all right.

"What about the house guests? Laura and Nelson? The other guy you don't want to talk about. What do they have to say?" I asked.

"I've been trying to flush out Laura and Nelson. But they haven't bitten yet. There are things I know Laura knows, things I was sure—" he shook his head. "It's just one dead end after the other."

"And the other guy, the one you don't want to talk about?"

"He's no damn help whatsoever," Joe said, not bothering to deny anymore that the guy was a cop.

He rubbed his hand across his forehead, like he was trying to make some thought inside his head disappear.

"You have no idea how long I've been after Littlejohn. Man, it feels like I've had a hard-on for that guy for forever."

"You've had a hard on for *him?*"

We both laughed, but he stopped laughing first.

"All I wanted was to nail him at first. Then I realized there were other people to be nailed. So I wanted to nail them too. And now, now I have to find out who it was that got Ricky. And I want to find out what happened to the big pile of money he was scarfing up. It has so completely disappeared and he was so damn fat that sometimes I believe he sat there and ate it for breakfast."

We both laughed again, but Joe's laugh turned bitter at the end, and the bitterness surprised me.

"I've been thinking I'd do anything to find out about the money and who killed the son of a bitch.

But I'm not so sure today. I'm not so sure the end justifies the means."

"It does if it means this much to you," I said.

It was the kind of argument I sometimes had with myself—does the end (me making my rent money) justify duping another old lady into believing her dead spouse really liked her new permanent wave? And usually, I reached the conclusion that it was justified because not ending up on the street was indeed important to me.

"It's that obvious how I feel, huh?" he asked.

"Pretty obvious, yeah."

"Here I thought I was being pretty mellow about my feelings. Maybe it's that psychic thing of yours."

His hand had returned to mine, and he was squeezing it like he didn't want to let go. And then he did let go and pulled me to him, and we kissed. It was the kind of kiss where your breath is just plain taken away and you start feeling like you're floating outside your body, even as every single nerve in your body is tingling and dancing and jumping and aching.

Everything we'd been holding back that morning went into that one kiss. I wanted to tell him to turn the car around and take us back to the motel.

I also wanted to tell him there was no psychic thing at all. At the same time, I actually wanted there to be such a thing, and I wanted to be able to use it to take the crease out of his brow and the bitterness out of his voice.

I had it bad for him. For a guy I hadn't even known two days ago, never mind that he was a cop with conflicted feelings. The thing was, I was pretty sure he had it bad for me too.

And maybe having it bad was a good thing, or it

could be, once this Ricky Littlejohn he was so obsessed with was behind us both.

When we came up for air from that kiss, Joe stared out at the ocean again. "Ricky wasn't much of a surfer even when he was young."

I twitched. I was getting very sick of big fat Ricky.

"He was never worth much," Joe went on. "Except for the fourteen million dollars that are missing today, of course."

Abruptly, Joe started the car.

I'd been thinking we were talking a couple hundred thousand maybe.

"Fourteen million dollars. Wow! That is a lot of money," I said, sounding almost as stupid as Ricky was supposed to have been.

Chapter Five

I told Joe I lived in a very nice pink stucco, three-story art deco apartment building a few blocks away from my Venice storefront. He asked which apartment was mine and made me point out the window to him. I told him I had the top left corner without blinking, but it did make my heart beat a little bit faster and my throat constrict simultaneously to think that I was lying.

He gave me one last kiss; it really had to be the last one now, but again, I got the feeling that he didn't want it to end any more than I did.

Still, he didn't ask to come up. He had to get back to work on the case, he said. That was a relief, all told, since I didn't have a key to the corner apartment, much less live there. He asked for my number though.

I hesitated to give him even that, but only for a second, and then I gave him the number of a pre-paid minutes cell phone I'd bought and registered under a phony name at a phony address; not the number of the cell phone I actually talked to Louie on; not the number of the cell phone I gave out to select marks; not the number of my unlisted home phone, the utility bill for which I always paid with a money order.

This was my spare, backup phone, purchased for just such a reason as this, if I could ever have imagined such a reason.

The only point in giving him a phone number at all was because I wanted to see if he'd call me, not because I ever intended to talk to him again. But it would be nice if he called me. It would be nice if he called me even if I wasn't the psychic solver of his case. If he liked me just for me, whoever it was I really was anymore. Sometimes, I wasn't sure.

As he drove away, I told myself sternly that he was already a sweet memory, and that was it and that was that.

I already wanted to cry, even as I waved from the front of the apartment building I didn't live in and slipped into the lobby and past the elevator and back out again through the garage.

He'd given me his number too. I threw it away in the first trash can I came to, and then I wished I had it back. I even stuck my hand down in the soda cans and wet newspapers, but I came up empty, so I figured it was a sign, and I let it go.

I was walking to the bus stop, planning on taking the local down Santa Monica Boulevard and home, but before I'd made it to the corner, I doubled back to my storefront office. There was something else I wanted to take out of the trash.

The telemarketers were in, and the sales supervisor was not exactly thrilled to see me. He was wearing a headset and listening in on his crew.

"Somebody came around looking for you last week," he muttered at me.

"I know," I said.

"I'm not sure we want to keep this arrangement going," he whined. "I mean if someone came looking for you once . . ."

"You didn't have to tell him you knew where or when he could find me."

"I didn't," he said, but his eyes were shifty, and I didn't believe him.

"If you increased the fee just a little—"

I cut him off. "Nope, actually; I need a different location anyhow. Thanks, though, for everything. I just stopped in because I left something here the other day."

He shrugged and gave up that easily. Joe must've flashed his badge.

"Hey," he said into the headset, "get off the phone with that wanker."

He crossed the room to some fat guy in a "Hot & Spicy Beef Jerky" tee shirt and smacked him upside the head. "Guy sounded like a lawyer or something, moron."

This was the perfect opportunity for me to rummage through the wastebasket until I found the article on Ricky.

After sticking my hand in a public trash bin, the greasy burger wrappers and cigarette ashes here were nothing. Still, I made a stop in the bathroom and washed my hands.

Even as I scrubbed off the muck I persisted in sticking my hands in, I allowed myself a satisfied look in the mirror. I looked good in that dress; my hair was windblown but still perky. Louie was right in calling the cut "insouciant."

I ran my fingers through my hair and put on some fresh lipstick. I stretched my lips into a welcoming smile. Voilà. A little loving agreed with me.

Then I pouted. It was probably the last I'd get for another six months. And if I ever, even in six *years*, found somebody I clicked with like I did with Joe, I would be very, very surprised.

I folded the paper under my arm and went back to the bus stop; while I waited for the bus, rather than pouting, I read.

After Ricky returned from a long, somnolent stay in Madrid, he hung around the New York loft scene, developing a taste for heroin, cocaine, and quaaludes.

"Stay high and fly like a bug," was apparently his favorite saying. Very catchy.

His first scheme was selling illegal drugs over the Internet back when that was a new idea, but he apparently never really had the drugs, and he was arrested, convicted, and incarcerated for interstate fraud. Somehow, it got pled down to a sentence of six months, and though he only served three, he was beaten up and otherwise abused in the penal system. At least, he filed a lawsuit against the state of New York for having subjected him to said abuse.

He lost. This experience, Ricky said, made him "hip to the way the world is now days. Play or be played. That's what they should put on the money now, not that hokey 'In God We Trust.' "

Ricky evidently considered himself a player.

"I'm too pretty for prison," he said, waving to the lone fashion magazine photographer who turned up to greet his matriculation from the college of iron bars. The photographer was, of course, Nelson, the one who had left the McDonald's bags in Ricky's guest room.

An attempt was made to sell Ricky as looking tough and world-wise in black leather and handcuffs, but the look had changed—the dim pretty boy variety was out, and a sort of intellectual, burning-eyed intensity was in for male models, at least those over sixteen. Ricky was now definitely over sixteen.

Although Ricky still imagined he could make a comeback, nobody else agreed with him, not even his mother.

"My son always imagined himself more than he was," she commented. "And now he also imagines himself thinner."

He apparently did not imagine himself by her bedside when she passed away. Still, he wore black for a year, and according to various acquaintances, "gazed at his old magazine covers and teared up, talking about how proud his mother was of him in those days," even as he was "fleecing you for every penny."

His new scam was running a modeling agency, whose chief contribution to the careers of its clients was photographing them, charging them a lot of money for the photographs. Sometimes, it would sell certain types of photographs through Ricky's Internet connections.

The girls who formerly had been flocking around him gradually disappeared, whether due to the weeping or the fleecing or the photographing, I wasn't sure. He began to drink heavily, and he really put on the pounds.

"You can't take apples and oranges, compare them, and make them into lemonade," he said after a stint drying out at Betty Ford.

He liked his mixed metaphors, Ricky did. He also liked illicit substances.

Ricky landed back in jail on a charge of forging medical prescriptions. This was before the general Hollywood population began routinely getting stoned on Vicodin from Mexico, and it seemed rather forward thinking of Ricky. He did a year this time, and he came out thinner and well-muscled from daily workouts in the gym.

"You gotta stretch the body, and then the mind follows," he said in an article about prison inmates in a local paper. "I volunteered to be quoted here so all my fans could see I've grown from my experiences. It's not always the positive things that make you wise."

He became wise enough to seek out a protective close personal relationship while he was locked up.

"He was all right. A little pudgy, but he looked okay," this fellow remarked from within the confines of his life sentence. "I always knew I could do better though."

To downplay this and his other prison relationships, immediately upon Ricky's release, he picked up a woman named Laura, who was ten years his senior. She had been married a couple of times previously, and she was the only heir to her wealthy father's family business.

Yes, the Laura whose mind I'd been attempting to climb inside. At least going by the photo in the paper, she had bug eyes and thin, stringy black hair to go with her short skirts. Her father, Carl Ordam, owned a chain of very profitable funeral homes in the greater Southland.

Laura's mother, Rosalyn, had wanted no part of the business, which she considered macabre, insinuating that her husband had brought the spirits of the unrestful dead into their home.

Divorced, she nonetheless encouraged her daughter's marriage, the third for Laura.

"Your father's never given you a big wedding before. Make it splashy. Hold it at the country club," she had reportedly counseled.

Splashy it was. There were the obligatory swans shaped out of ice and butter, flowing fountains of champagne, a designer original in cream satin wrapped around Laura's skinny frame.

Ricky contacted old friends. Old friends contacted the media. People who had never heard of Ricky nonetheless pretended to have heard of him long enough to drink champagne and eat lobster.

A swarm of fashionistas turned up, including Nelson with his camera. There was a spread, of sorts, in several fashion rags that showed aging, hideously skinny women in satin slit up to their spine and men whose faces were too frozen with botox to smile. Some young turks came to pose and posture, and Ricky acted like they'd come to pose and posture just for him. He slung his arms around the shoulders of the most prominent, and he kissed the cheeks of the youngest, men and women alike.

"I'm still in the body business," he proclaimed. "Gonna use my connections."

There was that phrase Joe seemed so interested in me saying, the body business.

Slurringly drunk before the end of the reception, Ricky reportedly confided to Laura's frowning daddy, "You know how it is, your business isn't so much different than mine. Make the bodies look pretty."

Ricky pushed a slice of wedding cake into Laura's face just a day shy of his thirtieth birthday. They stayed married for seven years, distinguishing themselves by running Ricky's so-called modeling agency and a nursing registry started by Laura out of one address. Their contract employees sometimes worked as nurses and then paid Ricky to get them work as models. Mostly, they worked as nurses.

The nursing agency did an inordinate amount of business and brought in so much money that a rumor floated through the neighborhood that the nurses serviced their patients in a kind of informal prostitution outcall service for the desperately ill.

"It's always important to keep a smile on a guy's face," was Ricky's only comment, and he was apparently grinning all the way to the bank.

And when the desperately ill did depart, chances were apparently excellent that their earthly remains would be disposed of by Laura's father. Apparently, Mr. Ordam and Mr. Littlejohn were now golf buddies.

Laura was reportedly pleased by the newfound harmony between her father and Ricky. She adored Ricky and even wrote him little love poems, paying for their publication in the classified section of the *LA Times* and the same alternative paper in the pages of which their lives were now being chronicled.

He returned her love by cheating on her, mostly with overweight, middle-aged nurses who were even more impressed than Laura by his old magazine covers and the occasional sweet young thing whose brains were addled by drink or drugs.

Although Laura and Ricky began to fight, sometimes engaging in public battles that escalated to throwing forks at one another in restaurants, they did well enough at their businesses.

Despite a propensity for bouncing checks like

rubber balls due to Ricky's refusal either to balance a checkbook or to stop buying expensive things like burnt sienna Hummers and a twenty-four hour rolfing session, they managed to buy the house in Malibu with cash.

Their house was the scene of jovial neighborhood parties at which too much liquor often flowed. Ricky's weight ballooned again and kept on ballooning.

It was probably not because of his weight that Laura left him, sued him for support, won in court, found the bank accounts emptied, and put a lien on the house, but never got her money.

No one could guess her reasons, and she wasn't talking. In spite of the divorce and what had to be acrimonious days in court, she continued to see Ricky, often spending extended periods of time at the Malibu house in the so-called guest wing.

She supposedly told her mother that "Ricky just does it for me the way no other man can," which was pretty pitiful, especially as his weight tipped the scale at over three hundred pounds; possibly she was after that prettier and less pitifully large fourteen million that Joe had told me about.

There was also speculation that Laura was interested in Nelson, the photographer who was also a drug dealer; that even though cocaine was no longer the must have party accessory it had been in the late '80s, Laura clung to it and thus to Nelson as a purveyor of the stuff. Since Nelson seemed to more or less live at the beach house, maybe Nelson and his stash were the reason she elected to live there too.

The article then speculated that Ricky put up with them both hanging around because he needed Laura and Nelson to validate the fact that once upon a time, they had both coveted him, even if now they were coveting each other.

Neither the nursing business nor the modeling agency continued to operate after the divorce, yet Ricky seemed to have plenty to party on.

Still, it was a lot harder for Ricky to meet people who coveted him toward the end, except the occasional failed hanger-on from Ricky's modeling days.

And a musician named Dennis Lane. The musician was someone new. Ricky met him while Dennis was performing at a seaside bar only a few months before Ricky met his bitter end.

Dennis Lane drove Ricky home when Ricky was too drunk or otherwise messed up to drive himself, and he presented himself as a convenient and favorable witness when Ricky was accused of harassing, manhandling, and stealing from certain female guests at this establishment.

For the favor he did Ricky, the musician lost his gig, but he did find himself installed at Ricky's place where because there was still booze and drugs, if no more major parties, pretty young models still occasionally found themselves sunning on Ricky's deck, and because Ricky reportedly now had various problems past the filthy talk stage of any sexual encounter, the musician found himself in receipt of much mutual pleasure. At least that was the reason posited in the article for him sticking around.

There was no mention of the possibility that Dennis the musician was an undercover cop, and that this was the reason he was sticking around.

The reporter seemed to believe that Ricky had passed out in the hot tub and died of a drug overdose, the culmination of a wasted life, the ultimate outcome of foolish misbehavior and the decadent eighties and capitalism, a perfect example of what happens when someone who lived entirely for the flesh made what small brain he had into Swiss cheese and his flesh into excessive corpulence.

Still, authorities said they were investigating all possibilities and that they had not ruled out homicide at the time the article went to press.

I crumpled up the paper, disappointed. I guess I was hoping that learning more about Ricky would help me learn more about Joe. For example, why was he so driven to uncover the circumstances of Ricky's death? And of course, most importantly, would he ever call?

It took two hours to ride the bus down Santa Monica Boulevard, a ride enlivened by a smelly old man talking about Satan and the significance of the bus route, which was 666.

A quarrelsome Russian family lugged a Christmas tree down the aisle to the back of the bus, its needles already turning to New Year's confetti from our heat wave and besprinkling my hair.

A large-breasted woman in a shorty Santa dress necked with a guy wearing elf feet. Some guy chatted on his cell phone about how his personal assistant hadn't liked his holiday bonus and had stolen his car and now he was riding a bus filled with nothing but losers.

I passionately regretted not calling Louie and asking for a ride, but I wasn't quite sure I was up to a lecture about my indiscriminate romantic adventure. Or maybe I just needed a while to detox from the illusion that romance was in the air.

At last the bus disgorged me, leaving its fumes rather than romance in my immediate oxygen.

Although he got off at the same stop, the old man didn't follow me with his rant about Satan; he disappeared instead into a tanning salon advertising "Only eight tanning days 'til Xmas."

As I rounded the corner toward home, I ran into Mrs. Marinak walking her poodle. She eyed me suspiciously.

"Why you not take your car?" she asked me.

"Can't a girl get some exercise?"

"You hiding your car from repo man?"

"No," I said indignantly. The car was ten years old; even I'd repaid *that* loan.

"You pay me this month's rent, that's good; you caught up on last month, that's good, but don't you be late in the New Year. That would be bad."

I reached in my purse, pulled out the envelope Joe had given me, and thrust it in her hands.

"Here, Merry Christmas; now I'm early," I said. "I was thinking of making you some cookies or a gingerbread house, but cash is probably better. The gift that's always in season. The one thing that never lies. Truer than love."

I left her looking after me with her mouth hanging open and her poodle lunging on his leash, I left her before the tears sprung to my eyes.

Chapter Six

I swiped at my face with the back of my hands. I then scraped the dates from the date palms off my shoes, and I was unlocking my apartment door when someone came up behind me and put his hands over my now dry eyes.

Panic wedged itself in my throat even as I struck out with my elbows and lifted my leg in a cross between the actions of a donkey in a bad mood and a Rockette.

"Ow-w, oh my, geez, knock it off," Louie said, dropping his hands and taking a step back, way back.

"You shouldn't surprise me like that."

"It was nothing like the surprise you gave me when you called saying you were spending the weekend with the police."

"Not the whole weekend and not the entire LAPD either."

"Although that could be fun," Louie said thoughtfully. He squinted at me. "I expected at least a phone call begging a ride." His squint deepened into a frown. "I've been home all day waiting for your call. And writing. And waiting for your call to rescue me from the writing."

"It's not going well?"

"It's going too well. I'd sworn off. I was clean! It's worse than being a needle freak. And it's all your fault I'm hooked again."

"My fault?"

"Without you to hang out with I went over to The Cat and Fiddle, and along with all the hard rockers who talk like Beavis and Butthead, there was this producer I met a while back. She remembered me, remembered my work, and told me she's looking for a picture for next Christmas, something fun, maybe a talking Christmas tree."

"A talking—?" I began, but Louie waved his hand at me and rattled on; clearly, he'd been holding all this in for the entire time I'd been letting it all out with Joe.

"She's looking for the project like immediately, already has a pitch set up at Fox Searchlight! So here I am, ready and raring to go, fill a need, all that. But it's a tough concept. I mean the tree's gonna die, right, so inherently, it's not a cheerful picture. Unless, I guess, it could be one of those potted trees? But anyway, you have to be careful, or it comes out *Wizard of Oz*, haunted forest, kind of creepy—'Don't hang the tinsel there, little girl, or you'll be sorry,'—you know what I mean?"

"Is it the same producer who wanted to do a movie about a talking pet weasel because there were too many talking dog movies?"

"Yes," Louie said defensively.

"I like your noir stuff better."

"It doesn't sell."

"Neither do pet weasels and talking Christmas trees."

"I told you—she already has the pitch meeting set! I confirmed it with the assistant this morning. All I have to do is write the script."

"That doesn't sound a little backward—meeting set, no script?"

"She had another writer in mind, but they had a falling out."

"Ah."

"His bad luck, my good if I can pull this off!"

"Maybe you could have a talking weasel living in a Christmas tree. The kid could be blind, and she could think the actual Christmas tree is talking."

"You're sick."

"Only tired. I took the bus."

Louie made little concerned clicking sounds with his tongue. "Come on upstairs. I have microwaveable French toast, Budget Gourmet mac and cheese . . ."

I knew I'd never hear the end of it if I didn't go, so I followed him upstairs to his place; flopped down on the faux cowhide sofa; plumped, if you can plump, lariat rope pillows; and kept my mouth shut.

"Breakfast or lunch?" Louie opened the freezer and waved frozen food packages at me.

"It's almost dinnertime," I pointed out.

"Don't be annoying," Louie said. "I lose all track of time when I'm writing about Christmas trees. That weasel idea isn't bad, by the way. I mean I already have weasel material to draw from."

"Breakfast," I said, "I want breakfast. Assuming you have maple syrup."

Louie waved a cow-shaped china pitcher at me. "I don't have just syrup, darling, I have kitschy syrup."

He shook the French toast out of its plastic packaging and onto a paper plate.

"Nothing says loving like something from the microwave oven," he said, tossing the paper plate into the oven and setting the timer. He dropped down next to me.

"You put up your tree," I said, gesturing toward a fake, white-flocked number studded with knitted, plastic, glass and cardboard cows, horses, six shooters, and spurs.

Some of them I'd helped him purchase at a toy store for adults on Melrose; some he'd found at garage sales and the Rose Bowl Swap Meet. On the top of the tree, there was a Ken doll dressed in cowboy regalia with silver wings pasted to his vest and a yellow pipe cleaner halo. Louie had made that himself.

"I thought the tree might inspire me," Louie said. "I actually asked it some questions like, 'where were you manufactured' and 'do you ever wish you were a real tree,' but it didn't say a damn word."

"I'm glad."

Louie walked over to his desk and typed. "Weasel lives in tree and talks. Kid is blind." He saved the Final Draft file he was working on and shut off his monitor.

I couldn't take my eyes off cowboy Ken. He sort of reminded me of Joe, the broad shoulders, boots, and all. I sighed. I was almost as nuts as Louie.

For a moment, there was only the hum of the microwave.

"Well?" said Louie, having turned away from his laptop; he was waiting for me to explain that sigh.

"Well?" I smiled, tearing my eyes away from Ken.

"Did you survive?" Louie asked me as if I'd just returned from a trek across the Sahara.

"Yes, obviously."

"You had a good time," he said accusingly.

"Also obviously. Why would I have spent the night with him if I wasn't having a good time?"

"He could've arrested you. Kidnapped you. Drugged you."

"I have no such excuse."

"You don't want to talk about him."

"I liked him; I'm not so stupid as to believe that I can have him long term; and it's making me petulant, okay? Isn't there anything else you want to talk about?"

The microwave dinged.

"Nope, but you just got saved by that proverbial bell."

He waved me over to the kitchen table and set out napkins and plastic cutlery. Louie liked meals to be not only consumable within minutes but also history within seconds. It was probably some kind of a reaction to all the fancy silver chafing dishes, china, and good cutlery he had to deal with at the catering company.

"So tell me about this case your detective needed help with," he said, whipping the paper plates of French toast onto the table and drowning his in syrup.

I ignored the little barb 'your detective' and launched into an encapsulated summary of Malibu; murder; Ricky Littlejohn, former model; and the information I had been able to present because I had read a newspaper the other day.

"Very clever," Louie said. "I should read more myself. Maybe I could get laid too."

I smiled, but I didn't laugh.

"There's something wrong with you," Louie accused. "Oh, my God, you're not going to sulk for days, are you? Oh, my God, you're not thinking of seeing him again, are you?"

"Of course not," I swore and passed my hand across my chest. But, of course I was.

Maybe a lunch that became a little regular noon-time thing? If he had only my fake phone number and my fake address and we didn't get too attached, what was the harm?

Too attached. This was already way too attached.

I stood up fast, making the cow pitcher jump.

"I told you I was tired, that's all."

I headed for the door but stopped at the tree and fingered one of Louie's crocheted horses, the saddle of which bore the name "Texas Red."

"He's from Texas," I said.

"Well, ostensibly. I mean, that's what it says. But I think honestly, he should be named Filipino Red because the tag said made in the—"

I cut him off. "I meant Joe. He's from Texas. Who knows, maybe you'd like him."

"Yeah, right," Louie rolled his eyes. "Now, not only did you date a cop, screw a cop, try to help a . . . a cop, but you also want him to meet me, and we can all go to Movie Theme Songs night at the Hollywood Bowl and pal around or something. Maybe he can write a testimonial to your psychic powers on the Internet. Or maybe he'll give us a squad car escort every time we work over a party."

"I had a good time, that's all. A one time, good time. Over and done with."

And I started to cry. I could blame it on too little sleep, too much tequila, and riding a bus in Los Angeles at Christmas time. I could blame it on Louie, for reminding me of who I was, I could blame it on the relentless sunshine streaming in the windows, reminding me all too clearly that perfect weather, even in December, was absolutely no guarantee, no guarantee at all, of a perfect life.

No matter what I blamed it on, I was really crying because here was a guy who was nice, who was sexy, who was real, and I had made myself the sort of life I could never share with him or, really, anyone else, for that matter. At least no one else who wasn't by profession, and probably by nature, to some extent at least, a liar and a thief. Who else could I possibly hope to meet, much less attract? And I had to face it, the odds of me finding happiness in such a relationship were slim to none, no matter how good I still looked in spandex.

"I guess I'm glad you had a good time," Louie said doubtfully. He pulled me against himself in an awkward hug.

I held on and cried myself out. I was fast about it; I knew Louie wanted to get back to his laptop and his talking Christmas tree. I also realized that despite my maudlin feelings about the dearth of possible positive relationships, me leaving my devious paths for the straight life was as unlikely as me finally landing an Academy Award.

So get a grip, I told myself, accept who you are,

and use it. Con your way into a good relationship with somebody just as cute as Joe but not a cop, and maybe rich too. There had to be someone out there like that.

I extricated myself from the hug. I had my hand on the doorknob now, but Louie took my arm and stopped me.

"If I hear any more sobbing or anything even resembling suicidal screams, I'll come down and haul you off to the triple bill at the Vista. All three *Terminator* movies, and if you come in a leather jacket and a Santa hat, they give you a free refill on any size popcorn."

"I'll try to keep it quiet," I said. I kissed his cheek. "I'm okay now, really. I'm looking at reality and trying to figure out how to turn it into my next and biggest score. I've hardened my heart, toughened my mind, closed all the windows and locked all the doors."

I knew Louie was watching me as I walked downstairs. I knew he'd be after me in a flash with a sympathetic hug and a new hairstyle if he had even a clue that as soon as I was safely inside my place, I was just just going to fall down on the sofa and have a much longer cry. But I'd bury my face in a pillow, and he'd never know.

And when I was done with the weeping, I really would shut this scam down. Falling in like with someone this fast—it had to be a scam, and worst of all, it had to be one of my own making. And I knew better than that. I knew better.

I opened my door and got ready to fling myself down, but the phone rang.

At first, I wasn't sure which phone. It wasn't the

cell phone turned to vibrate in the purse still hanging on my shoulder. It wasn't the land line. It wasn't the cell phone my marks sometimes used, as that phone was lying on the coffee table. It was kind of muffled. Coming from a drawer. The extra phone. The phone number I never gave out, the one I had a hard time even remembering.

It had to be Joe. Or a wrong number.

I ran into the kitchen, skidding on the linoleum like I was in junior high and this was the first boy I had kissed. Well, it was the first boy I'd kissed in a while anyway. Or a wrong number.

I picked it up. It stopped ringing. I waited, but no message blinked on the screen. I clicked on 'missed calls,' but it said 'no new numbers.' The call must have been an unlisted call, a blocked call, a private line—a wrong number. Or Joe. I cursed, a long, low, rumbling stream of invective. I could call him myself if I hadn't thrown out his phone number.

And then the phone rang again.

Since the phone was in my hand, the face plate glowing blue, I picked it up on the first ring, and it was Joe, and he was surprised.

"I just called," he said.

"I know. I couldn't get to it in time."

"Where were you?"

"At a friend's," I said.

"A close friend?"

"Close but platonic."

"Platonic's good."

"Is it?"

"It's great. I mean, we could be platonic if we wanted."

"We could, huh?"

"Whatever works. I just want to see you again. I mean, if you want to see me."

"Why wouldn't I want to see you?"

"I don't know. I don't know that much about you. You could be married."

"I guess my husband would be wondering what I'd been doing with you in Oxnard then."

"Would he be jealous?"

"If he was any kind of a husband."

We let it drop.

"You didn't leave a message," I said.

"No. I wasn't even sure if I should call. I wasn't going to call. So I hung up, and then I called back. I just wanted to hear your voice. See what you were doing. Make sure you're okay."

"Why wouldn't I be okay?"

"Because I'm not with you."

A silence fell between us, a kind of tingly, excited silence on my end because I had to admit I very much wanted him to be with me.

I cleared my throat. "Why weren't you sure you should call?"

"It did occur to me that I have no business bringing you into—" he hesitated as if searching for the right words, "—into my life the way it is right now. But I guess I've already done it."

He had indeed already done it, whatever it was.

I wanted to see him. I'd only been away from him a few hours, and I wanted to see him that badly.

"You have no business, you said. Well, can't this just be fun instead of business? We keep things light?" I said.

"You mean I don't drag you around to look at

murder scenes; you won't tell me about the dead people you've spoken to recently. We just tell knock, knock jokes or something?"

"I like knock, knock jokes. And yeah, I promise I'll make absolutely no mention of any conversations with the dead. It'll be as if such conversations never really occurred."

"I'm not sure we can keep things that light," he said.

We were both silent for a moment. Maybe we were both trying to think of knock, knock jokes.

"You want to see a movie?" he said after a while.

"I don't know."

Maybe we were both silent because we were rethinking our positions on whether keeping it light or not, this was really a good idea, us seeing each other again.

"You want to have an early dinner?"

"I just ate."

"A drink?"

"I'm still recovering from the tequila we had last night."

"You want to see me?"

"Do you want to see *me*?"

"Yeah," we both said.

My heart was hammering in my chest now, and I didn't care, I didn't care; he had called me.

"Should I pick you up at your place?"

Damn. "My" place was thirty minutes away by car, not to mention two hours by bus if I was still trying to keep him from seeing my license plate.

"Are you close by?" I hedged.

"Pretty close, yeah."

"I'm not though, actually. I mean, I was just at my friend's, like I said. This is my cell," I said.

"Oh. So you're not at home." He sounded almost relieved.

"I could come to your place . . ." I suggested.

"My apartment's being fumigated for termites. I was going to crash at the office tonight."

"You sure its termites you're concerned about? Not a wife you've got hidden away?"

He laughed. "If I was married, wouldn't my wife be wondering what I was doing in Oxnard?"

"Maybe she's not the curious type. Maybe she's fooling around herself. Maybe she thinks you're just on police business," I suggested.

"Wouldn't you 'know?' Wouldn't your psychic radar go up if I wasn't telling you the whole truth and nothing but the truth?"

"Nope," I said. "I'm blind to my own relationships. I'd probably think a talking weasel living in a Christmas tree was the Christmas tree itself talking to me."

"You should really explain that one."

"It'd take too long. We'd miss the movie," I said.

"So we are going to a movie. Which one?"

"Ones plural. There's a *Terminator* marathon at the Vista in Los Feliz."

"Los Feliz? That's where you are?"

I was a little annoyed about him trying to pin down my location.

"Close enough when they're offering free popcorn if you wear leather and a Santa hat."

"I'll have to buy," he said.

"Maybe *I'll* wear leather and a Santa hat."

"Maybe that's *all* you should wear."

Before we could get too excited, we picked a time and agreed to meet in the theater lobby.

I took a fast shower and tried on seven different things before I found something I liked. Too much of my wardrobe was a costume, the spandex for the parties, the baggy shirt and tee shirts for the 'tourist at the studio lot' disguise, the neat suits for showing up in a production office and looking like I belonged there, and the gauze and silk scarves of my psychic shtick. Other than that, it was mostly jeans and tank tops. He'd already seen my best sundress. I didn't have a Santa hat, and I'd pawned my leather jacket during this last long dry spell.

If I hadn't given Mrs. Marniak an advance on the rent, I could've redeemed it, but it was out of style anyway—it had shoulder pads. There were a lot of things I had in my closet that were out of style, and I just hadn't noticed or hadn't cared.

Now, with minutes to go, I was noticing and caring. At least my hair looked good, thanks to Louie.

I ended up with a white tank top, a black loose weave see-through sweater, a jeans skirt, and thigh high socks with little palm trees on them. It wasn't very psychic attire, every component predated the whole psychic gig entirely. It was simply an outfit I liked and still looked good in. Besides, I liked the idea of Joe peeling those thigh highs off my legs.

I left my car in its parking space and hightailed it up to Sunset, and for the second time that day, I took a bus. If I was going to keep seeing Joe, something had to give here; I wasn't really keen on busses, but I was even less keen on asking Louie to give me a lift to another assignation.

The bus was slow, and Joe was already waiting when I got to the theater. He was scanning the crowd, his eyes creased at the corners with the effort of looking for me.

He grabbed my arm and pulled me against him when he did see me.

"Wow," he said of my attire. "You are a sight."

He looked pretty good himself, dressed in a tight fitting blue tee shirt, jeans, and a denim jacket, and I think we both enjoyed simply admiring each other right up until our Governator says "I'll be back," in *T-1*, at which point we started making out. If Arnold did come back, we didn't see him.

Chapter Seven

"This is probably all sex," I said to him.

"Just because we're in another crummy motel?"

"That's one sign, yeah."

This motel was much, much crummier than the anonymous roadside chain ambiance of our tryst in Oxnard. The Sunset House Budget Motel was a rundown, two-story building with absolutely nothing to recommend it but its proximity to the movie theater. It had a half burnt-out neon sign reading like the ultimate enclave of ethnic diversity, *Sun Ho Bud,* and a clerk who not only appeared to speak no English but who also appeared to speak no language at all. The check-in was accomplished in grunts and gestures. He had a nose ring and three studs in his lower lip, which looked painful.

The room featured a dusty, chipped dresser and cigarette-burned orange carpet that was bald in places, kind of like my first agent's hair. The bedspread was a cautionary plaid. It was the kind of place they put a picture of in the dictionary next to the word "seedy." Being in a place like Sunset

House was weird in and of itself; weirder still, it was less than five minutes from the apartment I didn't want Joe knowing I really lived in.

Everything about this evening could be broken into degrees of weirdness. Regardless of what *sort* of place we were in when lying in bed, it was incredibly weird to be in bed with a guy and to not want him to know my address.

It felt even weirder to be trying to convince myself that I was in bed with a guy five minutes from my apartment and that it was all about, only could be about, sex. And that this would be a good thing.

Because it would be way beyond weird if it wasn't just bed that I was in with this guy, but love. Could that kind of thing really happen? Falling in love, not just lust, and falling in love fast? Could it happen to me? To someone as cynical as I?

Even as I was trying to convince myself that this was impossible, to scoff at myself, to make this into mere animal attraction, I had this very, very, very ultimately weird feeling that Joe was my model man or something, the guy I'd been waiting for all my life. Not that I was the type of girl to sit around waiting for anyone or anything. I wasn't that type at all.

"Lumpy mattress aside, this is a lot more than sex," Joe said.

My heart was beating far too fast, and I couldn't look at him just then. Instead, I looked around me—at the mattress, which was indeed looking, and feeling, mighty lumpy; at the snowy cable TV; and at a thick stack of yellowing discount flyers on the night table for the Hollywood Wax Museum, where most of the figures look like they melted in the last heat wave. Louie and I go in there sometimes for laughs and to pick up any tourists who needed psychic readings, cheap booze, or a reason to be parted from their vacation funds.

There was a sucker born every minute, right? A dreamer just waiting to have his or her heart broken, or at least his or her wallet lightened.

If Joe was in this with me for my money, he would be sadly disappointed. If he was in it to break my heart, he had another thing coming. Not only was I not the type of girl who waited around for some Prince Charming, but I was also not the type of girl to get her heart broken. I was a lot hipper and tougher and harder than that. Prince Charming could stick his glass slipper where the sun didn't shine. My pulse rate slowed. I was cool now; I was in control again.

"So," I said, keeping my voice light, "if it's not sex with us, what is it then?"

"We understand each other," he said.

My heart rate shot right back up again. That was it; that was true. He'd called it right. In some indefinable, crazy way, we understood each other, and not just physically either.

We had this . . . affinity. It was more like I was a real psychic, and I just knew. I knew I was going to have this electric crackling feeling down to my toes when we touched. I knew we were going to get all sappy and talk about our old hometowns.

Was it really possible to find someone you were connected to like that, a soul mate more or less? It wasn't something I believed in exactly, but then what had I believed in, other than my own cleverness, for a number of years now?

All my hardness and smartness and in controlness just vanished, pouf, like someone had waved a magic wand.

The guy who always dressed up as Glenda, the

good witch, and sold candy-flavored condoms at the West Hollywood Halloween parade had, in fact, waved his wand over me this past All Hallows Eve.

Still. "How can we understand each other? We haven't really done much talking," I pointed out.

When you came right down to it, the only subject Joe had extrapolated about at any length was Ricky Littlejohn.

"Does it have to be about words?" Joe objected. "You of all people should know that the important things go deeper than that."

Yeah, me of all people, the phony psychic. A small, impatient sigh escaped my lips. "A little less talk and a lot more action," I said, quoting a country song. "That seems to be our way of operating."

"Things I haven't told you, I know I *could* tell you. And you'd get what I was saying. You'd understand my reasons. At least, I sure hope you would. I'm kind of counting on that."

He was counting on me. I was getting all melty again. He seemed so sincere about it. But, after all, why would he be lying to get me to go to bed with him?

"Yeah. I probably would understand," I nodded. "I guess there's things I haven't said that I'd want you to accept and not get all bent out of shape about either."

Not that I was ready to rush into true confessions just yet.

He smiled. "I'm already bent out of shape. But in a good way, all twisted up inside. Common wisdom is that you get what you really want when you don't expect it. I certainly wasn't expecting you. I wasn't expecting you at all. I sure wasn't expecting to fall for you. And wham."

"I like you too," I admitted, which sounded kind of tepid, after his 'wham.'

"I probably like you far too much," I blundered on.

"Why too much?" he was rubbing my shoulders, and it felt so nice. Maybe it felt too nice.

"Why me?" I asked, "I mean really. What is it about me that you like, besides the sex and this understanding stuff?"

"How alive you are."

And truly, right then, I felt very much alive, tingly and warm and glad to be with him. Wasn't it all the better if it wasn't about talk and words?

"I'm tired of dealing with death. I just want to live again. Before—" He cut himself off, and his hands slipped off my shoulders.

"Before what?"

"Before it's too late."

Then he laughed, like he'd made a joke, but he hadn't.

"It's not just the Texas accent. You sure don't sound like a cop."

"How should a cop sound then?"

"Ma'am, you just ran that stop sign back there, are you aware of that?"

"Has that been your only experience with the police?"

Now it was my turn to put a lid on it. "Conversationally, yes."

But as Joe had so recently pointed out, a relationship didn't have to be based entirely on words. My relationship with the police was mostly based on wanting to avoid them.

When you came right down to it, it wasn't only cops I wanted to avoid. It was also the IRS; various credit card companies I'd borrowed from under names that were not quite my own; private security; security cameras; receptionists who demanded my business; bouncers who didn't think I looked like the name on the invitation or guest list; dissatisfied relatives of the deceased; or spouses, children, or siblings of the dissatisfied relatives of the deceased to whom I purported to commune; casting directors who didn't like my attitude; directors who wanted to show me the door; directors who wanted to show me their art collections; ex-boyfriends who'd married; anyone who had ever attended Improv class with me at Stella Adler and who knew anything about me; distant cousins; and anyone I'd ever known who could rat me out to the cops.

"The police make you uneasy," Joe said.

"No. Why would the police make me uneasy?"

"The whole idea of 'the law' makes a lot of people uncomfortable. Makes you feel like Big Brother is watching you. Like you have to be perfect. I used to feel that way myself. Listen, everybody jaywalks sometimes."

"Even you?"

"Especially me. I don't play by the rules any more than you do. Cops don't play by the rules all the time. Maybe they play less. They make their own rules because who's going to call *them* on it? And then sometimes, they even forget where the boundary lies between making some new rules and breaking the old ones."

"Have you forgotten?"

"Sometimes, I'm not sure I ever knew in the first place."

His face changed and hardened, and he fell stonily silent.

I'm not sure why, but I felt cold. The warm and tingly feeling left me, and cold and shivery came in, just as if the morning's coastal fog had returned and was writhing around me.

Maybe he thought we didn't need words, and maybe I didn't really want a lot of words either, but the lack of them at that moment gave me pause.

"I should go," I said at last.

"I don't want you to go home tonight," he said, and the hardness was still in his voice, but he covered it quickly, almost quickly enough that I didn't notice, or at least quickly enough that I could push it aside.

"We're going wrong here. And it's because we're not keeping things light. We agreed we'd keep things light," he stroked my arm.

The hardness fell off his face, and he looked perfect again, perfectly handsome, and sweet, and kind.

"Did we say that?"

He was kissing me now, keeping the kisses light too.

"You don't have to worry about anything," he swore. "I'm watching out for you."

Little butterfly kisses were landing on my nose, my ear, my cheek. "Let's get out of this place. It's a dump. It's bringing us down. It was just the first motel we came to that didn't have a wino sleeping in the doorway."

"That's because he has a room."

"Here we are, sitting inside these four grubby, thin walls and missing the star show," he said.

"The star show?"

"The stars are falling from the sky tonight," he said thoughtfully.

"There's some kind of celebrity skydiving event or what?" Perhaps Johnny Grant, the ever verbose, gnomelike little mayor of Hollywood, would be conducting interviews from Hollywood Boulevard when they landed.

Joe laughed. "The celestial kind of stars. The Leonid Meteor shower. Earth's closest view for twenty years is tonight. It was on CNN this morning. If we were in Texas, we could drive out on a dirt road to where the road ended and climb up on the roof of my car and just watch. Here though, with all the light pollution and the smog . . ."

He pulled me out of bed. "We have to get out of town for a while."

"Get out of town? We just got back from out of town."

"You consider Oxnard out of town?"

"I can't just leave," I balked.

"Sure you can," he said.

"No. And you can't either. Don't you have work or something? Responsibilities? Protect and serve? The Ricky Littlejohn case to solve?"

He looked defeated somehow, hemmed in. If I'd kept my mouth shut, who knew—maybe he'd have taken me some place really nice, even nicer than Oxnard.

Oxnard itself had been pretty damn nice. Even this rotten motel room had felt pretty nice for a while.

I wasn't sure why I said no. Too much too soon maybe. Maybe that cold hardness I'd seen on his face, even if I didn't want to admit I'd seen it.

"I kind of wish you weren't always acting psychic," he said, like I'd looked into him and seen even more than that look on his face.

But honestly, it wasn't something that I'd seen in him. It was what I saw in me that made me turn him down, my own limitations, my own fears. Still, I wasn't going to let him off that easily.

"I kind of wish you weren't a cop," I returned.

I expected him to ask me what I meant by that, but just as I hadn't asked what he meant when he said he wished I wasn't psychic, he didn't question me either.

I could've passed off our mutual silences as more of that understanding each other without words, except at least on my part, I didn't understand anything all of a sudden.

Since I was up anyway, I started putting on my clothes. I was plucking up one of those thigh high socks when he reached for my hand. I dropped the sock and let him take my hand.

We stood for a while like that. We were big on holding hands. It was really very old fashioned of us, even if the hand-holding led to other, more contemporary acts of expressing our interest in one another.

It felt safe and right holding his hand. But I had to let go this time, and not just to put on my socks. I had to get out of the motel room, and then things would be clearer to me, about me and him and how we felt about each other.

Yet I didn't really want to leave him. I didn't want to let go.

I had to let go. It was either that or move in with him, into this seedy motel. Or tell him I'd changed my mind, that he was right and we should just go away somewhere, go far away, never look back, and start over.

These were very dangerous thoughts for somebody like me. Very out-of-control thoughts to be having about a cop I'd met less than forty-eight hours ago.

No, I was getting out. I was getting out now.

I dropped his hand and picked up my socks and my jacket.

"We don't have to be anything but ourselves right now. We don't have to be anything at all," he said as I was walking toward the door. "Don't leave," he added as I opened it.

There was an urgency in his voice that made me turn back.

"Just don't," he said.

"We've spent way too much time together way too fast. We're not talking not because we understand each other so well, as nice as that idea is, but because every time we try to say one word, except about that stupid case of yours, we just start kissing. I need air. You need air. Go watch your stars. I'll settle for the ones pinned down on Hollywood Boulevard."

"They've got chewing gum and spit on them."

"I can't do this," I said.

"Do what?" he asked.

"Us."

"Give me one reason why you can't."

"I'm scared," I said simply.

And he walked over to me, and he didn't close the door; he led me outside. Only when we were outside did he put his arms around me.

"You don't have to be," he said.

And I more or less momentarily believed him.

We stood holding each other, staring down at the chlorine blue of the motel swimming pool, lit up for the night so that it was almost pretty, despite the peeling paint on the bottom, despite the dead leaves and palm fronds floating on the surface like dank dark lace.

"I might be falling in love with you," he said.

"Yeah, well." I absolutely refused to say I might be falling in love with him too, even if it was true.

But maybe he saw in it my eyes because he smiled the sweetest smile, just lit up, and that made me light up too, and then we were both laughing. Just laughing our heads off there on the motel balcony.

"Life's a damn short thing to waste being scared. Don't you know that? Haven't you had that conversation with the residents of the spirit world?"

"No, actually I haven't. I usually like to ask the deceased what the food's like in heaven, and if they get to watch their favorite TV shows, and are they reruns or first-run episodes never aired. Stuff like that."

He stroked my hair. I leaned back against him. Down the hall, a door slammed, and a belligerent man stormed out screaming in something that might've been Russian or possibly Greek.

"You're pretty down to earth for a New Age kind of mama," he said.

"You're pretty low key for a cop. Don't you want to go arrest that guy for disturbing the peace or something?"

The guy was trotting across the motel parking lot, shaking his fist at nothing.

I was doing the same thing more or less, railing at absolutely nothing just because it was my habit.

"That's not what I want to do. Not tonight."

"Why should I trust you?" I said.

"You shouldn't"—he smiled that smile again—"you should trust yourself."

* * *

So we agreed we'd go away together, but we wouldn't go very far. That seemed to satisfy both of our inclinations, mine unspoken, of leaving Hollywood behind, while still satisfying my somewhat futile desire to exercise some control over my life.

We stopped at the McDonalds on Highland and fueled up on million calorie burgers and fries and shakes.

Then Joe drove fearlessly up, up into the hills on Angeles Crest Highway.

"We'll get out of the city lights fastest this way," he said.

The road was dark and twisted, and it was lined with scraggly tall pines. I'd driven it once in daylight, taking what I thought was a short cut in rush hour traffic, to meet a mark at the home of the dead grandfather she was asking me to contact in Lancaster.

From that one trip, I knew that below us there were sheer drops and sharp edges, even though I couldn't see them now in the thick night darkness. There were no street lights and no stop lights, and in some places, no guard rails.

Joe's tires skidded on a patch of gravel, and my ears popped and my stomach churned. We shouldn't have bought that fast food. Or at least I shouldn't have eaten it.

"Watch out," I said. It was compulsion that made me speak, not because of any real, immediate hazard that second.

"Lotta people call Angeles Crest Highway Devil's Highway," Joe said conversationally. He sounded downright cheerful.

"Yeah, I know that," I said.

"There's nothing bad about this road," he said. "It's just some of the people who drive on it. People who want to, who need to get out of town, and this is as far as they get before their indiscretions catch up to them."

"You're creeping me out," I said.

"I am?" Joe glanced at me, and the car took a dangerous little pirouette closer to the edge of whatever was out there, probably only air heavy with smog, but not heavy enough to support a car that drove off the side of the road.

"Don't look at me," I said. "Not while driving."

"Oh, Lord, you're serious," Joe said. "There's nothing up here that can hurt us. Unless you're scared of teenage Satanists. Tagging everything from rocks to roads. Satan probably did invent spray paint. Big wife swapping club up here too. I don't think there's much danger I'm gonna swap you."

I laughed along with him; I wasn't afraid of taggers or swappers. I was only afraid of cars plunging off cliffs and falling, falling. I was only afraid to admit I was maybe, possibly, probably even falling some place more dangerous than off a cliff; I was falling in love with this guy I hardly knew and going off with him someplace, and nobody knew where I was, and even I didn't know where I was going, which was more or less a description of my entire life. No wonder my knees started shaking.

"You don't like heights," Joe said.

"I don't like not knowing how high I am."

"Oh, you don't like losing control." He laughed again, and the laugh was kind. "You've been up against it even longer than I have, I guess. You haven't let anybody in for a long time, have you?"

"Let somebody in, and there's no way out," I

said. "Let somebody in, and pretty soon they're about to drive you off a cliff in the middle of the night."

But Joe was having none of that. He got happier and happier the higher the road twisted. He patted my knee. "Can you tell, every time we climb a little higher, the sky gets a little clearer? Look at the moon. Not so yellow now."

I forced myself to look out the window at the white moonlight on blue-black pines. I had to admit it was pretty. Long shadows fell and wavered like dancers across the road. The pale moonlight made the edges of the trees silver.

But I liked yellow moons all right myself. And orange smog sunsets and neon signs and open gas stations and some place to run if you had to run.

In so many ways, right at that moment I realized there was no place to run.

Now we were descending, heading toward the desolate sprawl of Antelope Valley, the last community that could call itself a bedroom of Los Angeles. Any further, and you'd be establishing residency in a sleepaway camp.

Down, down, down. I wasn't sure I liked down any better than up. Joe was going faster now, touching the brakes only lightly, and the car seemed to be gaining momentum with every passing second. I gripped the bottom of the seat with my hand.

"It's like falling in love, isn't it?" he said. "Up and down, one curve after another, and you just have to go where the road takes you. I think it's useless not to give myself over to it."

"Over to what?" I asked.

He went on thoughtfully, as if I hadn't even spoken. "I can handle this. I can handle the stuff I've been handling, and I can handle this too. This . . .

curve in the road. This gift. You. After all, it's time for gifts and 'Joy to the World.' It's time."

I felt myself blush; I felt some of my fear slipping away, but maybe it was just the fact that the road had straightened out now. We weren't so very high up now, and my feet were a little closer to the ground than the sky.

Joe turned off the highway and onto a back road. Dark rocks stood like monolithic sentries; a few tiny bugs darted across the headlights, white as little insect ghosts. You could smell the pines and a soft dampness; the tops of the trees were rimmed by a strip of moon. I had to admit that it was beautiful. It was poetry.

He had his hand on my knee, not as a prelude to messing around, just comfortable, like we'd already gotten past that let's fool around stage—we could have it whenever we wanted, and in the meantime, just being together was enough. And maybe that was true.

"I've gone fishing at a little stream back here," he said. "There's a gate, but someone cut the lock."

"Was it you?" I asked.

"I'm taking the fifth," he said. His car rattled along the washboard of the road.

"You're mistreating this car," I said.

"I never mistreat a car. Or a woman. Or a kitten. Only bad guys," he said, "I only mistreat bad guys."

I shifted a little in my seat. I had that nagging worry that he could technically, coplike, consider me a bad guy.

Joe patted the dashboard of the Mustang affectionately. "Besides, my brother took his car on roads lots worse than this."

"It's your brother's car?" I asked.

"It was. He passed away," Joe said shortly.

"I'm sorry. Were you close?"

"Best friends growing up. One year apart, and there was a time people couldn't even tell the difference between us."

As he navigated the dirt road, he gave me a brief family history.

His brother Hallie, short for Hallidale, Joe's mother's maiden name, liked riding horses and making bull's-eyes on the firing range, just like Joe. But where Joe liked hunting for arrowheads and going fishing, Hallie loved the Texas Rangers and fixing up old cars.

"Before he was fifteen, he'd fixed up three old cars, sold 'em, started over again. Always thought he could fix just about anything."

Joe had to stop there; his voice just tightened up. I put my hand on his knee. He smiled at me, his teeth shining in the moonlight, and he drew in his breath and went on, his voice deliberately casual, holding whatever unhappiness he was feeling just then somewhere inside where I couldn't see.

"He liked to make things right, that was the thing about Hallie." Joe shook his head. "He always had a strong sense of fairness. He carried it with him straight through the police academy and into active service."

"So your brother was a cop too?" I asked.

"Yeah. Just like my father."

"Your whole family." I was dumbfounded, "In law enforcement."

"Right," he said after a moment.

I did my best to shake off the sensation of having disturbed an innocent-looking garter snake and then realizing I'd encountered a full nest of vipers.

Just then, Joe shut off the brights and brought

the car to a dead stop, seemingly in the middle of the road but actually in front of a State Park Service Gate.

"Come on," he said, and I followed him out of the car. He opened up the trunk and took out an old blanket, the kind you could use to roll bodies up inside. He had a big industrial size flashlight too, and he took that and fired it up. He shone it on the gate.

He fiddled with the lock until it swung open with a creak.

"Don't worry. I won't let you trip on anything in the dark," he said, clutching my elbow. "I promise you. I'm watching out for you."

Almost in spite of myself, I relaxed as he led me confidently down a path littered with pine cones. The soft night was filled with rustling, whispering things that might've been branches or night birds or nocturnal squirrels or maybe more family members of Joe's who were all cops and waiting to arrest me.

We came to a clearing, and there was the creek where Joe must've gone fishing.

It shimmered in the moonlight, and the rustling sounds became the water flashing over stones.

Around a little bend, there was a big rock, flat on top like a table. It was about twice as tall as Joe, with footholds in the side that had been worn by many feet over the years, nothing formal. Joe stopped by it.

"Guys panned for gold here a hundred and twenty years ago or so. No gold here now, but it's a great place to cast a line."

I looked up doubtfully at the rock. "You expect me to climb that?"

"I've got you covered," he said, and he just lifted

me up before I could argue, his warm hands on my waist and under my shoulders feeling good and strong.

When we reached the top, he spread out the big, itchy blanket and drew me down against him. I put my head on his shoulder. It sure felt good, leaning against him like that. Being covered by him. Even if he was a cop, a cop in a family of cops. Resting against him, feeling his heart beat, feeling how good it was there in his arms, it occurred to me to tell him who I really was and that I might change.

I wouldn't be changing for him; I wasn't that much of a sap, I'd be changing because wasn't I a little sick of the whole game? Wasn't it time maybe, to find a better, more acceptable scam? Sell real estate, go to law school?

But I was tired just thinking about the effort that would all take, the telling, the changing, or maybe I was tired because it was past midnight, and it wasn't like I'd had a lot of sleep the night before. I snuggled closer. Another time. I'd tell or I wouldn't tell another time. I closed my eyes.

"Look up," Joe said, his voice rising with excitement, echoing off the rock, "look!"

My eyes shot open, and there above the pines was a sky, if not quite perfect in its darkness, then close enough to perfection for anyone who'd lived in LA for fourteen years and rarely left the basin.

And into that dark sky now came dancing streaks, ribbons, shreds of light, stars—falling stars, shooting stars, spinning stars.

"Look at them fly," Joe said happily. "There's hundreds more meteors we can't see, but we're sighting a percentage anyway."

Ten, twelve, twenty went by. My eyes were

strained, looking, but I didn't mind. This sky was there before I was in LA and before Joe was in LA, and it would be there for us wherever we were and whoever we were. We were just passing through. Just sparks of light soaring through the darkness like these stars, just a few glorious moments of time.

I wanted to say something poetic like that, but all I said aloud was "Wow."

All the Shakespeare I had read, all the screenplays I'd devoured, all the vocal exercises I'd perfected, and all I had to say was wow.

I was a little disappointed in myself, but Joe didn't seem to be.

"It's perfect," he whispered in my ear. "And so are you."

Around four, the shooting stars shot less often, and a dampness rose off the stream and began to creep into my skin. I shivered.

Joe rubbed my hands. "I better get you back to civilization."

We hadn't talked for a long time, and I realized how little I really wanted to speak. He was right about not needing words. I needed them too much. I was talking all the time. I was selling myself all the time, whether it was a psychic con or cheap liquor for sale or birthday parties for children of privilege or what a great actress I was.

"You haven't said much," Joe noted as he helped me off the big rock and back down the path.

"I haven't needed to," I said.

"I was right about coming here." He had a self-satisfied smile on his face and the beginning of a five o'clock shadow. That little bit of scruffy beard made him seem just the tiniest bit disreputable. And that made me glad. It made me feel more at home somehow, like neither one of us was perfect but it didn't matter.

As we walked down the path, he put his arm around my shoulders, and he sang to me in a soft, surprisingly confident baritone. "Oh the yellow rose of Texas . . . she's where I want to be . . ."

I was singing along with him, our voices making pleasing, little echoes in the still forest.

We stopped as we reached the car, and for a moment, I heard what was probably the first bird of the morning take up our song. We listened to the birdsong for a moment before Joe unlocked the doors and we scrambled inside. When Joe started the car, the sound of the engine turning over seemed unnaturally loud.

As we bumped back onto the pavement of Angeles Crest, he turned right instead of left, and we took the prosaic freeway back to town. There was already some traffic on it, early commuters strung out on their jobs and coffee.

It was past five AM when we saw the city lights, and the moon was low and yellow again. If stars were still exploding in the sky, we couldn't see them now.

"Back to the motel?" I suggested sleepily.

"Kind of a letdown after seeing the heavens dance."

"Where then?" I was too tired to deal with it if he suggested my place. I made a quick prayer, *please let me get away with this just a little while longer.*

I've said that prayer a long time, longer than I care to think about, and I used to couple it with, *and I'll be better, I won't do this or that anymore,* but I figured both God and I knew by now that wasn't necessarily the case.

"Let's go some place nicer," Joe said. "I know.

The Mondrian. They have damn nice suites. Sunken tubs, all that."

I breathed a quick thank you.

"The Mondrian? What does a cop know about The Mondrian?" I teased him.

"I was there—working." He sucked in his breath grimly. "Ricky used to . . . party there."

"That Littlejohn case really is all you work on, isn't it?"

"For a while it was, yeah." he said. He smiled. "Now I'm working on you."

It didn't make an impression really when Joe paid me for my psychic powers in cash or for the motel in Oxnard, the Mexican dinner, motel breakfast, the triple bill movie, or the Sunset House Budget Inn, all in cash.

But it did make an impression when he paid for the Mondrian that way. That was the only place we got a funny look, and it was the only time that I wondered why a cop would have the cash to stay there anyway. Especially right there in his pocket, the means to book a suite. A five hundred and ninety dollar suite. But maybe we just got the funny look because now it was close to six AM, and we had no luggage.

I was sufficiently tired and sufficiently impressed by the beautiful art deco suite that the cash thing slipped out of my mind in the immediate moment. The fact that Joe swung me up in his arms and carried me over the threshold like it was our honeymoon or something was also distracting.

Since we had no luggage, we had no bellman and there we were, me still in his arms, opening the curtains to a view of fading LA lights and velvet dark hills, the same hills we'd driven through, with the first pink streaks of a fabulous sunrise blooming like a rose in the east.

Watching the sunrise with him, I realized we were going on a third day together and three motels. Okay, one was a luxury hotel actually. Surely spending three days in three different rooms with the same guy meant something incredibly significant, but what it was I couldn't say. I was having serious trouble even keeping my eyes open.

It was all a delicious blur—the LA view, the purple velvet settee we sank into to appreciate it, the enormous Jacuzzi tub and various scented bath products luxuriously arranged in a marble bathroom. We took advantage of the tub and the marvelous sensation of our two bodies rubbing up together in the warm, swirling water, as if the steam circling our heads was a product of the heat we felt for each other, rather than the water temperature. All rosy and sated, we also enjoyed the complimentary bottle of midrange Chardonnay—Louie and I probably wouldn't go to the trouble of stealing it, but it was nice all the same—deliciously decadent to sip it, naked, silky in the sunrise glow.

Then clean and fuzzy, we surrendered to sleep, and to what I believe is the ultimate expensive luxury whether the bed is in the Mondrian or the Sunset Budget House—sleeping in somebody's arms.

Chapter
Eight

Joe was gone when I woke up just shy of the one PM checkout time. The last time I had slept that late was when I was twelve years old and I had chicken pox.

On the pillow next to mine was a neatly written little note on hotel stationary.

"Have to get back to work today," he had written. "Honeymoon's over, so to speak. Let's have a second one tonight. Call me when you get this. I love you. Joe." And he had put double Xs and Os. He had also left me a twenty, with a scribbled note "for your cab back to Santa Monica."

The honeymoon thing gave me as many shivers as last night's drive up Angeles Crest Highway. Still, I had to admit I kind of liked this particular shivery feeling.

Even if I did have to lie to him for the rest of my life, maybe things would be fine anyway. Look at all the little, fat, bald rich guys walking around Hollywood who dated supermodels. They were liv-

Genie Davis

ing proof that relationships didn't always have to be built on truth.

I read the note again. On second read, I started to have some doubts. The "call me" part bothered me more than the honeymoon part. Was he forcing me to make the next move? Had he bared so many of his feelings while I'd held back that now it was up to me if we were to go on? If so, it was going to be tough to make that next move since I'd thrown away his phone number and never thought to ask for it again.

But if he meant what he'd said about falling in love with me, surely when I didn't call, he wouldn't stand on ceremony. Maybe even this very minute he was drumming his fingers, impatient for me to call, itching to pick up the phone. So pick it up, I whispered under my breath, pick it up and dial.

Or maybe this was the swan song. He told me he loved me, I almost believed him; I had almost told him I felt the same way. Because I did feel the same way. I was holding back with him, but not with my heart. Even though I knew better, even though I should be tougher and harder and more defended than this.

Everybody wants to believe, that's how people get suckered into a con. That's how people get suckered into love. Even people like me have a little faith. And you nurture that faith just the teeniest, tiniest bit, and there you are, lying in a hotel bed at one o'clock in the afternoon wishing your beloved would pick up a phone.

He had written those words, "I love you." That had to mean something. That wasn't just some expression, like "howdy" that they used along the Texas Gulf.

I stretched out in bed and allowed myself, just

for a few minutes, to feel really wonderful. I didn't think about my prevarications; I didn't think about not having his phone number; I didn't think I was a fool. I let myself believe.

It was all pretty unreal, this love business. But the feeling it gave me, the happiness, that was real. That was right. It had to be.

I took a shower and left the bathroom door open in case the phone on the nightstand rang. See, I sort of hoped he'd call me right there in the hotel room. Because if he called me on the cell phone number I'd given him, he wouldn't reach me. That phone was still in my kitchen drawer.

I cursed myself for not having it with me, and then I cursed myself for wishing that I had it with me. Couldn't I wait fifteen minutes until I got home? No, honestly, I couldn't.

I threw on my clothes, except I left off the socks this time. They felt kind of passé in the daytime without Joe to appreciate them.

Quite honestly, I felt kind of passé myself without Joe to appreciate me.

Was I really that far gone? Was I really this nuts? Was I really in love with a cop? Shouldn't I stop things before I did get really, truly, totally that nuts? Or was it too late?

I went out into the hall but that wonderful feeling I'd had lying on the bed only minutes before had fully faded, kind of like Anna Nicole Smith without her peroxide.

There was a maid's cart at the end of the hall, and I waited at the elevator until she went inside a room, and then I stole a terry cloth robe; three fluffy towels; and about a dozen little bottles of very expensive, imported from London Penhaligan shampoo and bubble bath. I stuffed them into a plastic laundry bag that also came off the maid's cart. The theft made me feel a little bit better. They were very nice towels.

But somehow, it wasn't as big a triumph as it might've been some other time. Stolen moments, stolen bath care products. They weren't all the same.

I just wanted to go home and check that cell phone.

I took the elevator down to the street. There I hesitated. Even though I wanted to go home fast and get to that phone, just because I momentarily had my rent covered, there was no reason to break that twenty on a cab. Waste not, want not.

Plus the sooner I got home, if Joe hadn't called me already, the worse I was going to feel. So, lugging my bulging laundry bag, I took a stroll east on Sunset, south on La Brea, to home.

By the time I turned down my street, I really wished I'd spent a slice of Joe's twenty on a cab. The walk took longer than it should've. I was wearing annoyingly high heels. It was a humid, gray day despite the promising early morning sunrise, and I kept shifting the awkward, heavy bag and actually wishing I hadn't taken the towels and the robe. Still, never pass up a score, that was me.

In spite of sleeping in late, I was exhausted. Some of it was due to two nights in a row of having my sleep disturbed, albeit in a very pleasant way, by Joe. But most of it was the exhaustion of effort required to be someone who I was not for an extended period of time.

I should just tell him who I was. I should just come clean.

Then the thought flashed through my mind that maybe I'd been pretending to be someone I wasn't for years; maybe that's why I was so tired.

And with that thought came another—that even if I wasn't telling Joe the whole truth and nothing but the truth now, at least not in words, perhaps I was at last truly who I was with Joe. Maybe it was just like he said, and words weren't everything.

And then I got scared. What if I'd talked in my sleep? What if I had revealed things I didn't want to reveal, the way Louie was afraid I would? How I made my living, how I didn't have a psychic bone in my body, my last name?

Most importantly, what if I had revealed just how much I wanted to spend another night in his arms?

I was getting really worked up thinking about all these things, especially the part about spending another night with him. Two nights in a row we had been together already—that was significant. That was even more significant than the words "I love you." Anyone could say that. Not just anyone could spend two nights with me. In fact, I couldn't remember the last time anyone had.

I wondered if Louie was home or if he was working at the catering company today. If he was home and he asked me where I'd been, or he guessed who I'd been with, I would never hear the end of it. And all I wanted to do was sneak inside and check that cell phone. Please let him call.

I took a quick look around me as I reached Mrs. Marinak's house, and then I hurried down the driveway to my place. There were a lot of freshly-squished dates on the pavement and footprints, which made me think Louie had gone out somewhere.

There wasn't a sound coming from Louie's apartment—no country western, no lightly tapping laptop.

I breathed a sigh of relief. I was fumbling with my keys and reaching for my doorknob when someone grabbed me from behind and put his hands over my eyes.

"Come on," I said, "Louie, please, not twice in—"

But before I could finish the sentence, somebody had pushed something smelly in my face. It was thick and disgustingly sweet, like nail polish remover crossed with Christmas cookies. I coughed on it once, but before I could cough on it again, I blacked out.

I was in my own hall closet, sitting on a stack of dog-eared *Backstage West*'s and *Hollywood Reporter Talent* issues. I was wedged between snow boots I bought for a weekend ski trip to Mammoth three years ago; a tiny black and white camping TV purchased for a Yosemite campout when Louie wanted to get back to nature two years ago; various cheap umbrellas purchased every time it rained in LA and caught me by surprise, which was virtually every time it rained; a flat of emergency water in case of earthquake; and an Exercycle I'd never used that its previous owner had also apparently never used that I'd found sitting shining and new by a curb in Hancock Park one trash night.

Well, I wouldn't get out of shape, and I wouldn't get thirsty, and I might even be able to get some TV reception if the antennae of the camping TV wasn't broken and hanging askew. I'd broken it trying to fit it into my car along with a very uncollapsible

collapsible tent in the middle of the night when a swarm of mosquitos found us and Louie discovered he had had enough nature.

My mouth was gagged with my own silk scarf, which made me realize someone had gone, or was even now going through, my dresser. This meant he probably had the six hundred I'd made on the champagne; the three gold coins my grandmother gave me before she passed away; and possibly my grandmother's ruby ring, which was not a real ruby and virtually worthless—I'd tried to pawn it several times in my acting days—but looked real and was pretty.

My wrists were bound behind me with an extension cord pulled scrupulously tight. I worked at the cord with my fingers for a while, but there was no point, I would have to see what I was doing, or have a sharp object and still be able to see what I was doing.

The closet was dim and stuffy and dusty, and I felt sick to my stomach from whatever had been placed over my mouth and nose.

I could not imagine why anyone would pick my place, of all places, to rob, especially in broad daylight, nor could I imagine why anyone who was robbing it would go to all the trouble of having chloroform handy to take me out of commission.

Wouldn't it have been a lot more efficient to just break into my place when I had been gone all night long and into the afternoon than to wait for me to come home, jump me, and then rob me?

Since efficiency was out and the guy hadn't personally attacked me beyond the chloroforming and the stuffing in the closet, I figured I was dealing either with someone whose motives were completely irrational or with someone who wanted to rob me first, then attack me. Kind of saving me for dessert as it were.

I had not seen my attacker, which was the only reason he or she had been able to take me at all. Knowledge was power and in this case, possibly a good swift kick in the balls since my legs were free. I was not going to be anybody's dessert. I was itching to deliver a kick or some kind of blow, but all I could do was stay wedged in my closet, listening to the rattling and muttered cursing coming from my bedroom.

The longer I sat there, the more it struck me that I wasn't afraid. I was pissed off, and I was going to be ready when the closet door opened. But having access to my legs wasn't going to be good enough.

Since I couldn't use my hands, I settled for my mouth. I rubbed the silk scarf back and forth against the closet wall until I loosened it. The gag slipped down to my chin and lodged there. It was annoying and confining, but my lips and my teeth, albeit with limited range of motion, were now my own.

I bent over the little camping TV and seesawed the loose hanging antennae back and forth in my teeth. I worked at them furiously until sweat ran down the sides of my cheeks and stained the silk scarf.

Up and down, up and down until my jaw ached. Oh, I could just imagine the dirty jokes Louie would tell. Louie, was he home? Had he heard anything? Had he called the cops?

No, it was unlikely Louie would call the cops even if he found my dead body being chewed on by Mrs. Marinak's poodle.

Thinking about cops made me think about Joe; made me miss Joe; made me think that if Joe knew I'd just been mugged in my own home, he wouldn't even have to call the cavalry to rescue me. He was the cavalry, more or less.

The antennae snapped off. They rolled on the floor with a clatter. A tiny clatter but still. I held my breath, waiting for the closet door to open, but it didn't.

I squatted down and twisted on my side, and putting my tongue as well as my lips against the dusty indoor/outdoor carpeting, I picked up the antennae again.

And I clenched them between my teeth, the jagged, broken ends out.

They were the best weapon I had, that and surprise, not that there was anyone around to use either on just yet.

I couldn't hold the damn things in my mouth forever. For one thing, I was going to start to drool pretty soon, and I didn't like drooling as well as sweating all over my silk scarf. So I decided to summon someone.

I lifted my foot and kicked at the door. I kicked for some time. I would've screamed, but I didn't want him to know about my mouth being free.

I heard the mumbled cursing grow louder; I heard the footsteps, the jiggling of the closet knob—it tended to stick—and then the door was flung open.

I didn't think, and he didn't have time to. I jumped on the little man with the very white skin, the reddish eyes, and the pale frizz of hair, and I jabbed the broken antennae in his nose.

I was aiming for the little red eyes, which reminded me of a pet rat a boy had shown me back in junior high.

"Shit, you," rat–man said and snatched the thing away.

But the element of surprise was good, he was little, and my hall was narrow. I body slammed him against the door frame hard enough that I knocked a framed Magritte print, the one that looks like the cover of the Jackson Browne album *Late for the Sky,* off the wall and onto the floor with the sound of shattering glass.

He flailed at me, but I smashed the top of my head against his already bleeding nose. When he ducked, I bit his ear and pulled really hard.

"Ow-w!" he wailed. Actually, it was more like an oink than a wail, and now, his little red eyes had the quality of a cartoon pig. Oh, if only my hands had been free, my fingers would be in those eyes.

"Stop it," he hissed, and he made a big effort to throw me off.

When I stumbled back, he was holding an intricately carved, very sharp, very long, Japanese-style kitchen knife up against my throat. The knife looked oddly familiar.

"Scream or try anything else smart, and you're dead," he said like he'd heard somebody else say tough guy lines once and he was doing his best to imitate them.

"What do you want?" I asked, breathing hard and eyeing that knife.

"What do *you* want?" he returned, breathing even harder.

"For you to get that knife off my throat, untie my hands, and get the hell out of my apartment."

He lifted the knife away. "Don't you try and hurt me again," he whined, "I mean it."

He rubbed at his ear and his nose, and now instead of a pig or a rat, he reminded me of an albino bunny rabbit about to cry.

"Look, let's cut to the chase here. Why did you have me trussed up in my closet?"

"I want to know what you found."

What I had found? Was he nuts? He was the one who had been rummaging around.

I just stared at him.

"What did you find?" he asked again.

I figured the best defense was a good offense.

"I know what *you* found. Six hundred bucks."

The little red eyes blinked—guilty. "I didn't come here to rob you of a lousy coupla hundred."

"No? But you did anyway, right?"

"I don't let opportunities just pass me by."

He gave a little giggle. Yes, he probably was nuts.

"Including the opportunity to tie me up, throw me in a closet for fun?"

"I said. I need to know what you know."

"I know many things. Like that you're an asshole."

I had my eye on that knife. It was still tight in his hand, even if his hand was now slack by his side.

He was silent, considering me. Considering what about me, I wasn't sure.

"What were you doing in the Colony?"

For a minute, I had to think, what colony? New England Pilgrims came to mind, followed by an ant colony inside glass in grade school. It then flashed to a hand-lettered sign on La Cienega that offered colon cleansing 'y purification' in butchered Spanish, and then I got it. Malibu Colony. The gated enclave of Ricky Littlejohn.

And that was where the knife had come from—Ricky's kitchen rack.

"You're the photographer?"

I was relatively certain he wasn't the wife, Laura, and nobody this weird looking could've made it as an undercover cop. He would've been hazed out of the police academy long before he went deep at Ricky's house.

His thin little rabbit mouth twisted, his rat eyes blinked, and he oinked his piglike confirmation.

I looked at his soiled jeans and threadbare tee shirt. "The *fashion* photographer?"

"I've been on the road," he shrugged.

I thought about the dirty sleeping bag and the rolls of film in McDonald's sacks in Ricky's guest bedroom.

"No, you're just a pig," I said, realizing how sometimes you look like exactly what you are.

He raised his hand, the one without the knife, to slap me.

The slap connected, and it made my head snap back, and it stung badly. But here was the good news. He was interested enough in delivering it that he more or less completely missed the wonderful female empowerment kickbox move I'd learned for the part of a superhero's sidekick in a kid's action movie. I hadn't gotten the part, but boy, that training came in handy now.

I got the knife out of his hand, and it skittered across the floor. And just as he noticed it fall, I sliced my instep into his knee.

He fell with a thud. I jumped on top of him. And jumped again. He'd really made a mistake when he hadn't tied my feet as well as my hands. I heard a satisfying crack. Ribs, I figured.

"Damn it," he gasped. "I wasn't going to hurt you."

"Right. That's why you jumped me, drugged me, bound me, and gagged me, and you keep on waving a knife while you ask asinine questions. That's why you slapped me. I don't get slapped."

I gave one more jump, and he groaned, and I thought I probably shouldn't kill him. For one thing, disposing of the body would be tough. So I stopped, keeping one foot on him, my own chest heaving with adrenaline and effort.

"I just need to know what you know. That's all. Just tell me," he was wheedling now and gasping at the same time.

"You're in no position to ask me questions," I said. "Besides, I don't *know* what you're talking about."

I sort of knew, but I wouldn't let him know that.

He struggled and squirmed beneath me; I wasn't sure, cracked ribs or not, that I could hold him down long.

"Saw you at Ricky's. I watch the house. I woulda jumped you there, but you weren't alone." A giggle escaped the thin lips.

I jumped on him again; maybe I could roll the body up in my bedspread. The giggling ceased, and he lay still like a broken toy.

"C'mon. We could work together, you know," he gasped.

"I doubt it."

"You went sniffing around Ricky's place for some reason," he said. "You're pretty enough to be a model, but I never took your picture, so that's out. You ain't a nurse. What I'm guessing is that you were brought 'cause of the body business. Am I right?"

I wanted him to say more. "Ricky's body?"

"Don't be cute. You know something about the

money. I found your business cards. You're scamming the old lady."

His lips were wet and loose, like he was drooling. He now reminded me of a slug more than a pig, lying there on the ground.

What old lady? I wondered. Was that what he called Laura?

"People have died for knowing what you know and not talking," he said, the little red eyes glowing demonically. A demonic pig–rat–rabbit–slug, that's what he was. "You'd better answer me."

I gave him another stomp.

"I'm the one asking questions now," I said. "Let's start with how you got in here."

His words came out in little fits and starts. "Waited behind that . . . bus every damn stop . . . breathing in the fumes. Been waiting . . . over twenty-four . . . hours. Damn poodle always barking. Don't spend much time here, do you?"

I shivered. He had been lurking outside my apartment since I had come home from Santa Monica. While I tried on outfits and talked to Louie and after I had left to meet Joe. If only I'd brought Joe home. Surely Joe would've bested the guy. And called in more cops and exposed me to their scrutiny and—

Boy, Louie was right. I really shouldn't have gone off with Joe in the first place. It was thanks to him, to his stupid case that this guy showed up at my door. And man, it was bad enough a bad guy knew where to find me; what if I had to let the good guys know too?

I shivered. I suppose Nelson saw me shiver because it made him bolder; he seemed to mind his messed up ribs less.

"Whoever you've been scamming, I don't care. Just tell me. What the hell were you doing at Ricky's? What did you find?"

"Have you forgotten so soon? I'm the one breaking ribs here—"

I was also the one with a sharp little .22 now pointed at my chest.

He must've pulled it out of his pants pocket or something while I was busy worrying about the police getting my address. Maybe there were worse things.

"Off me," he ordered. "Get off."

He cocked the gun. I stepped aside. He got up painfully.

"I didn't mean what I said about not hurting you," he sneered.

I opened my mouth, and I did my very best, guaranteed to reach the back of any theater anywhere, loud, bloodcurdling scream, pushing it out from my diaphragm and projecting it to the rear balcony, as if this were a ten-thousand seat auditorium and not my apartment.

My scream pissed him off. His red eyes narrowed, and he fired his nasty little weapon.

I ducked; I screamed again and ran, ran, ran down the hall, across the living room, and to my front door. And before I could address the very real problem of how I was going to open the door with my hands tied, I tripped. I fell on the plastic bag bulging with stolen hotel towels and a bathrobe. The irony was not lost on me. I had at last been tripped up by my own ill-gotten gains.

Nelson fired again from closer this time, and I heard Mrs. Marinak's poodle hit extended play.

My left upper arm stung and burned—he'd hit me.

If he got a little closer and missed, I could knock him on his ass again. If he got a little closer and didn't miss—I held my breath. I heard his footsteps coming toward me, and then I heard the welcome, yes, actually welcome, words, "Open up, police."

"Get the hell in here," I cried, and then something happened, something painful and bright flashed through me.

There was just a sort of swarming buzz, like a million bees were attacking me, and silence. I was out of it, just like when Nelson had thrown the chloroformed cloth across my face.

Chapter Nine

When I opened my eyes again, I was in a place that smelled like Pine Sol; beeped and hummed like the inside of a spaceship; and had pale green, grubby, industrial cinder block walls.

Horror coursed through me. I was either dead and in hell, or I was in a hospital. Maybe I dreaded being sick and hauled off to a hospital even more than I dreaded being arrested and hauled off to jail. It might've had something to do with my parents passing off this mortal coil during my impressionable years after making pit stops at hospitals, or my grandmother's lingering last illness, or it might've been simple paranoia, but people do die in hospitals. Everyone I'd loved and known had died in one.

Sure, sometimes people get well too; they have needed appendectomies, get a broken bone set, and deliver babies. But I was not having a baby, I didn't think I had any broken bones, and I was relatively certain I didn't need an appendectomy.

My head hurt, my arm hurt, and flourescent

light spilled down on me, making my hand, when I could focus on it, look as green as the walls.

There was a long-faced nurse nodding her head and a guy who was probably a doctor in worn-looking scrubs shrugging his shoulders. Their voices seemed to come from far away and maybe from underwater. Maybe this was a hospital under the sea, and SpongeBob SquarePants would walk in at any minute with a thermometer.

"How are we feeling?" asked the nurse.

"Terrible," I said, and my voice was hoarse.

"Can you tell me your name?" asked the doctor.

I was pretty sure that if I'd been taken to the hospital, someone somewhere knew me as Christine Harris. So I said so.

The doctor smiled and said "Very good."

The nurse yawned and walked across the room, pushing back a yellow curtain.

"You can see her now," she said to someone, and she and the doctor retreated. I was left alone with my tongue feeling thick, and my head feeling like it was stuffed with cotton balls instead of brains.

I couldn't move; I felt somnolent, drugged. I could barely keep my eyes open, so barely that I closed them. What could be worse than this? A man cleared his throat, and I opened my eyes again.

Well, apparently what could be worse than being in a hospital with something wrong with me and not knowing what it was was being in a hospital with a couple of guys wearing uniforms and another guy, short and squat like a fireplug and smelling of garlic, sticking a badge in my face.

I was in a hospital, and I was arrested. Maybe I was in a jail hospital.

Things came back to me, and they weren't nice

things. Nelson tying me up; me cracking Nelson's
ribs; me running for the door and Nelson shooting his gun; me inviting the police inside—who
knew what had happened next.

Whatever had happened had made my arm and
my head hurt and had given me this plague of law
enforcement leaning over my bed.

The uniforms looked bored; the fireplug guy
looked annoyed.

I tried to sit up, but it took too much effort, so I
just lay back on my pillow blinking and waiting to
hear how this nightmare was going to play out.

"Detective Handley," said the fireplug guy, intro-
ducing himself. "They said you could talk now."

I nodded weakly but kept mute because who
knew what he wanted to talk to me about. He filled
me in quickly.

"Want you to talk to me about last night. Your
neighbor heard you screaming."

"I don't . . . don't remember much—a man
grabbed me, had a gun on me . . ."

I lifted my right hand to my aching head. No
bandages, my head just hurt, that was all. My left
arm, however, was swathed in gauze.

"Did he shoot me?"

"Knocked you out cold with the handle of his
.22. Mild concussion. Shot at you. Grazed your triceps with a bullet from that gun. I'm assuming he
shot at you to keep you from running, but then up
close, he didn't have the heart to take you out, so
he creamed you instead."

More likely, he didn't want to kill me in case he
could come back some other time and get some
more information out of me.

"Do you have him . . . in . . . in custody?" I was

getting the idea that I wasn't the one in trouble here, although from the shifty look in Handley's eyes that could change at any moment.

"Nope. Guy climbed out your bathroom window. Knocked over trash cans. Ran but not too fast—"

"Hurt him," I said pleasedly. "I think I broke his ribs."

"Someone picked him up on Highland. Dogs lost his scent."

No stranger would pick up a guy who looked like him and who was limping along with broken ribs. Nelson wasn't working alone.

"Any idea who your attacker was?"

I thought it over. Of course I knew who he was, but if I revealed that I knew who he was and why, what else would I be revealing? My faux psychic persona, my real last name, unfiled taxes . . . the list could get a lot longer.

"No idea who he was," I said.

"How'd he get in your place?"

"He grabbed me from behind. Put something over my mouth that made me pass out. Stuffed me in my own closet. I broke out, fought with him, then he brought out the gun."

The detective was blunt. "Trying to rape you?"

"No."

"He ransacked your place, but I can't see much is missing."

I didn't mention the six hundred. "Maybe a ring," I said. "It looks like it's worth more than it is. A couple of gold coins."

"So he robbed you, and you jumped him, and he shot at you when you tried to run."

"Yes."

"Seems like an awful lot of trouble to go to."

"Yes."

"He wasn't an old boyfriend?"

"God, no."

"Business associate perhaps?"

O-oh, that one made me uncomfortable.

Had Mrs. Marinak made a comment? Did somebody have something on me as Christina Harris?

"Ugh, who would want to work with a man like that?"

"Give me a description."

The guy had trapped me! This Handley was smarter than he looked. If I gave a false description and someone else had seen Nelson, that would look bad.

"He was little and pale and rabbity," I said, which wasn't much of a description but was true.

"No distinguishing marks?"

He truly didn't have any. "His eyes were red."

"Drug red or albino red?"

The guy knew something. He had to know something. I shook my head and sighed like I was very tired. Actually, I was tired.

"Don't know," I said.

"See, it's hard to tell now."

"What do you mean?"

" 'Cause like I said, he got in a car. Dogs lost his scent. For a while. By the time we caught up to him, he was lying in an alley, and he was dead."

"He's dead? Look, I didn't—"

"Wasn't the broken ribs that killed him. Wasn't even the fact that somebody cut off his hands."

I felt a quick surge of nausea. "Cut off his—"

"Nope, that happened after he died. Shot in the mouth."

I tried not to gag.

"You said he might've gone after a ring. Was it a real nice ring?"

"No, it looked like it could've been nice, but it was really a fake stone, and I don't even know if he took it."

"See, maybe he was wearing your ring, and somebody else thought it was a nice ring and wanted it. It was tough to get off, so they just cut it off—"

"Both hands?"

"Well, maybe he was wearing other rings. Was he wearing rings when you saw him?"

"No! Not mine, not any."

"Okay. So much for that theory." Handley sighed.

Somebody cut off Nelson's hands? Someone had picked him up, then killed him and cut off his hands. Right after he'd messed up whatever it was he was supposed to be doing with me.

I put my own hand against my mouth and pressed very hard. I did not want to throw up. I especially did not want to throw up in front of this detective.

"It was a woman that picked him up. Don't know who she is either, but we've found witnesses who put your friend as a passenger in a yellow Caddy, female driver. She dropped him off in front of the Rite Aid on Sunset. What we don't know is if they knew each other or if he was just a hitchhiker."

"And you think this woman, she killed him, she cut off his hands?"

"No, I don't think a woman would cut off his hands. Too tough. Too bloody. Women get queasy even thinking about that stuff," Handley said, eyeing me.

I imagined that by now I was as green as the hospital walls.

"We found his body down near Long Beach. Pretty far away from that woman and that Rite Aid."

"You've been busy," I said.

"You've been unconscious," he pointed out. "And now that you're up and around and we have a guy who attacked you, then ended up with his hands hacked off, I was kind of hoping you could give me a little more information than you've given me so far. Could you try? Could you try to give me just a little more?"

His words were pleading, but his eyes were hard, and I had this feeling he'd keep asking and asking and never leave.

But at that moment, the hospital curtain around my bed flew back, and Louie flung himself in.

"You're up and around they said! You're all—"

He saw Handley, his smile faded, and he tried to scuttle away. "Sorry. You're already occupied. I'll come back when . . . later when . . ."

One of the uniforms leaned close to Handley and said something unintelligible, kind of like at the end of an overhyped Sofia Coppola movie.

"Don't go," Handley said to Louie when the uniform finished whispering.

He froze Louie in his tracks, using the kind of commanding tone that conveyed "don't go or else" that cops often use to make people freeze in their tracks.

"You're the neighbor." Handley looked Louie up and down, taking in his black leather pants and bright pink shirt with little ponies printed on it and not particularly enjoying the fashion statement.

"That's right," Louie said defensively, as if that alone made him guilty of something.

The guilty-of-something vibe registered with Handley.

"You know the guy who attacked your friend?"

"Know the guy? I didn't even know it *was* a guy."

"Have you heard or seen anything funny the last couple of days, anybody hanging around?"

"A few Scientologists, that's all."

"And you, Ms. Harris?"

"No, nobody."

"You were just coming home when this man grabbed you?"

"Right."

"From where, work?"

"No. From a friend's."

"Could the guy have followed you from the friend's place?"

"No. I walked home, and I would've noticed."

"Would you mind telling me where you were all the same?"

"It's . . . private," I said.

"Boyfriend," said Louie, rolling his eyes appreciatively.

"Married?" asked Handley, bored. "We can keep this confidential."

"No, no, he's not married, he's . . ." I gave up on not saying too much.

I gave up because all of a sudden, I just wanted Joe; I wanted him to know what had happened to me. I wanted him to know where I was. I wanted him to come to me and reassure me. I wanted him to rescue me or something. I wanted to tell him about Nelson and about how scared I was. I wanted to tell him that I didn't like hearing about the guy getting his hands cut off, not at all. He'd asked for my help, and now I wanted his.

Of course, wanting Joe to be with me now almost certainly meant that I had to come clean with him. But how bad could that be, really? He'd said he loved me. I'd tell him I loved him too, and maybe that would make up for the lies; maybe it would make up for who I was, instead of who I was pretending to be.

Yeah, I'd have to come clean to Joe, but I couldn't come clean to Handley. I was in just as much peril with Handley as I was with Nelson, just in a different way.

Joe loved me, or he said he did, and even if things blew up in my face, I knew he wouldn't hurt me.

Did I know that? I had this unreasonable feeling that he had already hurt me, getting me mixed up in this whole mess, taking me to Ricky's house. Maybe that was me preparing for the speech I might have to make about how he couldn't possibly hold my sins against me—look at the problems he'd caused.

But if he loved me? If I was falling in love with him? Everybody made mistakes, right? I'd made some; he'd made some. That was all there was to it. We'd be fine. I just had to see him, that's all. I just had to talk to him.

Oh, I wished I still had his phone number. I also wished I had my own orphan cell phone with me because by now, surely by now, he would've called, and he would've left his number. But as it was, I couldn't call him from here, and all of a sudden, I couldn't wait even long enough to send Louie home to get the phone. I had to talk to Joe right now, immediately.

What if he was worried about me, trying to reach me, and all he got was my voice mail over and over? What if he'd gone to look for me at the apartment he thought I lived in but didn't or to see the telemarketing guys and they'd said I'd vanished?

I could see the light spilling in through the hospital window, and I realized it was morning now. It was over twenty-four hours since we'd been together; if I needed Joe, wasn't it reasonable to assume he needed me too?

And what if Nelson had gone after him before he went after me? What if Joe was hurt, or worse still, what if he was dead, his beautiful hands missing?

What if Joe had just changed his mind about me and hadn't called? What if he'd found out about me, found out even more than this Handley guy had, and I'd never see him again?

Handley was staring at me as if I had spoken all my thoughts aloud. I looked at Louie for confirmation that I hadn't. Louie looked nervous but not like I'd done anything too nutty.

"I'll be in touch," said Handley, proffering a business card. I took it with my good hand. Louie breathed a sigh of relief.

"Wait," I said as Handley stood.

Now Louie's expression showed that I'd done something nutty.

"Do you know Detective Joe Richter?"

Handley's face creased with puzzlement. "No. What's he to you?"

"He's . . . my friend."

"Oh," said Handley and allowed himself a slight smile. "What division?"

"Homicide," I said.

Handley looked impressed.

"He work outta downtown?"

I realized I didn't know.

"I don't recall," I said, feigning bump on the head vagueness. "But I'm sure you could find him for me. I mean, I know he's working here in LA somewhere."

"Huh, yeah, somewhere in LA; it's such a small town," said Handley.

He shrugged, elaborately casual. "I'll make some phone calls for you. See if I can send him over. Comfort you in your time of pain, all that."

He left, followed by the uniforms who had to wait and file out of the room behind him because the door was only so wide and Handley filled it.

"What are you doing?" Louie asked urgently, sitting on my bed.

"The guy who attacked me, he's involved in the case Joe's investigating. I didn't want to talk about it with this guy. I want to talk about it with Joe."

The ugly truth was that I just wanted Joe, period. And that I was afraid, for one reason or another—that Joe had found out I had lied to him or that Joe was in trouble himself—I was afraid that for whatever reason, I wouldn't be able to be with him ever again.

"A cop sicced this guy on you, and now you're gonna talk it over with him?"

"He didn't sic the guy on me."

"He got you involved. You got yourself involved. Look what this has come to! You disappear to . . .

to Oxnard. Then you disappear again; you don't even call—"

"I didn't have reception. We were up on the top of Angeles Crest Highway. Watching the meteors."

"Oh, excuse me, but how incredibly romantic. Barf. And then you come home, and this guy mugs you—"

"No, then we went to the Mondrian. To a suite."

"Well, that makes up for Oxnard a little," Louie sniffed, relenting just slightly. "And *then,* this guy mugs you—"

"Yeah, it was my own fault. I wasn't paying attention. I thought it was you, putting your hands over my eyes."

"I was asleep. Fast asleep. Never heard you come home. Pulled an all-nighter. Almost done with the Christmas tree script! Almost done. I know it's horrible, and the producer is horrid—do you know, she pulls out her hair when she's anxious? She made a braided *mat* out of her hair, and she uses it as a mouse pad? But she has a connection at Fox Searchlight. Like a major connection. And look at *Elf* and *Miracle on 34th Street.* Nobody loses money on a Christmas movie."

"Okay, so you finished your script," I prompted, to keep him on track.

"Yeah, and I fell asleep about noon. And then I was awakened by this ungodly racket about three o'clock, and you screaming—you screamed so loud and so long that I grabbed my nine iron and headed downstairs."

"You didn't call the cops?"

Louie's eyes widened in horror. "No! Marinak did. She called them before you screamed apparently, said she saw some guy hiding in the bushes.

It took them a good long time to respond, and when they had, you'd just finished screaming. They got to you just as I was running down the stairs, and Marinak gave them the key. You were lying there, and I thought you were dead because there was blood because the bullet got you in the arm, just grazed you, thank God. I heard the guy go out the back window; I heard him go, and I told the cops, but they were standing around like they were waiting for donuts or something. What a mess, what a mess! You'll be in the paper. We should move. We should both move. Silver Lake maybe. Mt. Olympus."

I started to cry. I was already giving up my storefront and now my apartment? I'd lost my six hundred bucks too to a guy who no longer had hands or any way whatsoever to spend it.

"Oh baby, okay, don't cry; I'm sorry. I'm sure this, this Joe is very nice and worth all this trouble, and you'll have children and live happily ever after, and I'll sell the Christmas tree script, and we won't have to steal any more champagne—"

On these last words, Handley pushed back into the room, and Louie shut up like someone had clamped tape over his mouth.

I swiped at my eyes.

Handley cleared his throat. "No Joe Richter in LAPD Homicide. No Joe Richter in LAPD, unless you mean one Joseph A. Richter who works in traffic."

Could Joe have lied to me? Was he just some traffic cop hoping for a promotion?

I sat up. "Maybe that's him?" I said.

"He's older than you?"

"Yes." Maybe he was thirty-five.

"Much older?"

"No." I frowned.

"Joseph A. Richter is one week short of sixty-two and retirement."

"Oh."

A thought occurred to me. Joe was from Texas. Maybe he was a Texas cop just helping LAPD on the Littlejohn case.

"If police from another state come out to work on a case with you, then they wouldn't be listed through personnel, right?"

"He was from out of state, your Joe?"

Louie gave me an imperceptible head shake, like shut up already before you get in deeper and deeper.

Still, I plunged on. "Texas," I said. "And he was working on the Ricky Littlejohn case. And I think the guy who came after me was somehow connected to that case. I think he was this photographer guy named Nelson."

"Ricky Littlejohn," Handley muttered. "Never heard of him."

"He was a model. Long time ago. He died about a year back. In a hot tub. And there was a lot of money missing."

Handley looked blank.

"It was in the paper. A big story about him. In *The LA Free Press.*"

"In that street rag?" Handley was dismissive, as if a murder was described in that paper, it was no big deal.

"It was probably in all the papers. I only saw the one article. A long one."

"And this friend of yours, this cop, he was talking to you about this case?"

"Yes," I admitted.

"Huh," Handley said. And without saying anything more, he hustled his thickset little body right out the door again.

Louie scowled. "We should move out of state."

Chapter
Ten

I was told I couldn't move anywhere, not out of state, not to Silver Lake, not even out of my bed for a full forty-eight hours. I had to stay in the hospital another day and a half for observation.

I tried to get out of bed, felt a little dizzy, and lay back down again, and the nurse was right on top of me with words of cheerful encouragement.

"You never know when a concussion can lead to a coma and then death. You want to die, you go right ahead and leave."

Even though I took her at her word, another way to put things was that you never knew when an emergency room visit the price of a small car could turn into an observation that cost the price of a large boat.

On top of everything else I had to worry about, I was now worrying that the hospital staff would turn their powers of observation to the Blue Cross insurance code I gave them and discover it was not really mine.

Still, I stayed on threat of coma, and I sent Louie home for that all important cell phone.

I refused the pain pills I was offered because they made me feel even more out of control than I already was and forced down some cold mashed potatoes and chicken parts.

I was used to being the one in charge. I was used to calling the shots. And instead, the shots had been called on me. Down to and including how much I wanted to see Joe. I wanted to see Joe very badly.

When I finished picking at my lousy hospital food, I got the nurse to give me a plastic bag to wrap around my arm so I could take a shower without wetting the bandage. Then, feeling positively stunning in my crisp, fresh hospital gown, impatiently waiting for Louie and obsessively thinking of Joe, I was actually glad when Handley came back.

He had a different sort of expression on his face now than he'd had a few hours earlier. He looked like I might be someone worth taking an interest in, instead of someone who probably in some way deserved what she had gotten.

He was smiling, actually smiling, and he had brought a bouquet of cheap daisies with him.

My first guess was that Joe was on his way and that he had asked Handley to pinch hit for him, that Joe was more important either to the LAPD or at least to the Littlejohn case than Handley had known, so now Handley had to be nice to me.

"I have some really interesting news for you," he said, and his tone was almost gleeful.

As I hunched forward in my hospital bed, I realized too late that his smile had a little bit of a smirk to it. My heart sank, and my second guess was that

I should call Louie and tell him to forget bringing me the phone and to start packing right now.

"A Detective Richter of Mayville, Texas, was indeed working on this Littlejohn case of yours."

"Did you speak with him?"

"Did I speak with him, she asks."

Some of the smirk faded, and Handley put the daisies on my night table. He shook his head almost sympathetically.

"Lady, everybody's been wanting to speak to him since Littlejohn died. Because he was the last one to see the son of a bitch alive. Or, at least somebody who called themselves Richter was the last one to see Littlejohn alive."

"Someone who called themselves . . ."

I went hot, and I went cold. I could feel myself flush red, and I could feel my hands go clammy.

"He called himself something else while he was at Littlejohn's place. And when he disappeared and we figured out it was the same guy, we found out our Joe Richter wasn't a cop back in Texas."

"He's not a cop?"

I confess, a feeling not unlike relief washed over me.

"Nope."

"Why didn't you know he wasn't a cop?"

Handley went all squirrely on me. "Mistakes were made. Let's not compound them. Now. Why were you with him?"

I went elaborately casual. "Chance meeting. Liked him. Just met him on Saturday. We spent some time together. That's all."

But it was apparently too late for the casual act. Handley raised an eyebrow.

"So. You just meet the guy, but he talks to you all

about this case he's supposedly working on, and then somebody mugs you. The same somebody turns up gruesomely dead, and you think that's all connected somehow to the Littlejohn case? Why?"

"He talked about it. He wanted my opinion about the case."

"This guy you just met—he wants your opinion on a murder case?"

"It wasn't as odd as it sounds now. And I liked him."

I didn't want to get into the whole psychic thing or how Joe had heard of me if I didn't have to. And I didn't want to get into the part about us going to the Littlejohn house either. That last part was more for Joe, whoever he was, than for me, he didn't need a B&E hanging over him.

"So how would it be that the guy who attacked you was connected to the Littlejohn case anyway?"

"I don't really know that he was," I lied. "It was just an idea I had. You're the cop; why don't you solve the crime?"

"Is that what you said to this so-called Joe Richter when he wanted help?"

"No."

"So I guess he was a tad more persuasive than me. I guess you had more reason to discuss a case that at least supposedly, you knew nothing whatsoever about with this perfect stranger, than you do to discuss a case that completely and totally affects you with me when I'm only trying to help."

He looked indignant and genuinely wounded. I wondered if cops took acting lessons now.

I just shrugged. "I always try to help. When I met the other detective and now too."

He shifted his weight and his tactics. "So when

you and Joe met up, how'd he bring up this Littlejohn thing exactly? Did he just say, hey, can I buy you a drink, let me talk to you about a murder case?"

"It came up very . . . naturally in conversation. And we weren't in a bar. We were at the . . . the beach. Haven't you ever turned to someone for help on a case that was bothering you?" I asked.

"Not a pretty girl I picked up."

I turned red again; I could feel the flush rising.

"He didn't exactly pick me up. We just spent some time together, and we liked being together, so we spent some more time . . ."

"Some time in the Mondrian Hotel, I imagine," Handley said, and he pulled one of my stolen washcloths from his pocket. "Found this on your living room floor."

"A souvenir," I said.

"Of a romantic weekend," Handley sneered.

"There's something illegal about such a weekend?" I countered.

"Stealing's stealing," he said. "Regarding the washcloth. And the towels. And the robes. Not that we're gonna press charges or anything," he added hastily. "But in regard to your ah, assignation—no, that's not illegal. That's odd. We're back to odd. I mean, really and truly, why would a woman like you want to be with a guy she thought was a cop?"

When the bottom falls out of your life, it should feel like something, but maybe I'd been through so much in the last few days that I was numb to it.

After his little remark about a "woman like me," Handley outlined a couple of complaints filed against a Christina Alberts of Venice. I denied that I was her, and I hoped that the telemarketing manager who took my money at that address would deny that I was her too. I pointed out that I didn't live in Venice, that I lived in Hollywood; that my first name was Christine, not Christina, and that my last name was legally Harris. I did not point out that my actual birth name was Suzanne Christina Harbert.

He started making notes on everything I said. I think the note taking behavior was just to ratchet up the discomfort level. The complaints were lightweight stuff, "took my mother's money for bogus services . . . had grandfather's Social Security check signed over to her and cashed it . . . took money to conduct a séance and never showed up at the séance." Oh, I remembered that one. That was a suspicious son who called me up, the same one who doubtlessly filed this heretofore uninvestigated complaint, so the spirits called me away, and I didn't make the gig.

I denied everything with scornful disinterest, but the fact that Handley knew about these complaints and that I had to deny that I was who I was made me wild inside.

It wasn't beyond my comprehension, of course, that someday I might be caught at something. It *was* beyond me that I would ever be in such a position because I had been conned by someone else. And that was what was dawning on me now.

The relief that Joe wasn't a cop began to slip away under the realization that Joe, or whatever his name really was, had conned me into getting involved in the Littlejohn mess. For what purpose, I wasn't quite sure. If Handley would ever shut up,

I might have a chance to think it through and figure it out. I might also have a chance to think
about whether or not the "I love you" stuff was a
con too.

That was the part that was really making me
wild.

I ran the show. No one ran me. I watched other
people's body movements, the looks in their eyes.
Instead, someone had watched mine. Even now,
someone was watching, someone who for sure was
a real cop, and tired as I was, obsessed with Joe as I
was, with my arm hurting and all, I had to put real
effort into deflecting Handley.

I performed as outraged citizen for a little bit,
but I didn't think he was buying it, so then I did
the grievously assaulted victim being persecuted
by questioning. When that didn't shut him up, I
did the poor, confused, ill-used lover, which I suppose had enough of a ring of truth to it that he
bought that.

Or maybe he had better things to do that day
than harassing me, or maybe when the dour nurse
came in and said I needed to get some rest, that
did the trick.

She was apparently right about the resting because I closed my eyes with simple relief that
Handley was gone, and then I was asleep.

When I opened my eyes again, Louie was sitting
patiently in the chair Handley had occupied.

"You poor thing," he said.

I didn't think he had said that because I was in
the hospital and sleeping.

I sat up and reached for a glass of water on my
nightstand. I took a long swallow, girding myself

for whatever it was that made Louie call me a poor thing.

"Spill it," I said.

"We-ll. That phone you wanted? It's gone."

"Gone?"

"I'm guessing the guy who attacked you took it."

"Or the police," I said.

"All your cell phones are gone," he said. "But that ring of yours is still in your sock drawer, and the gold coins are too. Not the cash though. Still, we can replace that, right?" he asked brightly.

When I didn't say anything, he gestured to a duffel bag by his feet. "I brought you a change of clothes, a hairbrush, a protein bar, and a whole mess of vitamins. You should really take the vitamins. Build up your strength. You're exposed to so many diseases when you're in a hospital. I took a whole handful of vitamins myself, and I'm just visiting."

"I'm sorry you had to come here . . ."

"You're my best friend. What am I gonna do, stay home because I have this thing about germs?"

". . . and the cops and all," I went on.

"Well, if I'd known they were going to be all over you, I might just have sent chocolates." He smiled and patted my hand.

"Is there anything else missing at my place? Other than the phones and the cash?"

"Well, I think he took a box of your Madame Christina business cards and your Fox Broadcasting parking passes."

"I guess the cops could've taken them."

"The parking passes?"

"The phones! But yeah, maybe the passes too

and the business cards to check up on me. I don't know."

"Why would they care that much?"

"The guy who attacked me is dead, Louie. Dead with his hands cut off."

Louie looked properly appalled.

"They think your boyfriend did it," he said after a moment. "Am I right? He's not really a cop. You slept with a psychopath."

"I don't know what the cops think," I said. "And Joe's not a psychopath. How stupid do you think I am?"

Louie looked away discreetly.

"They said he wasn't a cop though," I admitted.

Louie reached for the duffel bag and pulled out the baggie full of vitamins. "You really should take these," he said. "Keep your strength up. I'll pick you up on Wednesday."

It was a long and restless night. There was the nurse checking on me. There were the beepings and bleetings of machines indicating the tenuousness of mortality that I didn't want to think about drifting in from the hall.

I had to admit that Louie was right—the solution was to pack up and get myself a new place of residence and with that, a new last name. I'd done it before.

But it was tiring to move, and it took money. My bandaged arm hurt, and my head ached a little, and I was broke again. I was certainly in no mood to run any sort of scam. I didn't want to pawn the gold pieces; they were my grandmother's. But what other choice did I have?

My life, such as it was, was over. *There* was a thought conducive to sleep in a hospital bed redolent with the odor of disinfectant.

And right on its heels came another sleep-inducing thought. Joe had said he loved me, and I'd believed him. But he had said a lot of other things too, many of which weren't true. I didn't know how to find him, and he didn't know how to find me, unless Nelson had told him. He wasn't a cop, and he could be a murderer. He was, at the very least, as big a liar as I was, and while I often had very good reasons for my lies, that didn't mean he had good reasons. It was a lot more likely that his reasons were all bad. And if he lied about one or two or ten things, who was to say he hadn't lied about the love part, about not needing words, about my being his gift, all of it?

Maybe I'd been right, after all, to feel afraid the night of the shooting stars. Maybe I wasn't afraid of surrendering to sudden love; maybe I was afraid of being taken.

The first gray light of dawn was spilling in through my hospital window. I must've slept again. I felt thick and loggy, but I couldn't remember any dreams. It seemed like it had been a long time since a nurse had come in to check on me, but now, right on cue, here one came, slipping into the half light, a shadow.

Maybe I was dreaming now because this shadow wasn't a nurse; wasn't a doctor either; I was pretty sure of that, even though he was wearing a doctor's smock and he had a stethoscope draped convincingly around his neck.

It was Joe.

I sat up and swung out of my bed just as he reached it.

"You son of a bitch," I hissed, and I was auditioning for the made for TV kid's superhero movie again or the second unit of the *Wonder Woman* reunion, one or the other, it didn't matter. I was aiming my kickboxes low and hard.

"Stop it," he said, grabbing for me.

I spun around and punched him in the jaw. That set him back on his heels.

"Stop." He got me around the waist, and I continued to flail at him until he locked my hands in his.

"Not that I don't deserve it," he said breathlessly.

"Let go of me; I'll scream," I said, my worst threat ever, and he'd know it too if he'd spoken to Nelson before he cut off the guy's hands.

"Christy, don't," he pleaded. "You have no idea how hard it was to get in here. First, the cops, then the night nurse, what a demon. Had to wait for the shift change. But now I can explain everything."

"Really? Like how the universe was created, and what the green flash is that people sometimes see when the sun sets in the tropics?"

I heard footsteps coming down the hall, and we both froze.

He dropped my wrists, and I lay back down on the bed.

An orderly pushed into the room with a tray of something that smelled like a simulation of breakfast.

"Not now," Joe said in a commanding yet irritated tone. He sounded almost exactly like the guy who was my doctor. "This dressing needs immediate attention."

"Sorry, doctor," the orderly backed out of the room again rapidly.

"He's got that wrong. You're not a doctor," I said, springing up again. "And you're not a cop either."

"You're not a psychic," he shrugged.

"Who told the lie that for sure lands you in jail?" I countered. "Who told the lie that probably put my life in jeopardy. Who—"

I didn't get to finish my rant because Joe pulled me tight against him, and he leaned down and kissed me. He kissed me for a long time, and it was wonderful. Standing there, pressed up against a hospital bed, breathing in stale antiseptic air and the leftover waft of bacon from the orderly's breakfast cart, this lying, troublemaking man whose name I wasn't even sure I knew was kissing me.

He was also running his hand down my spine and slipping it under my stunning hospital gown, and his fingers were moving warm and fast to my breasts. Then his lips were no longer on mine, but on my skin, my throat, my shoulders.

"Stop it," I breathed, but of course I didn't mean it. I was fumbling with his belt; he was stroking my thighs. All I could think about was how good it felt to have his hands touching me, how much I wanted him to keep touching me, to never stop touching.

"What is it with us?" I asked, even though I pretty much knew the answer.

We were both starved for connection. Not just sexual connection, although that was what we were using to reach each other, to hold on.

We rocked close. He buried his face in my hair. "I was so worried about you when you didn't call. I don't think I could've stood another day with no word. It was killing me."

"Killing *you*?" I pushed him away and pulled down my gown. I'd almost forgotten the very real possibility that this man busily undressing me in my hospital room was a murderer. "You mean like I could've been killed?"

A tired look fell over him like a shadow. "Poor choice of words I guess."

"For a murderer," I said, and I was shaking because of the acts I was afraid he might've committed and because of the one I wanted to commit right then, no matter what he'd done, no matter how little I trusted him.

"You don't believe that. I didn't murder anyone. And I didn't mean to put your life in danger. I didn't."

"You set me up."

"Unintentionally."

"Unintentionally? You don't strike me as that incompetent."

Joe sighed. "You were a name, a piece in a puzzle. I only wanted information from you; I wanted to see how and where you fit in."

"It didn't occur to you that other people might want information from me too? Information that, I might add, I don't even have?"

"I thought I could watch out for you, protect you, but damn you, you gave me the wrong address."

"Good excuse."

"It's not an excuse." His face twisted. "At least not a good one. And starting right now, I'm not letting you out of my sight until this whole mess is over with."

"Oh, wow, how incredibly gallant of you." I scowled at him. "And when the mess does magically end somehow?"

"And then . . . then I'm not going to let you out of my sight either. Unless . . . unless you want me to."

I softened. Joe took my hands in his again, and instead of him gripping my wrist to keep me from decking him, there we were just holding hands again.

I'd known men with big meaty hands and overwhelming, crushing hands. Men with sweaty palms. Men with skinny fingers, hairy fingers, cold tips. Men with palms not much larger than my own.

But Joe's hands were just right. Strong and ample, but not too big and not too small, and warm but not sweaty. Hands that could take care of you and hold you. His hands weren't lying—I knew that much.

"You feel just right," he said, which was the simple way of saying it all for me too. "So right."

"I guess you do too," I said.

He reached for me, and we kissed a little longer. Then we just stood there looking at each other, hands locked together. I was still mad as hell but I was ready to take as much of it as I could.

"I love you, Christy," he said.

"I think I need to at least know your name before I can say I love you too."

"You know my name. I'm Joe."

"And is that the name your mama gave you?"

"No. She called me James Joseph, actually."

I actually believed him.

"Your real name is Christy?"

"Part of it."

"Part of it. Which part?"

"No, no. We're not getting off on me. Whatever I've done and whoever I am, I haven't almost gotten you killed. I didn't murder anyone either," I said, returning like a pit bull to the bone I most wanted to gnaw.

"I did not kill Ricky Littlejohn," he said firmly. "Not that I didn't want to. I had other things I wanted to get to first."

"The fourteen million."

"That's some of it, yeah. Plus a confession I wanted, and some names and places the cops could run with."

"The cops. Like you have a relationship with them?"

"I do have. It's just not quite the way I told you." Joe looked down at his hands.

"And what about Nelson?" I demanded. "Did you kill him?"

"Why would I want him dead?"

"Gee, let me count the reasons—so he couldn't rat you out, so he couldn't come after that money, so he couldn't try to kill you, so—"

"I'll explain everything," he said. "Just give me a chance."

His eyes sought mine and held them. The sincerity seemed so real. But I knew he might explain for eternity and still not make anything clear.

I was usually the one that pulled the wool over the eyes of the world. Why was it that I felt like I was the one being blindsided now?

It starts, I guess, when you fall in love. To fall, to let go, to just plunge headlong into whatever it was

you were plunging into with no regard whatsoever
as to where you would land.

"Just give you a chance and you'll explain everything," I sighed. "That's what they all say."

"Do they?"

He lifted my chin with his fingers, his eyes so
open, so unguarded, so hopeful. Could anybody
pull that off as an act? Other than me, of course?

"One chance," I said. "Only one."

"One is all I need," he said. "Now let's get the
hell out of here."

Chapter
Eleven

When I first showed up in LA, sixteen, thrilled and scared and ravenous, I got straight off the bus at five AM with my backpack and my dreams and just about enough in my pocket for one last meal. Then, there were plenty of places open all night at which I could have had that meal, complete with free refill coffee too.

There were twenty-four hour Ships and Pann's restaurants all over the city, Google architecture classics with neon signs outside and orange plastic booths inside. They had toasters right on the table, and they served big, cheap, greasy breakfasts around the clock. You'd see people just sitting at those booths, no matter what the hour, eating those breakfasts, reading a book, playing solitaire, or sharing a game of chess.

It seemed so very quaint now, really. Now there were laptops instead of chess boards and palm pilots and cell phones instead of paperbacks, and they were utilized in coffeehouses with croissants and Mocha or Capa or some kind of chino.

So there were no longer a lot of choices of where to hear an explanation of the sort Joe was going to have to produce and have scrambled eggs before sunrise.

I'd dressed quickly from the bag Louie had packed for me in jeans and a tee shirt, ignoring how much my arm hurt when I pulled the shirt on.

Joe found a wheelchair; tucked my chart under his arm; and looking purposeful and determined, pushed me down the hall one step ahead of the morning shift nursing staff starting their rounds. We abandoned the wheelchair by the elevator and took the stairs down to the next floor, tossed Joe's doctor's smock into a laundry hamper, and took the elevator from there straight to the parking garage where Joe's Mustang awaited.

Lack of wee hours breakfast spots led us to the Denny's on Sunset right by the 101 freeway, which was frequented by gangbangers, late night revelers, transvestites, and bag ladies at such an hour. The traffic rushed by outside our window table, its sound like that of a tidal wave about to break over us, and the place had the stale smell of the cigarettes and marijuana clinging to the clothes of the other patrons. Compared to the hospital, it was fantastic, and so was the food.

Drowning my limp home fries in ketchup, I demanded to know why Nelson had come looking for me, what Joe had been thinking when he asked me to visit Ricky's murder scene, who was it that had killed Nelson, how was it that Joe had known to find me at the hospital—

But Joe waved my questions away. "We'll get to all that. But I think I have to explain myself a little first, or nothing else will make any sense."

I nodded, allowing that that might be the truth.

"Remember how I told you my father was a cop, and my brother—"

"You made that up?"

"No. That's true. Cross my heart. My grandfather was a cop too. Everyone *but* me. I went to the University of Texas, where I took drama."

"Drama," I said dumbly. "Like acting?"

"Yes ma'am," he said. "I think we actually have more in common than you know, you and I."

"Uh-huh," I said, "well."

If he was as good an actor as I was, he could be lying right now. How would I know?

"I may never have been, nor do I ever intend to be a real cop, but I played the part of a young, highly dedicated police officer in a movie that went straight to video and was, I believe, translated into Portugese. I was sure that would be my big break, my calling card, and in fact, I moved to LA on the strength of it."

He swirled an extra spoon of sugar into his coffee. I couldn't help but notice that both of us liked double sugar.

"That has been my biggest part to date. Oh, I got by with extra work, some voice-over here and there. But it was clear really quickly that I needed a steadier gig. Without, you know, giving up the dream."

He smiled, I smiled. I knew all about the dream.

"Police work *per se* wasn't for me, but I guess I had inherited the investigating gene or something because the work I ended up with was private investigating."

"You're a P.I.?"

"A pretty fair one too, if I do say so. I apprenticed to a fellow working divorce cases, and when I went out on my own, I ended up with most of his clients. See lots of guys are so clumsy at it, so you could spot 'em a mile away tailing you. Me, I put my acting to good use, especially all the experience I had playing background. Nobody ever saw me coming. It was a way to earn a decent living without keeping regular hours, still go on auditions, and not have to wear a uniform. It seemed cool. After a while, I gave up on the acting, but I was actually having a good time."

"A good time?"

He took a sip of water; then he looked at me.

"Look, I was young. There were lots of pretty damsels in distress. Their attention kind of eased the sting of my Hollywood rejections, at least for a while. Over time though, seeing what I saw in people, in their relationships and how easily they were discarded, it was more disillusioning than my former stab at a thespian career. I started to think I'd never meet anybody who actually cared about me or who I would actually care about."

He was silent for a long time, twisting his coffee cup back and forth in his hands and reflecting the flourescent lights on the ceiling. I knew exactly what he meant, and I felt for him, I really did. But did I trust him?

"Anyway, one angst-ridden day, out of the blue, my brother, Hallie, called me and said he needed my help with something he was working on. He very rarely needed my help, or anybody's, really. He was the one who helped other people out, fixed things the way he fixed up old cars. So I was glad, flattered even, to help him on a case."

"Ricky Littlejohn," I guessed, which wasn't really that hard of a guess to make.

"Yeah." Joe rubbed his forehead. "Hallie was working homicide when he came across a flier being circulated to geriatric patients at Houston area hospitals and nursing homes and to the loved ones of accident victims and those who had, or who faced the prospect of, exceedingly high medical bills. The flier read 'Donate your body to science and profit while you're still alive. It is incredibly easy. Get your money immediately, and enjoy Life! That's right. You can make $20,000 per year by donating your body to science while you are still alive. You make the money now, and help advance science.' It is good for mankind and great for your wallet.' "

Even though he'd obviously committed it to memory, Joe still had a copy of this flyer; he pulled it out of his wallet and handed it to me, all worn at the edges like a favorite photograph.

I frowned, trying to understand.

"That was my first brush with the body business," Joe said.

"The body business," I repeated. There was that phrase again. Bodies in funeral homes. Bodies in nursing home beds. Bodies strutting down the runway at Paris fashion shows. And now, bodies for science.

"According to Hallie, the flyer was passed around Houston. At the corresponding nursing and hospital facilities there and all across the U.S. where the fliers were seen, facilities with what seemed to Hallie to be an inordinately high mortality rate. These flyers were circulated by itinerant workers nominally employed by a company called LJ Research, which was dedicated to providing "medical subjects for study" to major teaching hospitals, which doesn't sound that bad in and of itself, even if their flyer was kind of sleazy. The company was affiliated with a firm that provided nursing services, and both companies were owned by a parent company that was incorporated in Delaware and headquartered in California, where they were headed up by one Ricky Littlejohn and his wife, Laura. Hallie's department didn't have the budget or the interest to send him out here to investigate, and it wasn't even convinced there was anything that wrong with the whole business. It seemed that the cops in LA weren't particularly interested either. But Hallie was convinced. He was convinced it smelled bad. So he asked me to investigate for him when I had some free time.

"Looking into LJ Research, I found out that the corpse business was a big one, that people made a lot of money. Not just selling bodies for so-called science but also heads, legs, arms, and torsos."

"And hands," I said, thinking of Nelson.

Joe nodded. "Parts is parts. And it's not just for science, either; not research, not transplants, not for first year medical students to dissect. The bodies and body parts are sometimes prized collector's items. Kinda like hunting trophies. People have them taxidermied. Hang them on walls. Use them for religious rituals. Witchcraft. Art."

I grimaced.

"It's ugly," Joe said. "But not as ugly as the rumors that when an adequate supply of naturally deceased bodies tapers off, the supply and demand gap gets filled in with a less natural supply in some cases. Some companies, of course, are completely above board. But not Ricky's."

"What a surprise," I murmured.

"Looking into Ricky, I didn't think he had it together enough to play it cool in the kind of environment the sale of the dead entailed. I knew he had to have partners, besides his wife, that is. I also knew the business needed some kind of powerful outside support to prosper so that people who might be inclined to look at the operation closely could be persuaded to look away instead. Hallie agreed with me one hundred percent. I promised him I'd tail Ricky until I came up with something more." He shook his head bitterly. "But I didn't."

"But you didn't?"

"Paying clients. A case got messy, and I went to court on it. Life. Hallie didn't push me about it, so the whole thing kind of got put on the back burner."

Joe shoved his coffee cup away from him as if he were repulsed by it. "Until Hallie's wife calls me one night. And she tells me that he's . . . gone."

"Gone," I repeated stupidly.

"Hit and run. A fluke. He was just getting off his shift. Wee hours of the morning. He was . . . going out for coffee. I couldn't believe it. My brother, my best friend, gone. I wished I'd spent more time visiting with him, more time on the phone, more time helping him out with that case. And then the real bombshell exploded through all of those regrets. Susan—that's Hallie's wife—was settling Hallie's affairs. He gave what he had to his wife and kids, of course, except the car—the car went to me. So I fly out to pick up the car, and we're talking about how much fun Hallie had working on it, but I get this feeling she has something else she wants to say. And finally she does—she asks me did I know anything about Hallie coming into some sudden money. And I said no."

"What kind of money?"

"A couple hundred thousand. Deposited in his bank account just a few days before he died. And I tracked it the way they must've known someone would track it, if anyone cared, to LJ Research. And it didn't look good."

"Hallie was in on—"

"No!" Joe's color was high, and I thought he was going to stand up and shout. "Somebody wanted people to think that."

"Why?"

"It was one way to play Hallie's interest in the body business. And then another way presented itself. A predawn parking lot and no witnesses."

"You think he was murdered?"

"I know he was. Ricky told me. He bragged about it. Said he knew the driver personally. Said the driver had an itchy trigger foot; thought it was a big joke. According to Ricky, Hallie wasn't the only one who bought it in the name of scientific research."

"He came right out and told you?"

"Ricky liked talking about how he could have people 'dropkicked into eternity' anytime he wanted. He could just snap his pudgy fingers together and boom, he said. Of course, he wasn't telling *me*. He was telling Dennis Lane, guitar player, lounge singer, and easily impressed hanger-on."

"And faux undercover cop?" I prodded.

"I talked to some acquaintances of mine at LAPD, hoping to find the right person to tell my story to about LJ Research. But they weren't that interested. I was, after all, a lightweight P.I. in the San Fernando Valley who once wanted to be an actor. If I was a cop, then maybe there'd be a little more credibility ascribed to my story; maybe then they could put me in touch with the right people and launch an investigation."

Joe stretched out his hands in front of him. "So I became a cop. I more or less took on my brother's identity. I got a cell phone with a Texas exchange, and I pretended to be my own superior officer. I

led the LAPD to believe, in no uncertain terms, that
there was an ongoing murder investigation connected to Ricky Littlejohn here in LA."

"And nobody checked out your story?"

"Cops take other cops' words. And I was a be-
lievable cop. I played one in the movies, right? I
had my brother and my father to base my performance on. And I wasn't asking for much, just some
information, just some backup if necessary. I just
wanted to clue them in on how dirty Ricky Littlejohn was and that he was connected to dirtier men
than himself. Some of that they already knew."

And so, Joe went on, the LAPD, thinking it was
working with an eager beaver from Texas who had
made promises to it about handing it the collar
when and if he got it, was happy to help Joe set up
another fake identity—that of Dennis Lane, musician in a Malibu lounge—and let him go deep.

In fast order, Joe was installed in The Blue Wave
Lounge on Pacific Coast Highway, biding his time
until he could step in and ingratiate himself with
Ricky and scope out the entire operation.

"At first, things went better than I could've
hoped. Ricky literally took me home with him and
left me there alone. I could rummage through his
papers and tape record his phone conversations.
And I passed whatever I got onto the police here.
But I wasn't getting much in the weeks I lived at
Casa Ricky. Yes, his ex-father-in-law, the mortician,
certainly called on the phone a lot. Ricky brown-
nosed the guy big time, and it wasn't exactly rocket
science to figure out that the mortuary assisted in
some of the arrangements for the transportation
of Ricky's, er, product. But there was nothing with
a big, flashing red arrow pointing to criminal enter-
prise. Ricky never talked facts; he talked big plans

and phony dreams. One thing that he kept saying, though, seemed pretty real—he claimed he was holding *aside,* somewhere fourteen million dollars from his still unnamed business partners. Money they all expected to see sometime soon in return for their continued cooperation and involvement in his business. In other words, it was payoff money, and he figured he'd paid off enough."

"Did you pass that information onto the cops too?" I asked, but Joe didn't answer me.

"See, Ricky had this scheme to keep the money hidden somehow. He'd entered into the body business in the first place because he was deeply in debt, and not to Citibank. He felt he'd worked off his debt ten times over to whoever it was that had bailed him out, that he'd been poorly treated in the bargain, and he didn't want to be anybody's patsy anymore."

"Get that money, I thought, and the whole thing will blow wide open. There were people that money was supposed to be paying off who weren't getting paid off; they'd start floating to the surface like dead fish very soon, and he'd cave. He'd be forced to get into his stash. Unless, of course, his stash disappeared."

"And besides," I said, "fourteen million would be a nice little party favor."

Joe's eyes flashed. "I wanted it for Hallie's wife and kids."

I shrugged. Maybe he did. "Revenge and fourteen million dollars," I said. "That must've been a lot of heat to carry."

"It still is," Joe said.

"Who ratted you out?" I interrupted.

Joe gave a funny little smile. He reached across the table, and he took both of my hands in his. "I thought maybe you did."

"Me?" I was so astonished that I dropped Joe's hands back on the table with a slap.

"If you were a real psychic. Which I thought you just might be. The way Laura talked about her mother going on about you."

"Laura's mother?"

"Rose Holloman. Married Charles Ordam. That marriage produced—"

We both said it together. "Laura Ordam Little-john."

"Laura said she was going to see you," Joe said. "She said she was going to ask you questions about her living arrangements, about the men in her life, and about what any one of us might mean to her. That's what she called us, Ricky, Nelson, and me. She acted like we were all in love with her or something, but suffice to say, she wasn't getting a lot of empirical evidence to support that idea. So she said she had to talk to you about us. She said it just like that on the very same day Ricky called me out."

Joe spoke casually, but I could tell even now by the way he just kind of dropped the words in there, like he'd been planning to drop them all along, that this was serious stuff, that he was calling *me* out.

"I never saw Laura. Although I do think Rose said her daughter wanted to meet me. All that did was send up a red flag. Relatives usually want to check me out with the Better Business Bureau." I racked my memory. "Rose and Laura. I had no idea they were even related. And as far as Rose went, I just gave her the usual line."

"I know that now," he said and stroked my fingers reassuringly. He'd taken his last shot, and he hadn't hit a thing, and he was glad of it. I saw the relief crease his eyes.

"It didn't take me long to find out you weren't likely to give Nostradamus a run for his money."

I sniffed. "You seemed quite taken with me."

"You *are* good at pretending to know stuff," he amended.

"And you were very good at pretending you believed I knew stuff," I threw in.

All that talk about my perception, my special psychic gift. I was worrying about lying to him, and all the time he was lying to me!

My indignation broke out, red as the flush I could feel growing on my cheeks. "What was the point of taking me to Ricky's house? In asking me all those stupid questions?"

"They weren't stupid, and just because you weren't a, shall we say, legitimate psychic, didn't mean that you didn't know certain things. Didn't mean that Laura, or at least Rose, hadn't consulted with you, spilled certain things, revealed certain information. People talk to psychics just like they talk to bartenders or hairdressers. You might've had valuable information. A couple of times there at Ricky's house, it sure seemed like you knew something anyway."

"And is that why you came on to me? To find out what I knew that I wasn't telling?"

"Before I kissed you, yeah, there was some ulterior motive. Even though I was, from the minute I saw you, very attracted. But after I kissed you, that was something different altogether. That was electric. That was . . . amazing."

So far he was saying exactly the right things. So I felt exactly the same way. He still wasn't getting off that easy.

"And why did you take me to look at the shooting stars?" I demanded. "What were you trying to get from me then?"

"I took you because I wanted to," he said quietly. "Because I guess I'm not too jaded after all to know the real thing when I find it. To know that in spite of my own lies, which were more or less born of necessity, and in spite of any lies you might've told, we both knew the truth about each other. I could look at you and you could look right into me and we saw who we were. And we liked each other."

I could feel my reserve melting away, but I didn't show it. I looked away from him at the ketchup drying on my plate.

"How we found each other might be a little strange, but the finding itself is nothing short of miraculous," he said.

Miraculous or not, I still wanted some facts.

"Get to Ricky biting it," I said. "I want to know how that went down."

Outside, the sky was full light now, sunshine streaking the fly-spotted windows. Around us, the dining crowd had changed; there were people on their way to work, people who looked like salesmen with cheap briefcases, tourists with backpacks and maps, and blue-haired ladies asking for senior specials. We'd been talking over an hour, and we still weren't through.

Joe drained his glass of water like he was out in the middle of the desert and parched, and maybe he was. Maybe I was too, both of us stranded in the middle of the nowhere of our lives. We could save each other if we only believed. According to Joe, he already believed. I was the salvation holdout.

He began to talk again. "I was taking a shower in the upstairs bathroom because Nelson had regur-

gitated the previous evening's drug and alcohol in-
take in the guest basement's toilet. Ricky was out
with Laura, visiting Laura's mother and ostensibly,
Laura's mother's psychic. But he came back ahead
of Laura and earlier than I expected. I heard him
thunder up the stairs—you couldn't help but hear
him since he sounded like a herd of elephants
stampeding—and I knew there was gonna be trouble. I knew it the way you look in the rearview mirror of a car, and you see there's a truck coming up
too fast, but you don't have any time to get out of
the way before it hits you. I got out of the shower,
wrapped up in a towel, and went for the gun I always kept strapped to my ankle that was now resting on top of my jeans, which were resting on the
toilet seat."

I raised my eyebrows.

"I know. Pretty lame. I left the shower running,
got the gun, and dove behind the curtain again.
Ricky kicked the door open and pushed the curtain back, and he was waving a fancy chef's knife in
his hand. I thought, okay, so this is how it goes
down, you asshole, and I shot. I shot right at his
fucking balls, but nothing happened."

"Nothing happened?"

Joe shook his head. "Maybe nothing happened
because the gun got wet; maybe nothing happened
because there was just something wrong with the
weapon I'd been so carefully concealing; maybe it
was the hand of God telling me not to be so damn
cocky. At any rate, it did not fire, and Ricky got in a
couple of jabs with the knife, and I fell."

"The bloodstains in the shower were yours," I
murmured.

"I closed my eyes like I'd been hurt much worse
than I had. 'You lied to me,' Ricky said, 'I'm the

only one who doesn't have to tell the truth around me.' "

My eyebrows went up again. Joe managed a smile.

"Yeah, he really did say that. He really was stupid. Anyway, I let Ricky move in close. I was gonna grab his pudgy ankles, knock him on his back, and beat the living crap out of him. And let him know he killed my brother, or had my brother killed anyway, and I was going to kill him, unless he gave up his partners and his money. When he did, and I was pretty sure the fat rat would, surprise, I was gonna kill him anyway."

"But that's not how it went down?"

Joe shook the ice in his empty water glass. "There was a knock on the front door, and a doorbell jangled over and over. Ricky cursed and just left me lying there in my own blood before he could get in close enough for me to grab him.

"He locked the bathroom door after him. And it was probably just as well. Because when I tried to get up and go after him and slam through that door and tackle the son of a bitch, I found out that I was hurt more than I thought. I had a hard time with just the getting up part.

"I looked in the mirror, saw I had a nice deep slash across the chest, and a wound I knew I'd have to get treatment for just above the appendix.

"I pressed a towel tightly against the lower wound and pulled on my pants. I felt dizzy, and I knew I had to get some help before I really did just pass out and put myself at Ricky's disposal.

"I opened the chamber on the gun, checked the bullets, and closed it up again, but I still couldn't get the thing to fire. Still, I had to get out of there. It took a ridiculously long time, but I kicked the bathroom door open. I was ready to hear Ricky come stampeding up again, but he didn't come.

"It was real silent in the house, except for the shower, which I just left running. I inched my way through the bedroom and down the stairs. The front door was open, but there was nobody in sight, and I took it as good fortune. As much as I wanted to take Ricky out, after all that time, I couldn't risk Ricky taking me out, and I was just weak enough and shocked enough and incompetent enough that I knew it could go down that way."

So instead, Joe made his way to the garage, took Ricky's burnt sienna Hummer, and drove himself to Santa Monica Hospital to get stitched up.

"In the glove compartment, I found fifteen thousand dollars in hundred dollar bills. I also found a vial of Vicodin. I used some of the Vicodin to ease the waiting time in the Emergency room, and I used some of the money to ease the pain of the hospital bill. The rest of it I've been living on.

"Maybe it was the pain pills, I don't know; I guess I wasn't thinking clearly. I thought about calling LAPD, but an assault charge wouldn't be much to hold against Ricky, and besides—"

"You still wanted the money. And whoever drove the car that killed your brother. And Ricky's partners."

"Yeah. I at least wanted to nail Laura's daddy."

"Mr. Funeral Director—he really is in charge?"

"He had the money in the first place to fish Ricky out of disaster and get his cooperation in establishing this new sideline. He wanted someone to take the helm, to keep things separate from the mortuaries as much as possible. Ricky was his front man. But I still couldn't prove that anymore than I could prove he had a lot of help in high places to keep his business unscrutinized."

So Joe left Ricky's Hummer where he'd parked it in a public garage on Wilshire. He took a cab to the storage garage where he'd kept the Mustang since he'd driven it back to LA from his brother's funeral.

He headed back to the Colony, parked down at the public lot at Surf Rider Beach, and walked up the coast. He was still weak, and he had to stop four or five times along the way; he almost got kicked off the beach by some overzealous security personnel, and then at last, he was at Ricky's. And talk about security.

"The house was a hive of men in uniforms and polyester suits, cops swarming over the place. There was Laura sobbing, and Nelson nervously denying that the drugs were his. It was almost funny.

"I walked out to the road, saw all the yellow police tape, and asked some guy with a reporter's notebook what was up, and he told me Ricky was dead. I asked how he had died. The guy said some kind of drug but that things were hush-hush and that there were bruises on the body. The rumor was that Ricky'd been poisoned. He had also heard that Ricky's car had been stolen. I hadn't wiped my prints off the Hummer, and I now realized that had been a mistake.

"I got back to my car, and I was feeling pretty bad. I wanted to go home to my apartment where the mail was piling up, but something told me not to, the same something that told me earlier to drive my brother's car, not my own. So I checked into the first motel I came to, and I crashed. I just crashed. When I woke up, it was a day later. A day too late."

"Too late for what?"

"For anything that made any sense. I brewed some lousy in-room coffee, and I called one of the cops I was more or less working with at LAPD. Before I could explain much of anything or ask any questions, I could hear this kind of nervous tension in his voice, like there was a wire running through his throat. And he seemed to want to know where I was calling from very badly.

"It concerned me enough that I said the connection was bad, promised to call back, and hung up. I checked out and found a pay phone."

At the pay phone, which he was careful not to stay on too long, he found out that he was suspect number one in Ricky's death; that Ricky had died sitting in his hot tub, died of ingesting a toxic substance that the police felt was forced upon him.

The cop wouldn't say anything more than that over the phone; he was trying to talk Joe into coming in and ostensibly 'fessing up to his involvement. The police had swiftly discovered that Joe was not really a cop, and they'd found the Hummer, found that vial of Vicodin, both with Joe's prints on them. Only the vial they'd found wasn't in the car, but lying next to Ricky. On top of that, they'd figured out there was a strong family motive for revenge because Joe's brother who actually *was* a cop appeared to have been involved in the schemes Ricky was running.

"It got as far as him accusing Hallie before I hung up. Then I didn't know what to do. I knew for sure I couldn't go home. I found another pay phone and called Hallie's wife. Susan told me the Houston police were all over her; she asked me what I'd done, and why I'd done it. I tried to explain that I hadn't done much of anything. Which seemed to make her even more upset. And that was the truth—all I'd done in two months of living with that hog Ricky was find out that he had a big pile o' money hidden somewhere and that Laura's father was very likely the brains of the business. But it was all conjecture. It was all based on garbage Ricky told me. All I had for my trouble was the right to proclaim myself as big a phony as the next asshole."

I knew that feeling myself.

Joe was lost, looking out on the tinsel wavering on the telephone wires above Sunset. It was me who took *his* hand this time. And my touch seemed to work like a tonic—he came back from wherever he was and talked faster now, like he was coasting into the final chapter.

"So I rented a monthly furnished executive apartment in the near Valley in an assumed name and kept on doing what I'd been trying to do all along. Get the goods, posthumously now, on Ricky; find the fourteen million Ricky had stolen; and move in on Laura's daddy, who looked on paper to be blameless, completely disassociated from Ricky, Laura, and LJ Research. And through him, to find any other names I could."

"And while I was at it, I might as well find out who killed Ricky and clear myself. I had to move really carefully though because somebody was watching me, not just the cops. I had to duck tails that were definitely not police tails. If the cops knew where I was, they would've just come and arrested me if they wanted, brought me in for questioning if nothing else. So it wasn't the police watching. And meanwhile, there I am trying to watch other people."

"I spent over a month like that, under surveillance and surveying, and it was a bad way to live; I didn't think it was safe even to call Susan or my folks. The one thing that made me happy was that Ricky was dead. I was glad Ricky was dead. I was maybe even just as glad that I hadn't been the one who killed him. Although everybody thought I did—the cops, Susan, Nelson, and Laura. Why everybody just automatically assumed that, I don't know."

"Maybe it was because you lied about who you were and what you were doing. Maybe it was because you had a motive," I suggested, but not unkindly.

He inclined his head, acquiescing.

"The news article I read about Ricky didn't even suggest he'd been murdered," I added. "Drug overdose it said."

"Yeah, well, that was the other shoe that dropped. Here I was, a wanted man, more or less, in a death by poisoning, and then, boom, a month later, everyone stopped wanting me. Whoever was tailing me stopped tailing. The police yawned and moved on. No arrest warrant. No stories on the local news. Ricky's death was ruled as 'most likely' accidental, but it could've been suicide. Now let me tell you, the fat idiot never would've killed himself—he thought far too highly of himself for that. And accidental? With big bruises all over the body?"

"Yeah, but he didn't die of bruises, right? What was the toxic substance they said killed him?"

"Whatever it was, they kept it out of the police reports and the press." Joe balled up his fists. "Somebody wanted everything swept under the rug. Somebody important enough to get what he or she wanted."

"The detective who came to see me in the hospital said they were looking to talk to you though," I countered.

Joe looked back out the window again. "Now that Nelson's dead, I'm interesting again."

"How do you know about Nelson heading off into the great hereafter anyway?" I asked.

"After I left you at the hotel, I was nosing around some leads I had on Laura, who was last seen down in Mexico a few days before I followed her and bought these boots. I wasn't having any luck at all in tracking her down. I started thinking about you and about how, in comparison, you weren't really that hard to find even if you thought you were. It made me smile, thinking how tough you played yet how vulnerable you really were, and then it hit me that maybe other people saw you as vulnerable too.

"So I went over to your apartment. Or what I thought was your place anyway. And you didn't come home; you weren't at the hotel; you didn't answer your phone; I got very nervous. So I found Jack James."

"Jack?"

"You know, the guy who owns the liquor store you sell—"

"*I* know who he is. He more or less pays my rent. How do *you* know who he is?"

"I wrote down his license plate after I left your storefront that first day in Venice. I thought he might come in handy, and he did. When pressed, he came up with a surveillance tape of his parking lot that had a picture of your car and your plate. I owe a friend of mine at the DMV a couple of nice bottles of wine—I suppose I should patronize Jack's establishment."

"So you got my plate."

"When I researched it, it led to an address in West Hollywood. It wasn't your address of course. But while I was in the neighborhood, I saw a certain increased police presence. Discreetly, I found out about the female assault victim, and how the assaulter had been found dead. I got the victim's street. I knocked on doors, and I asked about you. Your landlady knew you, all right. She doesn't like you much, by the way, but she knows you. She told me what hospital they took you to, and I went to the hospital. The rest, more or less, you know."

He lapsed into silence, as if he were considering something.

"What?"

"Just tired," he said. "Just tired."

"The cops weren't still at my place when you showed up?" I asked.

"They had moved on." He threw some money on the table. "I think we should too."

I nodded, and we left the restaurant, and then we just stood out in the parking lot in too hot sunshine. It was like fake December, nothing real.

It wasn't that after all these years in LA, I wanted snowflakes and pine cones and sleigh bells; it was just that the inflatable snowman swaying on the restaurant roof in the unseasonably warm Santa Ana wind and the bank thermometer across the street already reading eighty-six at seven-thirty AM just weren't right. I wanted a sea breeze, at least, and a reason to wear a sweater.

Or maybe what I wanted was a reason to believe in Joe, to really believe, the way I used to believe in Santa Claus, the way Joe said he believed in me. I wanted to believe in spite of my misgivings, and I still had many, not only in him but also in love. I wanted to believe he was my perfect match, my ideal, my model man. I wanted that so much that all I could do was just stand there wanting.

We stood looking at Joe's car like both of us were expecting it to turn into a sleigh and like it needed to before either of us would actually open the doors and get inside.

Somebody drove by screaming "Ho-ho-ho," and I jumped. Joe reached for me, but I sidestepped him.

"I don't know if I believe a word of what you said," I told him. And yet I was close to believing. I wanted to believe.

"I can tell every word of it to you all over again," he offered. "I've found that to be a sure sign of someone telling the truth. If they can repeat the same story twice."

"Maybe they're just good at memorizing lines," I said, and now I *was* being unkind. "At least maybe you are. You did say you majored in drama."

Joe smiled a tired smile. "I deserved that."

"You deserve this too. That accent even real?"

"It's real," Joe said. "Although I can lose it, I can flat affect Valley boy, surfer dude, cockney, Irish, and even a passable Italian. Whole time I was at Ricky's, not a trace of a drawl. It's work to keep it up though," he said.

The whole time he was talking, he was running through those accents. It was impressive. Maybe too impressive.

"Look, neither one of us has been perfectly honest. You're an actress using her talents and pretending to be something she's not to make money," he said.

"Uh, like any other actress. But you, you out and out lied to me. 'Specially and specifically to me. And then you left me to the wolves."

"I would've been there to protect you if you'd told me where you lived. I checked the mailbox at that Santa Monica apartment. It said Harris, so I assumed—"

"That's one of the reasons I picked that particular location."

"If you'd picked Smith for a name, you'd probably have an even wider choice of fake residences."

I stuck out my tongue. He laughed. We both felt almost comfortable again.

"Look, we both lied. But how much does that matter? Even if nothing else in this entire world is real, how we feel is."

"And how exactly is it that we feel?" I asked.

He looked at me steadily. "I don't want to lose you."

Of course, I felt much the same way myself, but I was loathe to admit it. Instead, I looked away, out at the freeway, at the thickening traffic, at the smog line rising orange above it.

He touched my arm. "All I really want is just to look up in a clear night sky and watch the stars with you every night for the rest of our lives. Crazy and fast as this all happened, I love you, and I think you love me; I think we both know that much is dead true."

I tried to harden my heart. I probably did love him, but I didn't trust him completely. "Funny how the mind can play tricks sometimes," I said.

But he more or less ignored me; he simply unlocked the passenger door of his car, and I just slipped inside. Sure, I thought about jumping right back out again while he walked around to his side of the car, but I didn't, and there he was sitting beside me.

It was hot as July in the car with the windows

rolled up, or maybe it was his hand on the gear shift, resting far too close to my knee that raised the temperature to steamy.

"So what now?" I asked, inching away from him and cranking down my window.

"I want this all to be over. And I want you and that starry sky."

His hand was on my knee now. I didn't remove it, but I just kind of sat there, like I didn't feel the heat from his fingertips pressing through the weight of my jeans.

I wanted him too. I wanted to just give in and be in love. And why not really? Why not do it?

"Is that all you want really—me? What about the fourteen million?"

"I can't say I'd mind. Would you? We could keep a little piece of it for ourselves. We could do anything, be anybody, with that kind of money. No more doing things we didn't want to do, things we are tired of doing, just to get by."

Sure, that sounded good. "We?"

"Well, I'm just assuming, even though you're plenty pissed, that you'll forgive me and that there'll be a happy ever after kind of thing down the line."

"Down the line?"

"I'd walk away right now if I could, but I can't. Not just because of the money, not just because I still feel duty bound to round up the bad guys, but because if I walk away now, we are in danger. More danger than I would've believed before the police found Nelson's body."

"No, *you* are in danger, and you've drug me there along with you."

I actually pushed his hand off my leg, and I opened up my car door, intending to get out.

"I'm going to disappear now. You enjoy that

fourteen million, and then you better disappear too; don't disappear anywhere near me."

It was a nice little speech, but before I could climb out and prove how much I really meant it, he grabbed me and pulled me back. He pressed me roughly against him, and he took me in his arms.

And I knew I was a goner, a believer, a dreamer of the impossible dream called love. Why had I cultivated all these years of cynicism and self-reliance just to throw all that away, to throw myself into Joe's arms?

Yeah, I was in danger all right—the most dangerous place to be is in love.

But as he kissed me, I knew he was right about the "we" part. I knew he was right about us. He was mine, and I was his, and that was that. A couple of liars in love, and whatever happened next, we were truthfully in it together.

Chapter Twelve

It was now officially the day before the day before Christmas Eve. Joe was in my kitchen, unselfconsciously singing some soft country song while he made us toast for a second breakfast. I was perched like a queen on the sofa, if a queen has fresh from the shower wet hair, a bandage on her arm, and wears an extra large tee shirt stamped Track and Field.

There is something absurdly and wonderfully right about being with someone you care about in your home or theirs. It's very different than spending the night together in some pricey resort designed to impress or a cheap motel when you just need a roof and walls and a bed on which to sleep and play. Sharing your space with someone means you have the space, to begin with, to share. And I did, and into it, I welcomed Joe. Any nagging little street-smart doubts I had about his complete veracity were tossed aside, stripped away like yesterday's clothes. We had now officially proclaimed ourselves a part of each other's messed up, lonely, lying lives. At least for one day and one night, we weren't just sharing a bed or a room or even our histories; we were sharing those lives.

There was really something to be said for actually telling a man where you lived and having him come home with you. There was something even more to be said for letting him into your room, into your bed with him kissing you all the while, never taking his lips from yours.

When Joe did lift his lips from mine, it was only for long enough for him to carefully, mindful of my bandaged arm, lift my tee shirt over my head. Then the tee shirt was on the floor and kicked aside, and he was shucking off his own shirt, while deftly unhooking my bra and tossing it away, too.

Then he stopped, and he sat me on the bed in nothing but my jeans and bikini underwear and said, "Just looking at you—"

Clearly it made things happen inside of him as they were happening inside of me. He tugged off his boots and tossed them on the floor, those funky, Mexican cowboy boots. He yanked off his chinos, and I wriggled out of my jeans—I couldn't wait to get them off, couldn't wait to have only my skin up against his skin. Then he jumped right on me, knocking me back against the pillows and making the little stuffed bear I kept there, one of the few things I'd brought with me from Pennsylvania besides the ring and gold coins, squeak.

"Sorry little fella," he said as he set the bear aside on the night table. "This brass bed just turns me on."

"I think it was part of a bordello," I said.

"Wallpaper too, I guess," he agreed.

And we stopped for just a moment while he touched the red flocking.

"So let's pretend I'm a desperado on the run—"

"Apparently, that's not so great of a stretch," I said.

"And that you're the lady of the evening who agreed to take me in."

"For her half of fourteen million dollars," I suggested.

We both laughed. Right then, it seemed like a joke.

Then he put his fingers first to my lips and then to my breasts, lifting them to his own mouth.

And when he'd made them hard and wet, his lips moved lower, down my belly. He slipped my panties off, and his lips kept moving down and down, warm and wet.

"Maybe I'll settle for just a third of that fourteen mil," I whispered. "A quarter . . ." I was barely able to shape the words now, feeling his tongue lapping against me.

"And he works hard to talk her down, and when she agrees, absolutely agrees to anything he wants, when she will do anything he wants—" he was climbing on top of me now, "—then he says, 'I'll give you all of it, if you just keep giving in to me.' "

So I gave in there on the bed, making the mattress creak the way it must not have done since the room's bordello days; I gave in again, knocking the sofa pillows all over the living room, when we thought we might watch a little TV.

We slept some back in my bed, blinds drawn against the daylight. He said I was having a bad dream, and my heart was pounding when he woke me. He held me for a long enough time that soon, we were both giving in all over again. It seemed like there was always some place new and tender and delicious to touch and stroke and rub and glide together and apart and then together again.

"Maybe the honeymoon will never end," he said. "We'll just pack the kids off to visit their auntie or something."

"Oh, we're having kids?"

"Don't you want kids?"

"Sure, sure I want kids . . ."

"Three," we both said at once. I didn't think it could get much better than this.

"Do you want cinnamon toast?" he was asking now as he rummaged through my kitchen cabinets.

I guess it could get better. I jumped up and threw my arms around him.

He stopped rummaging and put his arms around me too. He checked the dressing on my bullet-grazed arm, which he'd redressed for me, and then he kissed me gently, softly, tenderly. Of course, we couldn't stop at that. He was already lifting up the Track and Field shirt and hooking his fingers in the band of my underwear. I was preparing to give in just one more time on the kitchen table.

"You don't have any cinnamon," he murmured in my ear, moving me back against that table.

"That's okay. It doesn't matter. This is what matters . . ."

But my hand brushed the scar on his stomach, the wound still, after two months, raised. He drew back just a little, and I let him.

"I almost forgot," we both said, maybe meaning different things or maybe the same thing.

There was a knock on the door, and we sprang further apart. I pulled my tee shirt down again.

He went into my bedroom and came back with a gun in his hand.

I hoped it wasn't the same gun that hadn't fired at Ricky's, in case we did need it to work this time.

But when he looked through the peephole on my front door, he relaxed and tucked the gun into the waistband of his jeans.

"He looks like the picture on your dresser, only without the rabbit ears," he said. "Why were you dressed up like rabbits?"

Joe pulled open the door, and Louie lit into me so fast I didn't have time to say hello, much less explain about the children's birthday party performances.

"I can't believe you left the hospital without me." Louie wagged his finger in my face. "Don't you like my driving or what? You never call. I go there to pick you up this afternoon, and I guess you were ducking the bill. Anyway, they had no record of you checking out, as it were, and I got extremely worried, what with all the mutilations and deaths and muggings and police around. you can imagine how I felt, but well, here you are, all safe and sound and . . . not alone."

Louie's mouth dropped, and he took in Joe and gave an approving nod. "Nice hair," he said. "You must be this . . . Joe."

Joe extended a hand, and Louie hesitated but then took it.

"Louie," he said to Joe. "Good firm grip," he said to me. "And he is hot. What he's not, honey, is a cop; how could you not tell? They always have lousy haircuts. Even the chief of police looks like he just stuck a bowl on his head, but you Joe, if that is, in fact, your real name, you see a decent stylist."

"Joe is my name. And it's nice to meet you," Joe said.

"He's not a cop," I agreed.

"Former actor, private investigator, undercover pretend cop, and—" Joe began.

"Wanted man." Louie whipped a folded newspaper out from under his arm. "I took this from Marinak, so watch out—there's mushed date matter on the front page."

It was to the Metro section that he was directing me, or rather us, for Joe was peering as eagerly as I at the second section lead story.

"Private investigator implicated in brutal murder."

That was the headline, but there was no news in the story, at least nothing that was news to us. Nelson was dead, and his hands were gone. The police weren't talking except to say he'd been picked up by a yellow car. The license plate hadn't been seen, but anyone with information should call. A tip from an unnamed friend of the deceased had suggested police find one Joseph Richter, who was not at his apartment and who was wanted for questioning. A private investigator, Richter had disappeared months earlier. Again, anyone with information should call . . .

"An unidentified friend of the deceased," said Louie. "Any idea who that would be?"

"Laura," Joe and I said together.

"Or Rose," I added. "It could be Rose protecting Laura. I should go see Rose and find Laura; maybe I can get the kind of information you were hoping I had in the first place."

Joe nodded. "I was going to suggest that myself actually. When we got around to it."

Louie folded the paper again.

"Do you trust him?" he asked me, pointing a thumb at Joe.

"Yes."

"Do you love her?" he asked Joe.

"Louie!" I protested, but Joe had already answered.

"Yes. Very much."

"Because I believe she is falling in love with you, or that she has already fallen, hence her poor lack of judgement in trusting you thus far. The question is—can she trust you now?"

"Cross my heart," said Joe, and although he sounded amused, his eyes were serious, which more or less satisfied both me and apparently Louie.

Louie nodded. "Okay then. Where is this Rose person located?" Louie glanced at his watch.

"Pasadena," I said.

"You'll have to wait until after five to scope her out. I have a meeting with Fox Searchlight. Before their holiday party." His voice swelled with pride. "The assistant to the VP's assistant tells me I might get a green light. He loves me, says everybody does."

"Is his name Todd?" I asked.

Louie and I had recently discovered that the current crop of the most prestigious personal assistants were all named Todd, Fielding, or Whitney. Personally, since most of them were required to go fetch, I thought Spot, Buddy, or Cocoa would be more appropriate.

"His name is Tad," Louie said.

"He's not good enough for you," I said. "I thought we'd agreed. Todd, Fielding, or Whitney are the only acceptable names for love interests pursued for career reasons."

"Who says I'm pursuing him? I'm doing his hair.

He's giving me a little inside information. They love the weasel."

Louie grabbed my hand excitedly. "The weasel was your idea!"

"That's great," I said. "That's . . . phenomenal."

It really was; it was just that I had so much else on my mind that Louie being about to sell a movie script finally had descended several ratchets on what would normally be my phenomenal scale.

"It's not a lead part, but you could play the girl's young aunt. You could discover your own weasel!"

"Or my inner one," I said.

Joe looked puzzled. "Weasels? Weasels eat your crops and steal your garbage."

"Not in Hollywood," Louie said jubilantly. "Weasels are celebrated." He rattled on. "So anyway, after the meeting, I'll go with you. To see this Rose. I don't want you going anywhere alone," he admonished me.

"It's okay. I'll go with her," Joe told Louie.

"If the police are looking for you, do you really think you should?" Louie asked.

"It's safer if I go. I mean no offense, but I'm assuming your skills at fistfights and target shooting are not as refined as your writing."

"Oh, macho man," Louie said. He arched an eyebrow at me. "Who do you feel safer with, sweetheart, me or your Joe? Your call."

"I feel safe with both of you," I said, which was true as far as it went.

Still, in the event of an appearance by someone like Nelson, Joe would be the one to have playing backup.

"You have a meeting," I reminded Louie. "And what if they ask you to the Christmas party afterward? And this is my mess, not yours."

"*My* mess," Joe said gallantly.

"True," I agreed. "But now it's ours. What it isn't is Louie's. So you're the one coming with me, not him. Still, you can't go near Laura or Rose," I told Joe. "You'll have to stay in the background."

"I'm good at that, remember?" Joe said.

"So you say," I nodded. "When you know the right street."

We shared a smile.

Louie looked from me to Joe. He sighed. "Aren't we the couple." Then he perked up. "At least he's not a cop, right? Just a suspected murderer."

I drove to Pasadena in case anyone could i.d. Joe's brother's car by now. The plan was for me to visit Rose, question her under the guise of psychic advisor, find out what she knew, and figure out where we could find Laura. Or at least give that a try.

First, of course, we had to find Rose Holloman. The phone number Joe had copied from Laura's address book was disconnected, and the street address on Rose's DMV record Joe had long since discovered belonged to the house Laura had grown up in before Rose had divorced Laura's father. Like her daughter—well, like me too when you came right down to it—Rose exhibited a tendency to disappear when she wanted to. According to Joe, her credit card billing went to a post office box in downtown Pasadena, and there were no water, gas, or electric bills issued in her name or Laura's.

Joe had hoped I had some record or another of Rose, but any records I had ever had of anything were shredded into confetti. All I knew was what

Joe surmised—Rose lived somewhere in the greater Pasadena area, not that far from her post office box, more than likely. The post office box had not been emptied, according to a helpful post office employee, since Ricky had died. Mail contained in it was being returned to sender.

So Rose knew something, she had disappeared with her daughter, or she had joined the unfortunate participants in the body business. Or maybe all three.

There was a cheerful, last minute shopping frenzy in the air, people with big, bright paper bags spilling out across the cobble-stoned alleys and into the semi-hip chain stores and intimate boutiques of Olde Town.

It was late afternoon now, and the sunlight added wisps of gold to Joe's curly, dark hair. I indulged myself and ran my fingers through it.

We parked near Rose's post office box and went on a coffeehouse and teahouse crawl in the immediate neighborhood. I remembered Rose asking me if I had any tea before I read her palm; Joe knew Laura's mother often gave her presents of English tea in fancy boxes. That was the best we had for a lead.

"I'm looking for a friend of my mother's," we took turns reciting to clerks, coffee baristas, and bag boys. "I've lost her address . . ."

We gave her name and description, and in return, we got variations of "You're looking for the Rose Bowl? Other side of town," or "Rose parade isn't until New Year's," and things like that.

I rubbed the back of my head gingerly. It was still a little sore from the nice whack Nelson had given me.

I wished she were named something other than

Rose—Daisy or Iris even—because it was understandable that in Pasadena, home of the Rose Bowl, Rose Parade, Rose Queens, Rose Bowl game, with every lamppost bearing a banner announcing "New Year's Day, Annual Rose Parade!," all anyone heard was the word "Rose," and they naturally assumed we were tourists asking a standard question.

By the time I'd repeat myself and they'd hear me and shake their heads, saying that regrettably they knew no such person, I'd feel impatient and annoyed.

Ninety minutes and twenty-six tea and coffee purveyors later we had no information, and I had to pee, a direct outgrowth of consuming iced lemon tea, a vanilla soy latte, and a free sample of spearmint purifying elixir.

Joe kept drinking hot black coffee, so much of it that I began to wonder if he wasn't really a cop after all.

We were working our way east, and I was about to hit the ladies' room of a place called Parsley, Sage, and Tea Tyme, when my eye fell on a small bookstore and curio shop called Psychic Sensations.

"Hey, hey, hey," I poked Joe in the ribs.

He got it immediately. "Better plan," he said agreeably. "Although honestly, I wish old Rose was into donut shops or burgers or something to go with all that coffee."

"Rose was certainly very much into my services, and she hit the chat room I found her in already fully up to speed on all her auric fields. Let me work this one alone, okay? I'll meet you across the street at the tea place."

Stepping inside the shop, I immediately recognized the sort of incense I was always burning, patchouli, clogging up the air, which was also thick with the heat of more candles than are probably burning in St. Patrick's Cathedral. Used to the bracing tea and coffee aroma of the shops I'd been scouring, I felt briefly stunned, and I became more sympathetic to my liquor buyer Jack James, who had found the scent in my version of a psychic pleasure palace so repugnant.

Louie's script had better sell, and Joe and I had better luck into some money because with Joe leaning on Jack, I was probably out my buyer.

Determinedly, I coughed and cleared my throat and approached the type of woman I'm used to dressing up as: long haired, gauze enshrouded, crystal wearing, vague of eye.

She looked up from a book titled *Ancient Souls*.

"Yes," she breathed. "How may I heal you?"

Oh, that was good. I had to remember that.

Sunlight struck the silver pyramids and pentagrams hanging from a mobile over her head, making a halo around her.

"I'm looking for a friend of my mother's," I said. "She's very much into . . . spirituality." That's what we called it in the trade.

"Yes?"

"You may know her. She lives here in Pasadena, but I've misplaced her address. Her last name is Holloman, first name Rose, nothing to do with the Rose Bowl. Mid sixties. She loves tea—"

"Ah. We rechristened her. Violet Rose," the young woman murmured.

"Can you help me get in touch with her?"

The woman smiled, a liquid, lovely smile. "If the spirits are willing, you'll be united."

I tried to quell my impatience. "A phone number or address would do . . ."

"Leave me yours," she suggested. "And when

Violet Rose is in again, I'll give her the information."

"I'm just here for the holiday," I said. "I fly out again Christmas day. Is there any way I could reach her right now?"

She frowned. "I'm sensing some anxious energy."

Boy, this one really had it down.

"All right," I said, "I guess you can't help me. I promised my mother, that's all. And she's gone now. Into the other world. I had a reading done last week, and Rose's name came up so—"

"A reading done? Where?"

"The Inner Eye on Ventura," I said.

"Oh, they're very surface. I can do a read that goes much deeper."

I drew in my breath. I should've taken some cash from Joe. I only had about twenty bucks in my pocket, and it was just about my last twenty too, thanks to Nelson. "I don't suppose for twenty . . . ?"

She leapt on it. "Fifteen minutes, twenty dollars."

I couldn't resist a little jab. "You can go deep in fifteen minutes?"

"I do it all the time," she said, almost panting for that twenty.

"I should tell my boyfriend," I smiled sweetly, ignoring the sharp look she gave me.

She led me to a little velvet-curtained room, sat me down at a velvet-covered table much like my own, and stared fixedly into a crystal ball stationed on the table. Her affect was a little wooden, I thought.

"Shall we do cards or palm?" she asked.

"Cards," I said. I wanted to see what she could do.

She had me shuffle and pick three, and she laid out a very simple three card spread.

"Your mother meant a lot to you."

"Yes," I said, and that was certainly true as far as that went.

"There was an older woman in your life as well."

I blinked, flashing on my grandmother. It was only a fishing expedition, but still. I wondered what she'd make of my blink.

"You've been on a long journey to get where you are now."

"Yes, yes, that's true," I agreed. I relaxed a little. I was better than she was. She hadn't made anything out of the blink.

"There's a man you just met."

I went cold, as if this woman was real, any realer than I.

I was sure I was revealing something, stiffening up, widening my eyes. But I didn't say anything.

"He lied to you," she whispered.

I looked down at my hands and kept my gaze there. Boy, wild stabs in the dark could still sting when you got cut.

"He doesn't want to hurt you though," she went on. "Although I'm still not sure he's being entirely truthful, I believe he really loves you."

"Huh," I said, bristling at her, at the very suggestion he might still be lying to me, at having some two bit hack of a fake fakir tell me Joe loved me, as if I hadn't figured that out for myself.

"Don't feel so hostile," she said. "He really does care, despite his secrets."

"We all have our secrets," I said. I looked up now and smiled. "Love is a complicated thing."

"It can be," she agreed. "Sometimes you have to tap into your soul to reach its true reserves and unlock the last hidden recesses of the heart. Everything else is illusion."

Indeed. This chick wasn't bad. She made me feel, for half a second anyway, that she cared. Was everyone a fake and a liar and a cheat and, at the same time, so expert in making you feel that they really knew you? Was that Ricky Littlejohn's secret—as stupid and corrupt as he was, did he get people to believe he cared? Was it Joe's secret too? It was an awful thought, and I didn't believe it for a second, but for a half second, I was thrown.

So I had to wait a beat before I smiled again, turning on my own fake charm and innocence. "You have a real way of seeing into me," I told her.

Oh, she smiled back, happy as a clam and as vulnerable as one about to be scooped up in a big, old net.

"Could I ask about Rose?" I murmured almost off hand. "About why I'm supposed to contact her?"

She had me pick another two cards, and I picked. I saw with my own eyes that I was revealing a need for knowledge and support, so I agreed when she told me that.

"Do the cards say why it's so hard to reach her? Why, for example, you won't give me her number?"

My eyes teared up slightly, and I reached out a supplicating hand. She patted it.

"I'll tell you what. I can see that you have a sincere heart. If you want to come back later this afternoon, I can arrange a meeting for you both. Perhaps summon the spirit of your dear mother. So that both of you could speak to her and find wisdom. There's no telling what could happen."

"No telling," I echoed, pretending to be impressed. "Could you do all that?"

"Absolutely." She beamed beatifically. "I'll unite you all. You see, I just don't feel comfortable simply handing out personal information on the fly. But bringing the two of you together here in a safe spiritual setting; of course, it will be your choice and Mrs. Holloman's to reunite and that of your mother in the spirit realm."

"That sounds perfect," I breathed.

"Now, of course this will take a little bit more than twenty dollars . . ."

"Of course."

"Spiritual convergences such as these are usually several hundred dollars. But because I can sense your positive energy, we'll look at this as simply a full reading, and the charge is a minimal hundred dollars."

"Very minimal," I agreed. I imagined she'd make more off Rose than off me. Me she wasn't sure about; she just wanted to keep me in the game.

"Will I have time to go to the bank?"

"Indeed. How would five o'clock be, assuming Rose is available?"

"That sounds perfect too."

She asked my name to tell Rose, and I told her it was Sarah, but I asked that she not reveal I was there until we met. For some reason, she seemed to think that was okay. Probably anything that netted her a hundred bucks free and clear on top of a twenty was okay, not to mention whatever she was planning to charge Rose, which was probably more like two or three hundred.

I gave her the twenty in cash because everybody needed to make a living and left, enthusiastically proclaiming how much I was looking forward to seeing her again in an hour.

Then I crossed over to the herb and tea shop, where Joe had a raspberry iced tea and a dark chocolate biscotti waiting. More of that knowing what I wanted without having to tell him thing. I liked that.

Looking into Joe's transparently admiring eyes as I filled him in, I shook off the very suggestion that he still had secrets. How could a man who looked at me like Joe was looking at me, who felt like Joe felt stroking my arm with his fingertips be keeping anything from me?

We were both hungry, but while there was a seemingly unlimited selection of teas and coffees, the food choice was more limited. Joe got us a few more biscotti and a piece of carrot cake.

"I sure would like a burger," Joe said.

"Maybe Santa will put one in your stocking."

"Reindeer meat," he nodded.

"You're a sick man."

"No, actually, I'm a happy one," he said, stroking my hand. "Or, I would be if I had you *and* a burger."

As the clock moved closer to five and the street to soft dusk, I had it all planned. I'd wait until Rose was about to walk into the shop, jump out of the tea house and make known my presence, act surprised to see her there, and offer my own brand of spiritual convergence for less than the going rate at Psychic Sensations.

It could be awkward if the shop psychic looked up from her reading of *Ancient Souls* long enough to check out the sidewalk, but I was pretty sure she had me pegged as too easy a mark to be bothered. Rose could also turn my offer down cold, but she'd been into me so much, I rather doubted it. The plan was coming together pretty well. That was, of course, assuming there was something to be discovered worth the coming together.

"What if Rose doesn't give us any information?" I asked Joe.

"Maybe we can go talk to your psychic friend across the street. Maybe she's more adept than you at reading people's minds, and she'll solve all our troubles."

Before I could sock him, I saw Rose walking at a good clip around the corner and right past our window. She must live close by or park far away, I figured.

I stood up so quickly I tipped my chair, and I hurried out of the shop without even saying anything to Joe, who seemed to figure things out pretty quickly. He scooped up my chair and concealed himself behind a copy of the same free press rag in which I'd first discovered Ricky Littlejohn's story before I was even out the door. The irony of the newspaper would've been worth commenting on, but I had to apprehend brisk-walking Rose.

She sure moved quickly in her too-stylish pumps perched on small feet at the end of her delicate ankles. She wore red Chanel with her blue hair, which was cut in a stylish, but not too stylish, bob. She perfectly fit the appellation "old money" in more ways than one.

I stumbled on a rough spot in the sidewalk as I tried to sidle up to her gracefully, and I had to catch myself against a light pole, which sent little frissons of pain shooting up from my injured arm. It's tough to want to curse but to have to say instead, "My goodness, Rose, is that you?"

I was slightly out of breath, but I pulled off the

casual thing pretty well while still cutting her off before she trotted right into Psychic Sensations. I gave her a warm hug of pleasant surprise just as she came abreast of the shop.

A smile crossed her face. "Christina. What a pleasure."

"For me too," I said. "I so enjoyed working with you. Running into you makes it almost worth the drive I took to come here." I shook my head. "I came to purchase a book, a last minute present, and I was told that this shop was a wonderful place." I gestured toward Psychic Sensations.

"It is—" Rose began, but I cut her off.

"All that traffic and what a disappointment. It's very poorly stocked, and the owner wasn't very helpful ... I don't think she knows the first thing about any psychic sensation whatsoever." I sniffed.

"No?" Rose said uncertainly. "I've always found Geneece to be so lovely."

"I don't know," I said. "I don't like saying anything negative about another spiritual explorer, but ..." I paused as if considering a further confidence. Then I shrugged it off. "I'll leave it at the fact that she wasn't helpful to me, at least."

Geneece, I thought scornfully. It was no more a real name than Violet Rose. It was the kind of name some human potential movement guru or past life reading charlatan would assign to their clients, a combination of your given name and your last name or a flipping of syllables meant to plug into your own special chakra. Gag me. Geneece was probably really Jennifer or Janice, just as Violet Rose was Rosalyn.

"Of course," I went on, "maybe she was distracted. She was giving a ... sort of a reading to another customer that just ... well it struck *me*, anyway, as not reaching any great spiritual depths. I felt a discordance."

"Really?" Now Rose was concerned. "She just called me because she wanted me to join in a convergence with another believer. She had a sudden communiqué from the spirits, she said."

A communiqué. Geez, how pretentious could you get?

"Is she *charging* you for this?" I sniped.

"Well, yes."

"Hm-m. Are you experiencing a longing for connection with the other world?"

"I always am; you know that. I'd come to see you again in two seconds, but I haven't been able to reach you. Did you get the slippers?"

"I did, and thank you. I've been on . . . sabbatical for a while. Sometimes, one needs a cleansing."

"Oh, I'd love a cleansing," she said. "Is there a place you go?"

Yeah, the shower, I thought.

"I go to a forest," I said. "And I wait until the stars fall."

"The meteor shower the other night . . . did you see it?"

"Oh, yes." I allowed that I had.

"Astrologically, of course, there's great significance in such an event."

"Of course," I agreed. "But honestly, the stars have been falling for some time now." I dropped my voice, making it low and sorrowful. "We haven't been watching however. That was our wake-up call."

"Really?" she was amazed.

"Look," I said, "I'd be happy to do another reading for you. I think I could do one right now if we kept commerce out of it." I wrinkled my nose in distaste. "I've transcended all monetary gain."

"Have you?" asked Rose.

I could almost see her pulse throbbing faster against her pale throat. A psychic who wouldn't charge her anything? It was like a dream come true.

"What a noble accomplishment," she said admiringly.

"If there's a quiet place we can go . . ." I let my voice trail off.

She glanced at her watch. "I promised Geneece . . ."

"I understand," I clucked.

"Maybe after the holidays?" she suggested.

"I can't. I'm going away again. I only returned for my family, you understand. This time though, I might not come back again. LA's become so . . . overrun with dark souls."

"Indeed it has," Rose sighed.

I perked up. "Anyway, I've really only got a few hours. It seemed like such destiny, running into you. As if we were meant to spend the time together. Oh, well."

I took her hand in mine and held it gently. "Goodbye then."

She shifted her feet. "I suppose I could call Geneece. Reschedule. Would you come back to my place, have a cup of tea?"

"I'd love that."

"I'm close enough to walk," she said. "A little exercise always does one good."

She cast one last look at Psychic Sensations and then led me resolutely up Fair Oaks Avenue.

I didn't chance a look at Joe to see if he was following.

Her house was on a side street a few blocks away. It was a large, white wood frame. It had a big yard and an old black Mercedes in the drive in front of a freestanding garage covered in ivy. When she opened the front door, the place had the look of a 1950s *House and Garden* magazine, all crystal chandeliers, hardwood floors, and plastic covered Louis IV furniture. There was a dusty quiet over everything; the house was not ill kept, but it was as if no one spent much time here.

There was not, I noticed, a single sign of the holiday season.

She led me into her kitchen, which was sunny and which had yellow daffodil wallpaper that was faded from the light. The stove, the dishwasher, and the refrigerator were all in custom canary yellow.

"You have a lovely home," I told her.

"It's not really mine," she confided. "Although I did help in choosing the decor many, many years ago. I'm deeply fond of the sunshine shades though. The vibe is of brightness. Always go with brightness," she said. But her voice was not bright; it was dim and sad.

She looked around her as if gathering strength from her surroundings. "A friend is letting me stay here. I travel a lot myself, you see. I don't seem to have a need for a permanent address at this juncture."

We sat at the table, and I let her pour me yet more tea. A beer would be nice, or a Coke. The glasses were yellow too, and I could see my jaundiced reflection in them.

"How have you been?" I asked her when she settled across from me.

"I've been very good, really. Since you told me about my sister, quite content. I've felt all our old sibling rivalry resolve."

"You've been in contact with old friends," I said.

"Well, yes, I guess I have."

"Like the owner of this house."

She smiled at my perception.

"Is that because of this reconciliation with your sister? Has it allowed you to find your past again?"

"I think so," she said, "now that you mention it."

I took her hands lightly in my own. "And how are things with your own family?"

"Good too," she said, but there was a bit of hesitancy in her voice.

"The holidays are difficult for you this year?"

"Well, not exactly difficult," she said. "It's just . . . hard to feel like celebrating. So much going on with my daughter. We'll probably just have a quiet dinner together somewhere. She's the only reason I'm staying here at all. Her children are with their fathers and—"

"Their fathers," I said thoughtfully. "And yet I see that her husband is not of this world any longer."

Rose nodded solemnly. "My daughter has been married several times. Her most recent husband, he passed away not too long ago."

"He wasn't ready to go," I said. "And your daughter knows that. She feels . . . responsible."

"Oh, dear," Rose said, wringing her hands. "I'm sure she does, in a way."

"And there's a certain darkness around her. As if someone else she was close to, perhaps a friend, has passed even more recently—"

"Goodness," said Rose, and she just sat there. Her already powdery pale skin had paled noticeably.

"Am I wrong?" I asked gently.

"No, you're not wrong. Although he wasn't

much of a friend in my opinion. Trashy man." She sniffed her contempt. She drew herself up. "But what does this really have to do with me?" There was a quaver in her voice.

"A lot it seems. The darkness in your daughter . . . the negative forces, they're coming very close to you. You know something about them."

A fishing expedition, and I hooked the trout.

"Well," Rose said, pursing her lips. "I know more than I'd like."

"You also feel responsible for all this . . . darkness in your daughter. Due to a relationship with a man no longer in *your* life."

"Goodness," Rose said again. "You've hit the nail with the proverbial hammer."

Probably I had. "You mustn't," I said kindly, "blame yourself. Your daughter's sins are not your own. And hers . . . well, she could overcome."

"Could she?" Rose sounded wistful. "I'm not sure. The sins of the father, you know. It's her father you're seeing . . . I tried my best to raise her differently, yet all roads seem to lead . . . the path that's chosen . . . oh, I don't know anymore how you read the right signs."

"Indeed," I said solemnly. "The signs are everywhere and can confuse. You mustn't watch them too closely. I do believe our meeting today was incredibly fortuitous. This is the season of gifts, and this is the gift I can give to you and your daughter both. Peace of mind."

"Peace. If there's anyone who could offer such a thing, it would be you. You certainly gave me an olive branch strong enough to hold out to my sister even in another life." She sighed and rubbed her hands together as if she'd experienced a sudden chill. "I thought that once I overcame those problems that I had reached inner tranquility. I actually believed, you'll be amazed to hear, I believed that my struggles were over."

"These current struggles are your daughter's," I said.

"I thought she was happy with Ricky," Rose was practically wailing, and it all came out at once, tears reddening her pale blue eyes, streaking her soft cheeks. "He had . . . charisma. He certainly fooled her. He certainly fooled me."

"Your daughter's deceased husband?" I asked.

"Oh, yes."

Rose wiped at her eyes and her cheeks, and she pursed her lips. "Ricky reminded me of my ex-husband. So much more than I realized. But perhaps, that was part of our attraction to him. Ricky reminded me of those wild, passionate, sexually charged days of my youth. And for Laura, he represented her father when he was young and carefree. Not what he later became."

"No, of course not," I said, trying to get over Rose in her Chanel having wild, sexually charged, youthful days.

"But he was already just as bad as Laura's father at his worst!" Rose shook her head. "Ironically, Laura's father was adamantly opposed to the marriage at first. It was my idea that she go for it. Just go for it," she said.

Kind of like a Nike commercial.

"He was cruel to your daughter emotionally," I said. "He was cruel to many people. He didn't care who he hurt. I can see the void in him, a void that is still there in the spirit world."

"Doesn't surprise me in the least," said Rose with a matter of fact harrumph, as if I had said his insurance premiums had gone up because he was such a lousy driver.

"Your daughter separated from him, but . . . remained connected somehow."

"Too true."

"And his death was a part of the ugliness around him."

"Yes."

"And your daughter in some way precipitated his demise."

Rose wiped tears from her cheeks.

I sighed; I shook my head. I clicked my tongue against my cheek. Out of the corner of my eye, I saw a movement in the rusty garden outside the kitchen just past Rose's shoulder. The movement was wearing a dark tee shirt, and I was pretty sure it was Joe. It had better be Joe.

"And Laura's father. He encouraged Ricky in his pursuits."

"More than encouraged. More than," Rose said.

"Together they traded in the grief of death," I said solemnly.

"I suppose you could say that." Rose suddenly stiffened, and her voice lost its dreamy quality. I felt I'd pushed too far, revealed too much practical knowledge.

I hummed to myself as if seeing an inner vision and gave her time to relax. When I saw her small frame sinking back into the chair again, only then did I speak.

"It's all about money, isn't it?" I asked.

Rose nodded mutely.

"Money involving death."

"There's always been too much death around me," Rose said briskly. "It's a wonder I've lasted as long as I have. I've lasted for my grandchildren, I think, a second chance, another generation that can achieve life instead of death."

"We're all dying inside," I said. "Which is why it is all the more important to truly live."

I wasn't quite sure what I meant by that. I felt edgy somehow, whether it was because I thought Joe was watching or because I was afraid it wasn't Joe watching, I wasn't sure.

"Laura's too caught up." Rose shook her head several times.

"Your daughter must do as I've done." I paused dramatically. "It's not too late. But she must, she absolutely must, renounce the worldly aspects of this life."

"She'll never listen to me," Rose said.

"Let me tell her then. Bring her here. Let me tell her," I urged and tried to keep the urgency out of my voice.

"I still have the reading an astrologer did for my daughter when she was born . . . and that was forty odd years ago . . . some very odd years they have been, indeed . . . he was quite right, you know, about her marrying poorly . . . of course, I wasn't a very good example, her father being such a terrible person. I had to have an exorcism when I divorced Charles."

"That was very wise," I said. "And now we must perform another sort of exorcism. To get the darkness away from your daughter and you and your grandchildren."

I thought tossing in the grandchildren was an excellent idea, but Rose didn't seem to be listening. She looked distracted.

"I wonder if the convergence Geneece suggested is on Laura's behalf . . . a spiritual conjoining, that's

all Geneece would tell me. Would you excuse me if
I called her? Perhaps she'd let me bring you along
to our session. Oh, that might be wonderful! You
and Geneece working together! That might make
the perfect connection! Then, reinforced as it were,
we can reach Laura. Maybe even without her knowing."

She was already rising, heading for the phone.

"It's a wonderful idea, actually, but . . . wait . . .
I'm getting something powerful—"

I shut my eyes, and I gave a soft moan. I felt
rather than saw her drop down in her chair, riv-
eted.

"Your daughter is in danger. Real physical danger. Someone was violently hurt. I see a rending of
flesh, a man who cannot touch—"

I opened my eyes and made them wide and
wild. "It's terrible."

"Yes, someone cut his hands off," Rose said, and
she gritted her teeth. "This so-called friend of my
daughter's, a degenerate addict if you ask me; he
probably was involved in some unsavory drug deal
. . . but Laura says no. She says it's about the money,
her father's money and her husband's money, and
other people wanting it . . . and it should be hers."

"Is this a lot of money?"

"It's too much." Rose looked angry. "It's a point-
less amount."

Maybe to her.

"Is your daughter around?" I sat back in my
chair as if exhausted from the effort.

She frowned. "Well, I know how to reach her."

"Can you reach her by phone?"

"Yes, I can call her."

"Call her and ask her to come here and meet
with us. Right now, today."

"She won't come. That's what I was saying about making a spiritual intervention. She's in seclusion—first Ricky, then this friend . . ."

"Try to draw her near. I wouldn't tell you this if I didn't believe it was important. If I didn't feel very strongly, that this was the reason you and I met today. To help your daughter."

She sighed and nodded. She reached for her phone, an old-fashioned rotary dial.

"It's Mom," she said. "Can you come and visit? It's important, or I wouldn't ask."

There was a long pause, and a shrill voice spewed what sounded like invective over the phone line.

"Well, I know this isn't the best time, but what time is best, really? One of my advisors is with me."

Another pause, and the voice on the other end of the phone raised itself, sounding shriller still. I caught the words ". . . money . . ." and ". . . stupid."

"Not financial," Rose said, drawing herself up irritably. "Spiritual. She's the real thing, Laura. She needs to see you."

There was another pause, and she put her hand over the receiver and mouthed at me. "Can I tell her what you want to see her about?"

I looked solemn. "Yes," I said, without any real idea of what Rose was going to say next.

"It's the darkness all around you," Rose said into the phone, and she was talking over the voice on the other end of the line, steadily, doggedly. "The money. The people dying—you can't tell me this is an ordinary life. A life like yours calls for extraordinary measures, and this is the woman I've told you about before, the one I was trying to get you to meet when Ricky was still alive . . . before it was too late. Maybe if you had met with her, none of this would have happened. This business with that fortune, the police, two men dead, and one who betrayed you, and—"

I assumed she meant Joe, and I went hot and then cold.

"You're telling me *I* trust the wrong people?" Rose's voice cracked. "Look who you trusted. Look who—"

A long pause and just breathing seemed to be on both sides of the telephone line, and maybe from outside in the bushes, too; my own breath was rising and falling rapidly in my chest.

At last Rose shrugged, held the phone a little away from her ear, and shook it as if she could make a sound come out of it.

"Laura, just come over to the house."

"No!" rang out loud and clear.

Rose looked at me and arched her eyebrows. I dropped my eyes as if downcast.

"Call me back then—" Rose managed to get out before the phone buzzed in her hand.

She hung up.

"I'm sorry," she said, pursing her lips, "but my daughter has other plans."

Chapter Thirteen

"We stake out the house," Joe said, catching up to me as I rounded the corner from Rose's place. I'd left with polite chitchat about my travel plans to "unknown places, off the map" and a promise to get back in touch with her and try once again for spiritual closure.

Rose embraced me, but I had the feeling her daughter had made her wary of me. She stood at the door watching me until I turned that corner and was out of sight.

"We'll hook up with Laura," Joe assured me.

"And then what?"

"I heard just about everything you said in there, everything Rose said. I was convinced of it two months ago, and I'm more convinced now. Laura knows what we need to know. She could break for us; tell us everything about her old man, the money, his connections; tell us who killed Nelson. And my brother. I bet she knows that too."

"And Ricky," I said.

"Yeah," Joe said.

"Maybe she killed him," I ventured.

"I don't think so. She's too worried to be the one who killed him. She's hiding. Everybody's hiding," Joe said.

"Then why should we bother to watch her mother's borrowed house? Why would she even come here if she's that afraid?"

"Her curiosity is greater. She believes just as Rose believes in you, one way or another. That you know something. The belief is strong enough from mother to daughter that it made *me* interested. Just think how Laura must feel, knowing you sat in her mother's kitchen."

"So I'm still sushi," I said.

"Sushi?"

"Bait."

"Don't put it like that."

"Why not?" I asked airily. "If it doesn't bother me, why should it bother you?"

"It bothers me," Joe said. "And all I can tell you is that I owe you a debt of gratitude. On top of the other things I owe you. And will, I swear, make good upon it."

And he made brief, reassuring good with his sweet, warm lips.

"Now what?" I said, with a sigh that was half weariness and half pleasure.

"We wait, that's all. We wait. We get your car, we hunker down in it, and we wait."

So we drove to Rose's street, parking far enough away that Joe had to turn the passenger's side mirror and look back to keep her house in sight. He pulled a scrunched up baseball cap out of his jacket and pulled it low and tight on his head.

It was dark now, and I kept yawning and fidgeting. This staking out thing was pretty boring, even

with the occasional time out for kissing and dis-
arranging each other's clothes. We were both tired
from lack of sleep and watchful, so we didn't talk
much, and I found myself dozing off, my head
snuggled on Joe's chest. Who knows how long I
would've slept, but I thought I heard somebody
talking. I sat up, and Joe was flipping around on
the radio.

Still no Laura when dinnertime was over; still no
Laura when primetime TV ended; still no Laura
when Rose clicked off her bedroom light.

"We'll come back tomorrow," Joe said.

"Early," I agreed.

Joe pulled off his baseball cap and slapped it
back in his pocket.

After sitting behind the wheel without moving
for so long, it felt almost unnatural to actually turn
on the ignition and drive my car. I slipped onto the
freeway and maneuvered my way through downtown, bright lights clumped up along the freeway
though we were long past rush hour—there were
plenty of shoppers and holiday revelers driving all
over to somewhere they could celebrate.

Although this morning I had felt like there was
plenty to celebrate—me and Joe, Joe and me—I
felt kind of empty now. We'd made some progress,
found Rose, but we weren't any closer really to
clearing Joe; to finding the bad guys, Laura, or all
that money. We weren't any closer to me not having to worry about some lunatic new man in Laura's
life showing up at my door with a fist full of chloroform. On the other hand, Joe was with me now. He
could take on the lunatic. Maybe that was enough
for the night.

Not for Joe though. He still wanted his burger.

"There's not much food in your 'fridge," Joe reminded me. "Maybe we should stop at the grocery
store."

I nodded and swung into the parking lot of
Jon's Market on La Brea. Joe put an arm around
me as we loped across the parking lot. I felt comfortable and tired, like we were an old married
couple returning from a shopping expedition. Even
though it was past eleven o'clock, the store was
crowded with people buying last minute Christmas
hams and turkeys; in this neighborhood, they would
be buying salsa, beans, and kimchee to go with
them.

Joe disengaged himself from me and took out a
shopping cart. Usually, when I was this hungry and
this tired and this broke, I'd go straight to the deli
counter; order myself a really nice six-inch tuna
sandwich on a french roll with cheese, pepper-
ocini, and tomato; and eat it while I browsed the
store as if fascinated by each aisle. I'd throw the
wrapper away in a trash can near the bakery, buy a
thirty-three cent on-sale candy bar, and check out.

It felt odd to fill a cart with items I was—well,
Joe was—actually going to pay for. With items we
weren't going to just stand there and eat in the
store, but actual food for a meal. Steaks, prestuffed
frozen baked potatoes, and a ready salad for tonight;
the fixings for stuffing, fruit salad, and Cornish
game hens, "enough for your friend Louie and
any friend of his," Joe said. He seemed to be taking
it for granted that we would have Christmas Eve
dinner together, that we would be able to make a
meal for my friend, that we were planning not only
for a holiday dinner but also for a future together.

Maybe it was all that sitting around in the car

down the block from Rose's place, but I just didn't quite believe it. I felt as if I was still suspended in the dark cocoon of my car. I didn't quite believe the bright flourescent lights of the busy grocery store or that we'd ever eat all the food in our cart, the hens, the frozen asparagus, and the out of season overpriced strawberries we'd surely have to dump half a box of sugar on to make edible despite their price.

I couldn't have gotten this lucky. My life couldn't be this normal. What about Rose, and Laura and dead Ricky and ill-gotten gains and the police and murderers who chopped off people's hands? Were they all going on holiday while we shopped and dined?

Just for old times' sake, while Joe paid for our bags of groceries, I picked out a thirty-three cent on-sale candy bar and paid for it myself, humming along to a Muzak version of "Grandma Got Run Over by a Reindeer." I munched the candy as we started across the parking lot toward my car.

"Don't spoil your appetite," Joe said. "I have something special planned for—"

There was apparently little chance of me spoiling my appetite because as I crossed the parking lot, the candy bar dropped right out of my hand.

It dropped out of my hand because something had hit my injured triceps hard enough to really hurt and make my fingers slip open and loosen my grip.

I spun. A can of green beans rolled at my feet next to the just opened candy bar. I picked it up, puzzled.

"What?" Joe asked me.

"This can. It . . . hit me."

"Show me," Joe ordered.

Joe and I both examined the can for a moment like it was a nuclear bomb or something, and we had to figure out how to deactivate it quickly.

Had the general manager seen me eat and not pay for sandwiches in the past, and had he been waiting for me to appear again, only now I was with someone who actually *bought* groceries, and this was the best he could exact in revenge? Was this what they did now to people who pilfered from grocery stores as opposed to calling security?

Another can sailed at my head; I ducked—this was cream of mushroom soup. If the next weapon of choice was dried onions, we could have the kind of vegetable casserole my grandmother used to make at both Thanksgiving and Christmas.

"Watch out!" Joe shouted and grabbed at me like he'd forgotten all about my injured arm, and maybe he had because more pressing things were upon us.

It wasn't a third can sailing at us now; it was a car aimed at me, or maybe at both of us, careening across the parking lot at top speed. And it wasn't a ripped off, pissed off grocery store manager behind the wheel of the canary yellow Cadillac hurtling toward us.

Maybe it was her mom's car, or maybe she'd bought it for Laura, looking for brightness. But it was obviously the same car that had picked Nelson up and dumped him in front of a Hollywood drug store, and it was driven by a dark-haired, middle-aged woman who could only be Laura.

The bug eyes gave her away as she bore down on the gas pedal. Her protruding eyes caught mine. She lifted something from her front seat, and even as she tried to flatten me like a pancake, she was hurling the accompanying can of Spam in my direction.

Joe had his gun out, and he aimed carefully, mindful of all the shoppers scurrying around in the parking lot. What he winged was not Laura, but the spam, which spurted superior canned juices all over us as it expired for the second time in the parking lot.

People ducked behind their cars and screamed. I screamed too; it just felt like the thing to do.

Joe fired again and got one of Laura's tires and a sizzling hiss out of Laura's radiator.

Laura spun the wheel. Thrown by the loss of a tire, she was heading now not for us but for a plump Hispanic woman pushing a shopping cart brimming with groceries and small screaming children in the direction of a minivan.

"Watch out," Joe and I both shouted, but the woman froze.

This was one of those life moments where either you do the right thing or you're damned to the same hell as bill collectors, politicians, and mass murderers.

Even as Joe fired again on Laura, I jumped on the woman, grabbed her and the cart, and slammed us all up against the minivan and the woman half off her feet. All this with a bad arm.

I heard her eggs break in one of the grocery bags, but there was only so much good I could do that quickly.

Laura's yellow car skidded harmlessly past us, grazing a light pole with an excruciating metal on metal squeal. She was wedged against the pole, spinning her wheels.

And Joe was striding toward her, his gun straight, telling her, "Get out. Get out of the vehicle."

He sure could still do that cop thing pretty well. I would've gotten out. Especially with that gun pointed at me.

The kids screamed louder, and the mother shook me off, fiercely swinging her purse and getting my arm again, which hurt too much not to shout about it.

I turned the shout into an admonition. "Hey! Knock it off," I yelled. "I just saved your lives!"

The woman was cursing in Spanish, but through it, I heard Joe say again, "Get out of the car!"

But Laura was having none of that. I heard her back the car up, and I peered around the minivan just in time to see her free the car. Joe jumped back just in time to avoid her rear wheels.

She swung that Caddy around so fast it almost tipped on its side, but she righted it and aimed it at the rear of the minivan.

Joe fired again, and I heard Laura yowl.

"Get out of the vehicle," he shouted.

"You'll never get the money," Laura screamed. "You'll die. Just like your brother d—"

Then there was another shot, and there was silence. I thought, Joe killed her, and we weren't any closer to anything now, not to the money; not to the big bad guy; not to clearing Joe, who had now, in front of many witnesses, just upped his body count. I sagged.

I sagged too soon because there was the revving of an engine, and Joe began cursing and shouting a warning, "Christy, run," but I was moving in slow motion—the car was almost upon us, and I was sidestepping like a tired dancer.

Luckily, the Hispanic woman got it now, and it was her saving my behind this time, sending me and the cart with her screaming kids and broken eggs sailing around the minivan and against the back of a pickup.

Laura's car smashed into the van, crumpling it in folds like an accordion. We would've been caught right up inside one of those folds if we'd stayed where I'd led us.

The kids stopped screaming as glass shattered around us like hail or Hollywood special effects crystal snowflakes. We all kind of ducked down and closed our eyes, and that slow motion feeling sank in deep, got into my bones, except now I wasn't just slow, I was frozen.

It took me forever just to look again, just to hear through the ringing in my ears from the crash, to hear Joe calling "Christy, for God's sake, Christy, are you—?"

The woman picked her kids up in her arms, shouting for the policia loud enough that I couldn't hear Joe anymore.

People were streaming out of the grocery store; two lithe bag boys were racing toward the Caddy, which was wedged up against the side of the minivan, shooting smoke from its exhaust pipe and steam from its engine.

And still, Laura wouldn't get out of the car; she was pumping the gas pedal and rocking it back and forth, back and forth.

Joe was reloading his weapon. Police sirens were screaming nearby.

"Everybody back," he said in a voice filled with authority.

"Get out of the car," he said with even more authority to Laura, but I could see his hands—even as he expertly slipped bullets into the chamber, they were shaking. "I *will* take you out this time," he said, "and that'll be doing the world some good." He sounded less authoritative, and more like he was losing it. Really, I thought, she didn't want him to lose it.

But she was already lost herself; her head was down on the steering wheel as he stepped up to her and reached for the driver's side door. Her head was still down, and Joe was just about to yank her out of the car when she backed up suddenly, shockingly, and rapidly. Disengaging her front end from the minivan, she hit a couple of other cars with her fishtailing rear before she zigzagged wildly onto Sunset.

Joe just stood there, as stunned as I felt. There wasn't much else he could do because firing after her could've taken out who knows how many other people gawking on street corners and what would that accomplish; she probably would've just kept on going as she was going now—disappearing tail lights, lopsided car, two tires blasted to their rims.

Joe shoved his gun inside his jacket and gave a jerk of his head toward my car. I snapped out of my freeze.

"I've gotta go," I told the Hispanic lady with the crying children, the smashed up eggs, and the equally smashed up minivan.

She let go of my arm, and it was only then that my arm really began to hurt. Tears from the pain of it or maybe tears of relief that Laura was not, at the moment, trying to kill me spilled down my cheeks.

I rummaged in my bag for a pen, and I scrawled Rose's address on the side of a paper bag in the woman's cart.

"That's the owner of the car, the mother of the woman who did the hit and run," I said, talking fast. One of the woman's kids translated for me. "Her name is Rose Holloman, and the killer in the car was Laura Ordam Littlejohn, her daughter. Personally, I think you could get a brand new van out of her and anything else you can find a lawyer to think of."

The woman started to thank me, but I waved it away. "No thank *you* for saving me, and I'm sorry that this happened to your car."

The police sirens were whirling through the air like Santa's sleigh bells would've in some kinder, gentler time, and I dashed over to Joe, who was sitting behind the wheel of my car with the engine gunning. I thought how appropriate the pop holiday song I hated most and seemed to hear the most had just become. Except it wasn't Grandma getting run over by reindeer; it was me and a Cadillac nearly getting it on.

With my arm throbbing and my heart pounding, I jumped into my car, and we skidded out of there fast.

"You okay?" Joe asked me.

"Fantastic," I said, swiping at my eyes and trying not to cry, but I wanted to cry.

He bounced over a curb and hurtled down an alley, and I heard those police sirens squeal to a stop in the parking lot right behind us.

We'd just gone from being the hunters to the hunted, I thought, not only by Laura and whoever else she was involved with, but also by the police, who we were one step ahead of. I hoped no one had thought to get *my* license number.

* * *

Joe swung down to Santa Monica Boulevard, then off it, and down some more alleys with scenic views of garbage cans. He had the baseball hat on again, pulled low on his forehead, and his eyes were narrow and hard and determined as he circled through not one, but two, bank lots and a Del Taco drive through before bringing us back up Highland to Hollywood Boulevard, where he took a detour into the parking garage for the Kodak Theater, where they hold the Academy Awards. You can also park there at premium prices to take a look at the celebrity handprints in the sidewalk in front of Mann's Chinese down the street or to hang out in the wanna-be-a-mall mall just to the right of the Kodak.

Unless Joe wanted to buy some new jeans at the Gap, get me some sexy lingerie at Victoria's Secret, stare up at the commercials running on a California slender version of the jumbo Times Square TV screens running soft drink commercials out on the street side of the mall, there was no real reason for hanging out there tonight.

"What are you doing?" I asked.

"Following Laura," he said, "I'm gonna nail her."

He skidded down a parking lane, around a corner, and at last, past the yellow Caddy parked crookedly in a fire lane.

"How—?" I asked.

He plucked a little black thing that looked like part of an i-Pod out of his ear and pulled off his baseball cap. "Tracked her," he said.

"You put a tracking device on her car while she was trying to run me over?"

We both got out of my car, Joe stopping to pull a

little glowing light, adhesive-strip thing off the driver's side door of what was left of Laura's car.

"No. I put a tracking device on her car while it was parked in the freestanding garage behind her mother's kitchen. I wasn't just sitting around eavesdropping while you did all the work."

"Then why didn't you know Laura was there and following—"

He shook his head impatiently, interrupting me. "I didn't think Laura was hiding out at Rose's house; I just figured she'd left the car. Which I didn't think anyone would be driving tonight or maybe ever again since the police had the description of a yellow car picking up Nelson. Low probability she'd take it out for a spin. So I took off my baseball cap and the monitoring device."

He was tugging me through the parking garage so quickly that I didn't have time to formulate my doubts, much less express them.

"You see her behind the wheel? She's a killer. A hit and run killer. I'm not gonna wait around for the cops to get her."

The light slowly blinked on in my head. "You think she killed your brother?"

"What are the odds Ricky was close to two hit and run drivers? Come on. She's on foot now, won't be so easy."

The pain in my arm began to dull out, but not all at once. The steady throbbing ache felt like an endless bass riff vibrating through my body.

"We've gotta find her," Joe said. "So help out here, okay?"

"Yeah," I agreed. "I'll try."

I was surprised to hear how shaky I still sounded, even to my own ears, and to feel more tears springing to my eyes even now. Mostly, it wasn't fear anymore; it wasn't my arm hurting anymore; it was anger that made me shaky and weepy, anger at myself.

Had I become the single most oblivious person in the universe in the last week or what? I, who could tell across a crowded dance floor if anyone was even glancing my way. I, who could spot a plainclothes store detective or a phony talent scout a mile off.

Two days ago, high on love and dragging a plastic bag full of hotel linens, I fell prey to an attacker lurking under a date palm.

Now, I'd completely missed a bright yellow Caddy tailing me from Pasadena in heavy traffic. The only reasonable explanation was that this love thing was even more dangerous than I knew.

Still, who would've expected Laura to try to kill me, to try to kill us, in the parking lot of a grocery store in a lower middle class Hollywood neighborhood two days before Christmas. All I'd done was ask her mom to call her, and her mom had invited her for tea and psychic phenomena. And this was the reaction that phone call had raised? Didn't she care about witnesses? Was she crazy? Who was this woman?

I wanted to ask Joe, but he was busy scoping out the recesses of the parking garage.

Who Laura was didn't matter much anyway. It was what I was that mattered, and I was lame, despicably lame. I was sloppy. I was a distracted, lovesick fool who had better start dealing with the distractions before I got seriously hurt.

Although I doubted anything could hurt as much as believing I had the right to fall in love. Look where that belief had gotten me. My life was in shambles. The longer I continued to believe such a ridiculous thing, the more in shambles my life would become. I was convinced of that now.

"She went into the mall," Joe mused. "The street would scare her. She's scared a lot."

"What are you, a shrink now?"

He didn't answer. He was paying no attention to me at all; I was just this appendage he was dragging around. I supposed I'd served my purpose as bait.

I couldn't help it. I sighed.

"Are you sure you're all right?" Joe asked me, still without looking at me, as he led me, power-walking, through the aroma of stale exhaust fumes and staler fast food that permeated the garage.

"Just fine," I said. "Just fine."

People like me, people like I had chosen to become, had to be a little bit more defended against loony emotions like love. Of course, that sort of smart, cynical thinking was beyond irrelevant now. Too late to be smart or cynical, too late to commit myself to more celibate emotions.

My life itself was about to be irrelevant if I didn't watch out.

Chapter
Fourteen

Joe and I reached the outside escalator and pushed our way past bag ladies and Japanese tourists and gangsta types.

We stepped off the moving stairs so fast I felt dizzy, and I had to blink a few times to fully take in the mall that was supposed to revive Hollywood.

From discount plazas to sleek, high fashion enclaves, every mall in the greater Los Angeles basin shortly before Christmas and Chanukah and Kwanza was a mad frenzy of shoppers carrying bulging bags and lines of children squirming and wailing to see Santa. But not this mall.

Here, amid a spectacularly strange reproduction of the set of D.W. Griffith's famous silent film *Intolerance*, beneath the quasi Greco–Roman sculpture that reminded me more of Caesar's Palace, Las Vegas, than the time of Caesar, the place was just about barren of consumers.

Maybe it was merely the lateness of the hour, or maybe it was the lack of actual stores. Except for the chain anchor shops purveying preppy jeans

and push-up bras respectively, most of the storefronts were shuttered and sported signs reading
"Going Out of Business Sale" or "Coming Soon!"
True, there was a make your own stuffed bear factory, which was popular with tourists in the daytime, and apparently, the designated destination
for the gangsta types with their oversized beverages
to cruise at night. Maybe it was just the lack of
other cruisable locations that steered them to the
bear shop, or maybe they selected bears in their
gang colors and gave them to each other for the
holidays or chose bears in rival gang colors and
left them on doorsteps as a kind of warning, sort of
like the horse's head in *The Godfather.*

We took a quick walk through Build a Bear, past
the bins where you could select eye shade, hair
bows, and vocalization buttons that allowed your
bear to say "I wuv wu," but Laura was not among
the bear makers. Nor was she browsing the aisles
of the anchor stores, where clerks were wearily
closing up.

A mild Santa Ana had sprung up, and it set the
metal security grills on the fast food stands to rattling and caused rumpled napkins to skittle across
the food court like nascent tumbleweeds.

A few sleepy-looking people shuffled about like
they'd come from different time zones, probably
tourists who had, looking lost and disappointed,
the way I felt.

A small group of teenagers threw food wrappers
and fistfuls of coins into a big upside-down wedding cake of a fountain with murky water. A costumed Superman and Batman stood at its edge,
holding flyers promoting tours of Hollywood and
movie stars' homes but mostly talking with each
other. A security guard strutted around like he was

doing something other than strutting, which he wasn't. One of the bag ladies from the escalator set up camp near the fast food court, and he didn't stop her.

The superheros tried to hand us flyers for a midnight screening of *Little Shop of Horrors,* a flick that, though the location would seem appropriate, was not located in the mall.

"Maybe Laura went to the movies?" I suggested.

"She can't sit still that long," Joe shook his head. "There Ricky would be, sitting like a Buddha gone bad, nodding off over his breakfast beer, and ogling bikinis walking down the sand, and she'd be hopping around talking on a cell phone, microwaving soup, painting her nails . . . never breathing in."

We glanced inside a few speciality shops exuding their own doom, selling overpriced 'exotic' makeup, batik pillows, and enormous wooden animal sculptures—I mean who buys a ten-foot-tall factory-carved giraffe for their living room? We peered in a Popcorn Utopia offering many flavors, including Cajun; and on the otherwise empty top floor of the mall, we glanced inside the two chain restaurants, which featured gimicky pizzas and many topping burgers, which explained that fast food odor in the parking garage.

Only then, our skin reeking of garlic, did we pay attention to the flashing neon sign with cascading red balls on it, a sign that pointed irresistibly to Twilight Town Bowling, black light and virtual bowling 'til 2 AM.

We both said at once, "She went bowling."

Or possibly to hell. If you viewed the recently revamped and already empty Hollywood and Highland mall itself as Purgatory, lost souls waiting for nothing much, then it stood to reason that enter-

ing the red-carpeted, red-lit entry way to the crash
and boom of bowling pins and intensely scatologi-
cal hip-hop cranked up to deafening was hell.

The place was cavernous, and it was decorated
in a kind of caveman motif with fake stalactites
and stalagmites and glowing tubes of pink and red
neon.

We slipped past the front desk and a line of people sporting nose, cheek, and lip piercings waiting
for their bowling shoes. They seemed to all know
each other.

Joe kept looking over his shoulder a little bit,
cocking his head to one side as if he was hearing
something only he could hear about the crash of
bowling pins and the rumble of rap.

Twilight Town was divided into two sections,
one for real bowling and one for the virtual variety,
the latter tucked inside a smoked glass enclave. Joe
nudged me through a thick door of sliding glass in
front of a jumbo video screen, on which virtual
balls were rolling down steep San Francisco streets,
through the New York subway, and crashing over
white water rapids. The crowd was slightly more
wholesome than that in the shoe rental line, and
even in the half light cast from the screens, it was
quickly obvious that Laura wasn't there.

We went back through the sliding glass again to
the sixteen lanes of authentic, old-fashioned, ball
striking pins type of bowling. It must've been sur-
real bowling night. The lanes were doused in black
light that made my skin glow purple and Joe's
jeans green. There were sparkling, strobing stars
playing over the ceiling, and along with the post-
punk crowd from the shoe rental line, there were
big, heady groups of Europeans speaking in excited Romance languages; an enormous and ugly

family sporting tattoos; a very wasted group of pale, louche transvestites; and a couple of guys wearing Santa suits with skulls on the back. Amid a crowd of teenagers in tee shirts labeled "South Bay Christian Bowling League" was Laura, disguised in her own SBCBL tee shirt.

The kids looked rabitty and out of place, but Laura looked decidedly out of place among *them*. Her small body was curling forward, her shoulders hunched as if her bones had all but melted away. Her hair looked thin and dull, and she had pouches under her protruding eyes.

She was a spineless Methusaleh in a crowd of yipping puppies. She had a flip phone pressed to her ear, or a better way of putting it might be that she was pressed against a flip phone.

"What?" she asked. "What? It's noisy in here; I can't hear you. All right, I'll meet you—"

She snapped the phone shut and slammed it in her purse. I stood at the side and watched Joe come up behind her and tap her on the shoulder.

"My turn to bowl?" she asked brightly, and then her eyes bugged out more when she saw it was Joe. She got up fast, but he held her tighter, gripping her arm in his hand.

He nodded at me, and like we'd planned it, which we hadn't done in words at least, I was right next to her on the other side, gripping her other arm. Yes, she still had bones, thin ones encased in flabby flesh.

"I'll scream," she said.

"Won't that bring the police?" I asked innocently.

She pressed her mouth closed, her thin lips disappearing into the disapproving folds of her face.

"Why her?" she asked Joe. "You and I could've—"

Joe must've squeezed her arm tighter because she gave a little yelp.

"Yeah," I said, "I've heard about the 'three men in your life.' I know you're the hottest chick around. I'm totally threatened."

Laura, on the other hand, looking at the bad ass look in Joe's eyes, was kinda freaked.

"Who were you talking to?" Joe asked her, propelling her across the room toward the door. "Daddy?"

She just kept her lips clamped shut, and her eyes were looking me over.

"Your mother was quite worried about you this afternoon," I said. "I bet she's more worried now."

I knew that would get something out of her. "You're nothing but a con artist. Working with him." She jerked her head toward Joe, and she tried to yank her arm out of Joe's grasp, but he held her firm. "You're nothing," she said, to both of us. "You're nowhere."

"To think my mother believed in you. To think she wanted me to meet you. And all along you were working with *him*."

She spat, missing Joe but shooting phlegm on a guy with a purple mohawk. He didn't like it much, and he glowered at Joe like he was going to take him out just for dragging Laura along. Joe seemed too absorbed in pulling Laura to notice.

He had, I realized, ever since we'd gotten into the car, been pretty quiet, like there were voices in his head he was listening to, and for all I knew, there were.

"She's crazy when she's drunk," I apologized. "If there's a cleaning bill—"

The mohawk guy shrugged it off.

We were back in entranceway now, in the cheesy red glow.

Laura kicked Joe hard, and Joe stumbled. He didn't let go of her, of course; it just pissed him off, so that he pressed her up against the red wall. Juvenile was blasting nasty sex talk through a speaker right near my head.

"I didn't kill Ricky." Joe was shouting to be heard over the back beat. "You know I didn't kill him."

"You screwed us though," she said.

"Look at all the people you screwed," Joe said. "All the people you hurt."

"The dead don't feel any pain. But you will," she sneered.

"Some of your victims were still alive," Joe said. "Some of them knew who you were. Unlike me, you are a real 'somebody.' "

I pushed her and Joe pulled her, and then we were outside, out in the now even emptier plaza. We were moving toward the escalator.

"What do you want with me?" Laura asked.

She wasn't shouting now; she was quiet, looking around her, edgy. She was probably more worried about the cops than we were after her grocery store stunt.

"I don't want anything *with* you," Joe said. "What I want *from* you is information about all of Ricky's business associates. And your father's. I want to know where that money is. I want to know who ordered Det. Hallie Richter of the Houston P.D. killed and who drove the car that hit him, although I have a pretty good idea of who that was now. And if I'm right, crazy lady, you should be glad I want some other information because I wouldn't have to think too long about getting you off the street. Permanently. So you better start talking."

"And what do I get?" Laura sneered.

I had to agree with her there—what did she get? And in spite of her trying to run me over and all and Joe's suspicions regarding his brother's death, didn't strong-arming her out of a bowling alley and hustling her into my car at gunpoint constitute kidnapping or something?

I had a profound feeling of unease that was exacerbated by Joe's reply. "You get to stay alive. At least a little while longer."

"Really?" Laura asked, and her voice was equal parts sarcasm and hope.

The unease rose up and gagged me. I tugged at Joe's sleeve, but he was already stopping at the edge of the escalator, like he was thinking over what we were about to do too.

But probably, it wasn't thought so much that stopped him as the sight visible at the bottom of the escalator just where we would enter the garage. Down there, a whole bunch of red and white lights were flashing, not unlike the interior of the bowling alley, except that these lights belonged not to Satan's interior decorating service but to a quintet of police cars.

"Great plan," Joe muttered to himself. "Something a little more subtle maybe."

I had no idea what he was talking about; in fact, right then I had no idea what he was thinking about, what he was feeling, whether he even knew I was still along for the ride as he pulled Laura back from the edge of the escalator. What had happened to him not being able to keep his hands off me?

"We'll take a cab," Joe said to her and to me.

"To where?" I hissed at Joe.

"I don't need you to take him out," Laura sniffed. "He'd never hurt me. Not really. Not much."

"And yet you're scared of him. You're hiding from him, not me."

"Of course I'm scared of him," she agreed like it was only natural. "I've always been scared—"

"Who are we talking about?" I asked, but neither of them answered me; they just glared at each other with undisclosed hatred. I was starting to feel like the chaperone on a bad date.

"Later," Joe said to me or to someone off in space. He acted only half aware of the fact that I'd said a word.

We hurried down a long flight of dirty marble steps onto Hollywood Boulevard.

I couldn't see any cabs around. There were buses and prostitutes and drunks and the neon dinosaur eating a clock across the street on top of the Ripley's Believe It or Not Museum. There was the requisite soft drink commercial blaring from the giant video screens on our corner and a guy with dreadlocks proclaiming the end of the world on the opposite curb, but no cabs.

Laura was looking around her like she expected to meet somebody, and maybe she did because she'd said on her cell phone that she was going to meet someone.

"Joe," I said, "we can't just stand here."

Joe nodded his agreement, and when the light changed, we crossed the street and headed toward the smog-fuzzed skyscrapers of downtown. "We'll go east on Hollywood," Joe said very pointedly.

It was darker here, away from the neon dinosaur and the TV commercial screens; there were street people settled in the door-ways of the wig shop; the magic store; and the Frederick's of Hollywood lingerie museum, its lavender walls streaked silver with moonlight.

Kids with more bizarrely pierced body parts than what we had seen inside the bowling alley strutted around smoking cigarettes. There was a smell of urine and rotting fruit.

"Where are we going?" I asked Joe. "You know, other than east on Hollywood?"

But Joe just shook his head at me, his attention somewhere inside himself, his words directed at Laura.

"The cops are going to arrest you sooner or later now," Joe said. "And you'll talk then. And you'll get hurt then. Think about it. Nelson's hands are missing."

"He put them where he shouldn't."

"Where was that?" I asked.

"In my pockets." The voice was right up behind us, and there was hardly any fight.

Laura was pulled free of Joe, but she was holding on to him now, not he to her.

Joe had his gun out, and he was readier than I would've guessed to use it, but he didn't seem nearly as upset as I was by the two brutal-looking thugs fencing us in. They wore cheap suits and good ties, and one was blonde, and the other, black. Joe seemed more concerned with the skinny, cranky-looking, bald man who had a hold of Laura now. He was probably eighty, and he was definitely mean.

"You better watch out *now,*" Laura said to me, her eyes bugged out in a mixture of fear and triumph. Her whole body twitched like she had stuck her finger in an electric circuit. Then, in a polite little girl voice like she was making introductions at a party, she added, "This is my daddy, Charles."

And Joe seemed to think better of whatever he

was going to get going; instead, he just let one of the thugs take the gun away. He was half-smiling.

"We should probably go somewhere and talk," Joe suggested, "Charlie."

"Like you have a choice in the matter," Daddy Charlie laughed. He looked at me not unkindly. "Guess you'll be coming along for the ride too."

Joe sent me a steadying look, and I didn't suppose that I had much choice. Well, the choice I had was to try to run and scream and hope all those cops massed around the mall parking garage three blocks back heard me, which besides being unlikely would screw up whatever it was Joe thought we were accomplishing here. And there was a steady look in his eye that told me that he at least thought something was being accomplished. All I could do was hope that whatever that something was, that it would be good not only for Joe but also for me.

"It'll be okay," Joe said as if he was reading my mind. Boy, we were both good at that fake mind reading stuff.

Although Laura and her father both laughed like Joe was the crazy one for talking like that, I climbed in the massive black car that glided right up to the curb next to us, driven by a third thug, this one freckled.

It went against all my scratch and claw and fight principles to get in that car. I was really sealing my doom now. Or maybe I'd already sealed it the day I'd climbed in Joe's car, accepted his coffee, enjoyed his flirting, and pretended I knew something about Ricky Littlejohn.

The black car wasn't really a limo; it was a hearse, which I didn't recognize until I had slipped inside it and smelled the formaldehyde odor. The smell, combined with Joe making an almost, but not quite, imperceptible lick of his lips, shook me, but I pretended I was cool with whatever was going down.

I noticed that Joe had pulled off his baseball cap or maybe lost it in the struggle, brief as it was, with the thugs. He looked behind us once and only once out the rear window, and then he kind of sighed and settled in between the two thugs. Lucky me, I got to rub knees with Laura, who twitched and giggled every few seconds.

Hollywood Boulevard streamed by our darkened windows. The Church of Scientology blazed with spotlights; Kaiser Permanente Medical Center hummed with an ugly flourescent glow; the rest was all darkness—dark storefronts; closed fast food shops; empty streets, except for a guy wearing a piece of indoor/outdoor carpeting as a loincloth and pushing a shopping cart. Then we turned north on Normandie, and we were driving past emerald lawns and neat stucco homes with tile roofs and sprinklers hissing like a snake chorus and splattering the sidewalks.

"You've made quite a mess, Laura," Charles said as we all—me, Joe, two of the thugs, and Laura—stepped into a walnut-lined study. There were bookshelves filled with crisp bound books, big leather chairs, and a fire in a massive stone fireplace.

"Do you know the people I will have to pay off just to keep your . . . your . . . antics in the parking lot out of the press?"

"Sorry, Daddy," she said, but she didn't sound very sorry. She laughed. "You know me. Put the pedal to the metal."

Joe's fists were clenched at his sides, and I knew it took some effort for him not to just deck her.

The room we were in was like a movie set for a masculine den. The books—I took three off the shelf, and no one tried to stop me—were just phoney cardboard covers. The fire in the fireplace consisted of gas flames issuing from plastic logs. The leather chairs, when I sat after being gestured into one, were plastic.

The den itself wasn't even in a house; it was in the Ordam Mortuary, an equally fake white-columned antebellum mansion, of which there were ten locations around the Southland. Throughout this particular outpost, at least, the faint formaldehyde smell I'd detected in the hearse lingered like perfume. I longed for some patchouli incense.

Laura crossed and uncrossed her legs. She made twittering sounds like a little bird. Her father snapped his fingers, and one of the thugs brought her a bottle of Evian and a white pill in a dixie cup, both of which she chugged. A few minutes passed, and she seemed to calm down.

Joe didn't appear at all nervous, but I sensed, rather than saw, that his calm demeanor was the best performance of his admittedly spotty acting career. The thugs were patting him down, and he just stood there like, yeah, try your best, you're not going to find anything. I wondered what it was they were hoping to find. Surely, if they'd figured he had another gun, they would've disarmed him before we'd gotten in the hearse; before the hearse was parked by the back door of the mortuary; before we got out of the hearse on a quiet Atwater commercial street, all shuttered cafes and boutiques whose windows displayed hand woven sweaters and hand spun glass and hand thrown ceramics, any of which would've shattered quite nicely and set off an alarm that would've brought the police if Joe had, in fact, had another weapon on him.

"Laura did," Joe said softly, "make a mess."

"Just like Ricky," Charles smiled and nodded as if he and Joe were pals from way back.

"Yeah, they shared that," the blond thug said, getting into the act. But Charles scowled at him, and he shut up and pushed Joe aside like he was done with him and then took his place toward the back of the room with the other thug. Both of them shut up and folded their arms, not that they'd done much more than shut up, fold their arms, and look muscularly ominous since I had first seen them. They were stock types out of central casting.

Of course, weren't we all? Laura was the ditz. Charles was the ancient, evil villain. Joe was the edgy noir hero.

I couldn't stop thinking that this was all a movie. Okay, if it was a movie, if this was an act, what exactly was my role? The innocent ingenue? As my backlog of head shots over the years would attest, I was getting a little past the prime for that one.

There was a long and steady silence except for the slight sizzling of the gas fire, which made the room uncomfortably hot. A line of sweat trickled down my back, and a drop of perspiration ran like a tear down Joe's cheek.

Nobody seemed to want to break the silence. There was a clock on the wall that was lined with a rim of pink neon like something out of a diner, like something that might've worked on the wall of that bowling alley, but it didn't fit here.

But then everything seemed a little off, a little

false, a little wrong. The groceries Joe bought, spoiling in my back seat. The transmitter Joe put on Laura's car but paid no attention to for a while. Joe going along with these thugs, with this act, whatever it was. Were the thugs the ones who had cut off Nelson's hands? Or had skinny, bald Charles done it? I studied him. His malevolent eyes were every bit as buggy as his daughter's, opaque and unreadable. Why had diminutive Rose married him; how could she have ever, in her youth, had wild sexual excitement with a skinny, mean-looking man with buggy, unfeeling eyes? Rose, who seemed so soft and vulnerable, who believed in changing her name to improve her spirit. Of course, there was no explaining really how one person ended up with another person, what the exact chemistry of attraction was, and how it formed the elixir of love. Look at me and Joe. Look at us sitting here in this room. Nobody talking. Everyone just sweating and waiting.

It was Laura, Laura who couldn't sit still even after taking whatever pill she was fed who jumped up and started babbling at last. Yes, of course the ditz would steal the scene.

"He's my Daddy; he won't hurt me. I don't need anybody's protection . . . he only hurt Ricky because he was stealing from him. Daddy can't abide stealing, can you, Daddy? That's the only reason— you know, an eye for an eye, a hand for a hand . . ." she began giggling convulsively. "Nelson's problem too, right, Daddy? I told you he was greedy, that he would not help—"

"Shut up," Charles roared loudly enough that his voice strained inside his scrawny neck.

More silence while he made an effort to compose himself. Laura was crying now, her shoulders, still inside the South Bay Christian Bowling League tee shirt, shaking silently.

"I didn't kill Lardo the Magnificent," Charles said, referring to Ricky and attempting to assuage Laura, but Laura sobbed on.

He gestured at Joe. "He killed him. Just like the cops said, or didn't say, because I told them that it was too much publicity, to lay off."

"You have a lot of pull," Joe said. "You and you alone. But I didn't, in fact, kill Rick. Which you knew. If I had killed him, it would've been a statement. Not punching him around and getting him stoned in a hot tub."

"A statement. Like a bank statement?" Charles asked, his voice rising.

Joe rose out of his chair, ready, thugs aside, to kill Charles. "I don't have your money. If I had your money, I wouldn't be hanging around LA."

"Why would the cops lay off Joe just because you told them to?" I asked Charles, curiosity getting the better of me.

"Always ask politely," Charles said, and whether he was correcting my tone or telling me why the cops laid off, I wasn't sure.

The thugs both stepped forward like they were robotically controlled to move at once, a synchronized dance step. I noticed the nice, heavy-looking brass lamp on Daddy's desk. Of course, like everything else, it was probably a prop that was made of cheap, light aluminum. But maybe not, in which case, it would function quite effectively as a club.

"Didn't grease your brother quite enough, hey? You were supposed to shake me down for more?" Charles said to Joe.

The ugly look that flashed on Joe's face passed off so rapidly that it was like someone had taken a rag and wiped it off. I might've been the only one who saw it. He was calm again and sitting back in his chair. He was even smiling.

The thugs returned to their first position like someone had flicked an off switch.

"You wanted it to *look* like my brother was made an offer he couldn't refuse, right? But he refused all the same. He discovered the dirty money you stuffed in his bank account. Did Ricky send somebody to threaten him, one of those goons?"

"They're bodyguards," and Charles laughed at his own joke, "get it, *body*guards; my, that is good."

Laura laughed too, exuberantly; shifted around in her seat; and shot me a little glance of triumph. "See. He's my daddy."

"My point is, none of the usual tricks worked," Joe said to Charles. "So you just decided to take my brother out."

It was a statement, not a question, but still, Charles shook his head. "No such decision was made." And intentionally or not, he looked at Laura. Joe looked too.

"Put the pedal to the metal, did you, Laura?" Joe asked very quietly.

Laura threw back her head and laughed. "You go fast enough, nobody ever catches you."

"Shut up!" Charles screamed at her. His bald head looked purple on top; maybe it was the light, or maybe it was all the veins sticking out like a topographical map that detailed the mental pathways of the truly evil.

Laura started to cry again, this time less quietly.

"Always the loudest one with the biggest mouth," Charles rumbled.

I got the feeling that if Charles murdered anyone tonight, it would be his daughter. But then we'd be witnesses, and he'd have to get rid of us too.

I would've been more upset just thinking about the no witnesses thing, except I had to pee. I really, really had to pee. When I was a kid, when I watched movies about people whose lives were in jeopardy or who were about to embark on some life changing adventure, I always wondered what they did when they had to pee. Now I knew. They held it.

"So you say you didn't kill Ricky," Charles said amiably to Joe, who was still coldly staring Laura down. "I tend to believe it because you had ample opportunity and you never used it, not one least little bit, so I think you were waiting to see, even as I was waiting to see, what it was that Ricky had done with that fourteen million you pretend you're too good to want."

"I'm not pretending I don't want that," Joe corrected, using an equally amiable tone. "I just wasn't that interested in a couple hundred thousand here and there. And just in case there's any doubt in your mind, neither was my brother. My brother wanted justice."

"Then he and I had something in common," Charles said with a sneer.

"Nelson didn't take the money," Laura was shrill, and she spoke so fast that her words all ran together like magic marker in the rain. "He would never have taken it; you didn't need to go off on him. He loved me . . ."

"Yes, yes, so many men find you irresistible." Charles didn't seem in the least bit sarcastic. He smoothed his own bald pate. "Like father, like daughter in some ways, I suppose. Nelson merely wanted it for you," Charles said smoothly. "Would've killed this girlie here for you."

"As if," I said. "I broke his ribs."

Charles ignored me.

"I just wanted to send you a message, Laura. That this isn't a little game; this isn't Daddy, buy me a new fur coat. That this money is important. That other people are expendable in order to retrieve it. I thought you'd received my message—" Charles spread his hands out flat, playing to the back row, the thugs.

"Instead you let these fools lure you in," a quick flash of his eyes took in Joe and I, "and get you to trail them, just as they *expected*—"

Just as the ugly look had passed over Joe and was gone, now there was a guilty look, quickly gone too.

Damn. He'd set me up again, set us both up this time as a target for Laura, so that once she was on us, he could be all over her daddy. If that's what was going on now, and he was truly all over Charles, instead of Charles and his goons being all over us.

The point was, Joe had lied to me again. He must've known Laura was in Rose's house or somewhere nearby. He had been playing me as much as her. He just hadn't counted on her being nuts enough to run us down. Or maybe he had known that too, maybe he had known she was the one who had run down his brother long before tonight's attempted hit and run.

Laura and her father screamed at each other about who had let the other one down for a good long while.

I felt tired now, along with having to pee. The

whole deal with Joe not telling quite all of the truth all the time just like that charlatan Geneece had suggested, that business was getting old. Apparently, in his quest for his brother's killer, or revenge, or the fourteen million, or clearing his name, or even happiness with me, he had put us in danger again without coming clean about it. Maybe he was so obsessed with his mission of vengeance, with that fourteen million, that danger just didn't matter.

He was showing a reckless disregard for his own life and for mine. Of course, if you came right down to it, wasn't that what had drawn me to him? What made us make out maniacally in a car on the Pacific Coast Highway only twenty-four hours after we'd met, but that reckless disregard? Wasn't I tired of always watching my back, always hiding, always holding everything in?

Or maybe Joe was merely performing the ultimate con, making me believe he was that reckless, wild, passionate person. But really, all along everything was planned, contrived, like a script Louie could've written while some platinum blonde sat under the heat lamps at his old salon.

It was hard to tell the difference anymore between what someone appeared to be and who they really were. I should know that better than anyone. And all at once, I was so tired I didn't care anymore about anything except the having to pee part.

I felt Joe looking at me like he knew I'd gone some place he didn't want me to go, like he knew me better than I knew myself, and he was sorry that I was feeling badly. Compassionate knowledge and concern were written on his face.

I looked down at my hands. I'd had enough of

him looking at me like that. I'd had enough of him knowing me when obviously I still didn't know him. Right then, I'd had enough of loving him and him loving me. I had just absolutely had enough with following the script, or doing improv, or whatever it was we were supposed to be doing. Enough.

Laura and her father stopped yelling long enough to breathe in.

"I have to pee," I announced flatly, breaking whatever character I was. "And I am not in the least bit interested in any of this. Joe and I've had a little thing going, that's all. I tried to help him out; sorry to involve you, Laura; or you, Charles; or you guys back there in the cheering squad. Where's the ladies'?"

Charles pointed vaguely out of the den, like I'd just written myself out of the scene and it was okay by him, but maybe he was still catching his breath.

"Right and right again," he said, half gasping, and for a moment, I wasn't sure if he was agreeing with my speech or giving me directions.

As I headed for the door, he added "Alarm's set; no one goes in or out without noise, and my driver's waiting at the exit. And interested party or not, I'm not quite ready for you to go home, young lady, so . . . freshen up; take a look at the casket selection down the hall; do anything you want to do, except exit the premises."

And so I just left the room. I just left the room and went to the bathroom. I scrubbed my hands of the grocery store parking lot and the bowling alley, washed my face, combed my hair, and put on lipstick. I found a water cooler, used about six of those little dixie cups Laura had her pill from, and drank. I looked around, but I couldn't find where the Evian had come from.

I was angry, angry at Joe. I was more angry at him than I was scared of being more or less held hostage in a mortuary. I wanted to stamp my foot and smack a few walls, but I didn't want anyone to see me. I practiced taking deep breaths instead.

Gradually, I began to calm down. After all, a mortuary at night is actually a pretty peaceful place.

I thought about going out the front door, alarm be damned; of going to the exit, pretending I was hot for the thug guarding it, and getting in close enough to gouge out his eyes; but still, there were those other two thugs back in the pseudo-den, and who knew what small sound would summon them.

I had to think things through a little while longer. While I thought, I went into first one showroom and then the other. I looked at all the caskets in their different colors and styles and sizes, propped attractively on tables draped in floor-length velvet. I suppose it's not unlike picking out a car, except it wouldn't be much fun to take a coffin for a test drive.

Some were pink and white and frilly; some, rich mahogany and velvet lined. There were expensive, gold-plated ones and cheap ones that still cost several thousand and looked like they were made of plywood.

Above the coffins, which were in black lacquer, stainless steel as well, there were discreet seasonal decorations—somber green wreathes with dark purple bows, a dull silver Star of David, pine boughs crisscrossing the door sills.

I drifted from room to room, clicking on lights and stroking caskets. I was probably right behind the den now; I was probably sharing a common wall with the back of the room right where the thugs were standing. I might say I didn't care anymore, that I was tired and angry and fed up, and that all I wanted to do was figure a way to get out of there, but I was lying. I still cared. About Joe and what was going down, and anyway, if I didn't care enough to figure this whole scene out, I might never figure out my exit cue.

I wedged myself between a copper-colored casket lined in satin, which cost more than most Mercedes, and a custom-designed double wide sample inlaid with some of kind of red stone with its lid closed. I pressed my ear up against the wall.

"So we'll leave it at that," Charles was saying in a crafty voice, like he was pulling something good. "I had the means, and Ricky was an excellent front man, charming as long as you fed him the right lines and the right pills. I made some excellent business moves with him to shake hands for me. Unfortunately, Laura, you could never control his greedier impulses, and I could never control you. If it wasn't Ricky, it was Nelson, or you yourself flying off like the angel of death. One thing you learn in this business is that you have to move slowly, carefully. The dead aren't going anywhere, see. And the truth of it is, most of the living aren't going anywhere either. But you, you could never just wait. So, directly because of your impatience and your husband's greed, we have the nosy detective who wants something. We are not sure what he wants; you lived with him, you had hopes for him, so we let it lie. The lies—" here he laughed. The thugs laughed too, and I heard Joe laugh a beat late.

"There was no point, after all, in rushing things. I had ears where I wanted ears; I had eyes where I wanted eyes. Yes, everything was just status quo until one day, I gather, he rejected you."

"I rejected *him*," Laura sniffed.

"I thought we were, uh, friends," Joe said in the time-honored tradition of cute boys who got stuck with geeky girls.

Was this really all so simple? I wondered. Was this huge incredible mess we were in all predicated on Laura having a crush on my Joe? How easy it was, really, to think of him as mine.

"So you decide to spill the beans, as we say, to your dearly beloved Ricky, inform him of a spy in his midst, of your and my knowledge thereof, and everything blows up . . ." Charles cursed a charmingly evocative blue streak that shook the very wall I was listening through and then picked up his narrative again in an even tone. ". . . before I can handle things. And when I take umbrage at your foolishness, you hide from me. You perpetrate the basest lies about our relationship. You tell your feeble-brained New Age mother that you have to hide from me. You tell everyone who will listen how afraid you are of *me*, and then when you mess up yet again, who do you call to save you?"

"You, Daddy," Laura said meekly.

Charles exhaled so sharply it sounded like a late train was coming straight through the mortuary. "You're exactly like your mother except that you are just so exactly like me. And you did give me grandchildren."

"Daddy," she said, "I don't have the money."

"I know," he said. "The question is where has it gone? Ricky left this mortal coil before I could pump him. Nelson would've spoken up, I'm sure, if he'd known."

A chill settled over me, and I could feel it settle all around the room on the other side of the wall. Charles sounded like a cliché of a cranky old mortician, which he was. But how many cranky old morticians added to their casket sales count by creating their own customers?

Charles cleared his throat.

"Come on, don't everyone speak up at once now. The money was kept in cash, the easier to hand out to our allies and associates, who are now suffering through a rather thin holiday shopping season. Mexico? Safety deposit box? Trusted advisor? Con man? Investigator?"

"Don't look at me," said Joe.

"Do you really want to take me down?" Charles asked. "Because there's nothing to take me down for. No one gave a body that didn't agree to give a body. I have all the paperwork. And dead people can't tell you if they felt the least little bit, shall we say, intimidated. There was nothing illegal in the sales of even those terribly politically incorrect body parts. To make a living, dying people do sign up to sell themselves as parts, just as they undoubtedly did all their lives. Take my heart, or my mind, or the strength of my back, and leave the rest to come home to dinner. What does it matter? And poor old Nelson, no one much liked him alive, not even you, my daughter, yet now we all mourn his pasty white hide?"

Although I thought he shouldn't really be going on about the pasty white quality of anyone's skin— he was pretty pasty and white himself, and wrinkly on top of that—I had to agree that Nelson wasn't a real likeable fellow. Although likeable or not, cutting off his hands seemed pretty harsh.

Charles began to sound mightily aggrieved. "You want to nail me on that scumbag's demise? I was nowhere near the scene!"

"I'm sorry I defied you," Laura interrupted

meekly. "You would've left Nelson alone, wouldn't you, Daddy, if I'd—"

"Silence," Charles roared in a voice loud enough to wake all the dead lurking around.

Then, more quietly, "It was a drug deal gone wrong. We have that nice and clear with the police."

"I don't," Joe said after a moment, "want to take you down. What's the point anyway? All I'm going for is the gold."

But I knew, through the wall, through the sincerity he was virtually oozing, that he was lying. Yes, he was a pretty good liar, Joe was, but he couldn't fool me. Not anymore. He wasn't just after the money; he was after the justice his brother wanted. He was, he had to be, a good guy after all.

So, just like that, I snapped back into character again, and I knew exactly how I was going to play the role I was destined to play—that of Joe's lover. I would play it so that when this was all said and done, even if we said goodbye, this would come out right, right enough that we could at least have another night together under the pines, watching the heavens do their thing, oblivious of us as the heavens always are.

My brain started working again; my heart started hoping again. I drew my ear away from the wall, and I plucked at my purse and shoved my hand past the sugar-free gum, the rumpled tissues, and my little cannister of pepper spray, and I snatched up my cell phone, the only one Nelson hadn't stolen.

All my aversion to police intervention aside, I dialed 911 without even having to think about it. Because I hadn't thought about it, I didn't realize at first that I had no cell signal inside the casket room.

Holding the phone aloft like it was the Holy Grail or something, I wandered out into the hall, into the other casket room, and all the way back into the bathroom. Still no signal.

Cell phones are wonderful—you can send photos on them, and get prepaid plans with identities that aren't your own, and chat on weekends for free to nonexistent relatives on the East Coast. They're absolutely wonderful except when you have an emergency, and then you can never use them. I couldn't very well step outside, activating alarms and thug number three, to get service. I thought about using the pepper spray on thug three and then dialing, as I ran down the street with the other two thugs chasing me, but even playing the scene out in my head, I saw far too much commotion and risk.

Instead, I gave the bathroom a quick once-over. There was an air vent in the ceiling, which I had a feeling led outside. So I put the toilet seat down, climbed up on it, and then scrambled up on the tank; propping myself against the wall, I held the phone aloft right under that air vent. Standing on tiptoe, with the tank lid rattling under me, I got one wavering service bar. Good enough. I dialed 911 again.

Now the call went through, but it wasn't time for rejoicing just yet. It went straight through to a recorded message, which indicated the police knew I had an emergency; I should just stay on the line, and help would be with me in under ten minutes.

Under ten minutes! Even though I'd been wandering around in the casket showrooms for at least that long, I was seized with fear that if I waited now, someone would come and find me standing on the toilet in the bathroom and would take my cell phone away.

I hung up, and I called Louie. His cell phone rang so many times I thought I was going to get the voice mail playing "I'm an Old Cowhand," but at last he picked it up, saying hello off the end of a laugh.

He sure sounded like he was having a good time. At least a better time than I was having balancing *en pointe* on top of a toilet in a mortuary.

"Louie," I said. "You've gotta help me."

"Where are you?" he asked, "You sound funny? Like you're in a bathroom or something."

"Listen. I'm in the Ordam Mortuary somewhere off Glendale Boulevard, okay. Somewhere near Highway Two in Atwater. I don't have the exact address, but I was watching the street signs. And you need to call the police, yes, the po-lice, and report that there is a hostage situation going on. Do you understand? A hostage situation. 911 has a hold time, and I can't get caught waiting. Do you get me?"

"Yeah," said Louie, "I get you, but—"

"I'm one of the hostages! Call the police, okay? Put your personal principals aside this once."

I thought I heard footsteps, so I hung up and left the bathroom. I didn't know what to do now except wait for Louie to reach the police and the police to reach me. If there was a ten minute hold time to answer the phone, there was probably a thirty minute show up at a mortuary in Atwater time.

Out in the hallway, there was no one around. I

must've imagined the footsteps. It was just as silent, as . . . well, the grave. I couldn't hear any conversation in the den from the hallway, so I went back into the casket room I'd used as a listening post before, and from there, I could hear voices again. Charles, Joe, and one of the thugs—their voices were low, like they were worn out with all the shouting and accusing and acting; it was all murmuring denials. Nobody sounded like they were happy, although at least Charles wasn't screaming.

I was pressing my ear up against the wall for another good listen when the lid on the red stone, double wide casket shot up, and before I could even scream, an enormously obese guy had his arm around my throat and was pressing down on my carotid.

I struggled. I refused, I absolutely refused to black out. He was so big he couldn't get out of the coffin, but he was so big I couldn't get his arm off my neck either.

But, oh yeah, the pepper spray. I snatched it out of my bag and sprayed it over my shoulder in the guy's face. Of course, some of the spray got me too, stinging my eyes and burning my throat, and I fell back against the wall with a thud. Ricky, for it could only be Ricky miraculously risen from the dead, started shrieking like a little boy in a high-pitched voice from inside the mound of blubber that he was.

I decided that now Joe was entirely off the hook for killing him.

His face was red, and tears were streaming. "You bitch!" he cried. "You absolute, total—do you know who I am?"

Of course I knew, and so did everybody else.

Whatever plan Ricky had in mind for leaping out of a coffin and yelling "Surprise" like he was at a macabre, large size bachelorette party for vampirettes or something was finished now because Joe and Charles and Laura and the thugs, the entire gang, tumbled pell-mell inside the display room.

Chapter
Fifteen

There was bug-eyed and now glaze-eyed Laura and her bug-eyed, purple vein-headed dad. There was fat Ricky, popping out of his coffin, eyes red, face puffy from my pepper spray. There was me, mildly afflicted from the same pepper spray, teary and gasping. Charles way too easily wrested the pepper spray out of my hand.

There was Joe, who was not sure what was wrong with me, straining to go to me, but held back by one of the thugs, both of whom finally had something to do. The blond one held Joe, something pressed up against his side, which I gathered was a gun that I couldn't see from where I was standing. The black one kept Ricky still in his coffin, although I suspect he wouldn't have been able to wiggle out just yet even without a Baretta held against his cheek.

I looked at Joe, and even though I was still wheezing, I mouthed at him, "I understand I think." My heart did anyway. My mind was still sifting through the stack of reasons my heart was feeding it for understanding.

"I love you," he said, nice and clearly, but then, he hadn't ingested any pepper spray.

"He's alive," Laura said gleefully. "Alive, alive, alive," pointing at Ricky. Laura was so thrilled to see him, she was jumping up and down.

"I've been using those pills you swallowed on clients not quite willing to give up the old ghostie for years now. I was careful with the dosage for your weight . . ." Charles mulled over the improbability. "Stupid Nelson. Despite his protestations to the contrary, not only did he feed you those pills before I could properly resolve my fiscal uncertainties, but he also somehow made a hash of the dosage. Still, I was certain you weren't breathing."

A chill passed over me, much as it had earlier when Charles had cavalierly dismissed any implication he was involved in murder. To him, helping the grim reaper was merely one part of his job description.

"But I didn't take no pills. Nelson didn't give me that crap at all," Ricky sneered. "We were friends a lot longer than you knew the dude. We worked out an understanding."

"Funny. So did Nelson and I," Charles said. "And we were *never* friends. Doesn't matter now, of course. He's been, shall we say, effectively cut off from any agreement."

"Yeah, he'd screw anybody." Ricky winked at Laura. Laura blushed like a school girl.

"So, Nelson was actually telling the truth, not bravely sticking to a lie," Charles mused. He shrugged. "All right then. He didn't feed you any pills, yet you managed to play dead. How?" he demanded of his son-in-law.

"Fubu," Ricky said, or at least, that's what it sounded like. "Woulda tasted better if I'd had a little marinara to put on it; a good red sauce makes almost anything more palatial."

"Palatable," Charles corrected. "Fubu?"

"Found a word you don't know, Charlie? It's a fish. A zombie fish or something. Nelson knew this sushi chef who owed him a favor, could create this special dish to put me in a state of suspender animation."

"Suspended," I muttered, but nobody cared.

"Man, oh man, that little Japanese chef sure was busy with the chop-chop. With assuring me that 'it not too much, not too little, mister Rick, sir.' Afterward, at the wake, I heard him laughing about it. I was a lousy tipper, he said. Go back to Tokyo, you don't like it. Whole world was passing by, and I couldn't even move, frickin' zombie fish venom. Kinda itronic, considering how so many people, supposedly friends and family and hell, even my wife, wanted me dead. Nelson and me come up with this plan, and it goes array. Yeah, real itronic it was."

Awry, ironic. I wanted to deck him; I really did.

"There I was all laid out, people comin' to see me, and I couldn't open an eye, twitch a limb. Lucky for me, I been overindulging one way or another all my life. Talk about a near death experience. Zombie crap had the half-life of plutonium, I swear; almost ended up underground in spat of everything."

"In spat?" I said, wiping at my stinging eyes. Having held back on the itronic, in spat was just too much to let slip by unremarked.

"Yeah, I've always been lucky. Not gonna change now," he said in a tone that could be a threat, which belied his present situation with a gun at his face and his lower body stuck in a coffin.

"Oh," Laura bubbled. "Daddy, let him go, let him go!"

"I thought you were after the musician–policeman–actor–thief," Charles said with a sneer at Joe. "I thought you were going to chuck Rick for this career-challenged individual, and that was the reason for my allowing him to continue breathing."

Joe sighed deeply. Laura shook her head vigorously back and forth like a bobblehead doll. "Daddy," she said. "Come on now, Daddy."

Ricky looked around at all of us, a look of cunning in his little pig eyes. Then he blinked once and focused on Charles. "We can still make beautiful business together, Charlie," he said.

Charles ignored him. "You don't seem very surprised to see him," he remarked to Laura.

"Why would I be surprised?" Laura demurred. "Knew he didn't take the pills. Nelson told me he would never betray Ricky, not when he promised more money than you did, Daddy. And Nelson told me how he took Ricky to little Tokyo. I'm the one who took the Vicodin container out of Ricky's car, put one of your pills inside, Daddy, and left it by the hot tub. I'm the one who insisted on a moment alone with the so-called corpse. I'm the one arranged the so-called cremation. Used the hearse and switched coffins. Easy sneazy. You never give me enough credit."

She giggled and drummed her fingers on her arms and shifted her feet around like she was perfecting a new dance step. Then her feet stilled, and she looked dejected. "But then he ran away on us."

She turned such an evil eye glare on Ricky that if I were him, I'd run away again and fast. Assuming, of course, I could wriggle my large behind out of my coffin.

"Just needed a little vacation," Ricky said, his voice taking on the wheedling tone of a small child caught eating a cookie before dinner. "You were getting kinda demanding, Laura, baby. I wasn't really sure if it was gonna be me or Nelson you decided on, or maybe neither of us, maybe just you and the big bucks. I needed a little space to think on you. Remember all our good times."

The wheedle apparently worked on Laura. The black stare went brown and then dewy. "Ricky, I'd never—"

But Ricky cut her off and turned to Joe. "Had you fooled, didn't I, Dennis?" Ricky smirked.

"Not Dennis. Joe," said Laura, obviously miffed that Ricky had lost interest in what she had to say so quickly. "The fake cop."

Joe wasn't that interested in Laura either. He was checking out all the guns in the room, the one on himself, the one on Ricky. He was sending me a steadying glance.

"Hallie," said Charles firmly.

At the mention of his brother's name, Joe's interest level rose, and he turned to Charles and met the old man's mocking eyes.

"You're a real cop, aren't you, Hallie? Taking your brother Joe's name, pretending to be him, then pretending to be an imaginary musician, Ricky and Laura's friend and confidant. If you weren't a cop, I would've killed you two months ago, no matter what little crush my daughter had developed."

My head was spinning. ". . . may not be entirely truthful." Maybe old Geneece was really onto something.

But Joe laughed bitterly. "I set things up very

carefully with LAPD to *look* like I was really Hallie
'cause I was pretty sure somebody over there was
chatting with you. Figured if my lounge singer cover
was blown, you'd at least consult somebody higher
up to see if it was okay to blow away a cop. Guess it
doesn't matter now if you know I don't really carry
a badge."

"Nope. What you are doesn't matter a damn
now," said Charles. He was already waving his bony
finger in his daughter's face.

"As for you, I disown you," Charles said to
Laura, his voice dripping cold fury. "You said you
wanted your husband dead, and you were glad he
was dead, and you've known all along he's alive."

"Perfectly natural a woman should want to kill
her espoused from time to time," Ricky said soothingly. "I realize I wasn't exactly the model man."

Laura pleaded for Charles's understanding. "I
figured *I* could find the missing payoff money . . .
not for me, but for you, Daddy."

Laura could really use a few acting lessons. She
wasn't in the least bit convincing with that finding
the money for daddy line. Charles's scowl deepened, and Laura hastened on.

"So I thought if I was just nice to Ricky—"

"Hey now. You were more than nice. And sometimes, you were nasty, shorty. But in spat of that—"
Ricky said.

He was just too annoying. "It's in spite," I said,
"you idiot."

"Maybe for you," he frowned. "Hot but not
bright." He shook his head at Joe.

Any other time, it would've been worth a laugh.

"Anyways," Ricky went on, "whatever his name is
here, Dennis, Joseph, Hale, or whatever, for him,
it's just the money. For me, it's about—" he had to

think for a minute, really think hard, to come up
with "—family. Values. Stuff like that. So take the
gun off me and put it where it should be put.
Family fooballs can be forgiven. Not incidence of
money. Betrothals of friendship."

Foibles, incidents, betrayals, I thought, caption-
ing as he sputtered.

"I never liked you," Joe said. "So there was no
friendship to betray. Naturally it's about money.
Just as it is for you."

"You're a dirty cop," Laura said, smiling. "A
very, very dirty cop. If you are one, that is."

"I have friends. I have influence. I know more
than you know I know," Charles said in a singsong
voice. He was laughing in Joe's face. Laura's craziness was obviously her birthright.

"You're not as mobbed up as you might think,"
Joe said. "That *I* know."

"Who needs the mob? When, as you surmised,
I've got police protection. The long arm of the law
stretches outside LA and deep into the heart of
Texas."

"You don't have as many friends in blue as you
believe," Joe said stolidly.

"I have enough. After all, I didn't find out about
you using psychic powers."

He threw me that nice, soft one, and I took it
and hit it right out of the park.

"Oh-h-h . . ." I made a great moan, and my hands
rushed to my head. "I see death everywhere!"

Everybody looked at me, which was what I
wanted.

"What?" Laura said. "Who cares, you fake."

Nobody did, really, but this was my way of telling
Joe, or whatever his name was, that I loved him
too, my way of buying him what I hoped he needed

right now, more than he needed that fourteen million dollars, more than he needed the names of every corrupt cop who helped Charles. What he needed now was just a single moment.

And he used it. Joe grabbed at the gun the blond thug had lodged in his side and twisted it, firing down into the guy's knee before anybody knew what was happening.

As Blondie fell with a bang and a groan, I fell too—self-preservation. Injured arm forgotten, I rolled myself right under the velvet covering of a casket display table, just as the other thug, the one with the weapon on Ricky, turned it to Joe.

I lay there with the dust bunnies, watching as Joe ducked wildly, an unnecessary action because Ricky shoved his body, at least the upper part of it that was mobile, against that second thug, and that thug's bullet missed Joe by a wide arc.

Then Ricky pulled the same move he'd made on me, a Jabba the Hut-like lunge, drawing the thug against him, his arm around the guy's throat, the gun loosening in the guy's fingers until it fell right into Ricky's puffy palm.

Laura crouched down in a corner and started rocking herself.

Joe was firing again, and he hit Ricky's thug and Ricky himself, both in the arm—Ricky low in the forearm, the thug at the shoulder. And he managed to blow a hole in the lid of the big red coffin.

The thug just stepped back politely, doing his little robot walk, clutching at his shoulder, and then sliding to the floor; Ricky yowled, but since his gun hand was unscathed, he kept his grip tight on the .38 he'd snagged. Plus, I was beginning to gather he was feeling no pain, probably due to the months later aftereffects of fubu.

Then Charles slipped his hand in his jacket and came back out again with a gun of his own in his hand, and everything stopped because he had the drop.

"Someone's about to get seriously hurt," he shouted. "Drop it, Tex," he said to Joe, rechristening him yet again.

And Joe did.

"Rick," Charles commanded.

But Ricky had managed at long last to extricate himself from the coffin. He groaned as he climbed out, still holding the gun. He turned it calmly on the thug who'd been holding him and fired through the chest at point blank range.

He ignored the messy splattering and groaning, focusing only on Charles.

"Don't you punch me in the face ever again," he said to Charles with his whiny, little boy petulance, so out of place in such a big man. "You punched me when I was totally in zombie land there in the hot tub, and I won't forget that."

"Don't you tell me what to do," Charles said. "You're a dead man already, a dead man again if I want. Besides, I only hit you to make sure you were a goner. Guess I should've hit you harder. Now toss the gun."

Still Ricky did not toss the gun, even as blood oozed down the fingers of his free hand in a copious stream. Laura was looking from Charles to Ricky and back again, her eyes darting and popping, and she was breathing as hard as if *she'd* just engaged in a gun battle. At least she'd stopped rocking herself.

Joe just stood there, kind of midway between Ricky and Charles, both of them holding guns, looking like he sure wished he was still holding his.

Of course, his was lying on the floor not that far from the table I was hiding under.

In fact, the first thug, the guy Joe had shot cleanly through the knee, was reaching for it.

"I'm not giving the money back," said Ricky. "The guys expecting it as payment for services rendered, well, they ain't rendered nearly as much as me. It's mine. You'll never find it. All you people in this room been trying to find it. I'm not as dumb as you think I am. I have ideas. I have plans. I have dreams."

Laura clapped her hand over her mouth and then lifted it off again like she could no longer keep the words from spilling out.

"Ricky, when you called me up from Peru—"

Ricky shook his head irritably. "Potato land. That's all you get for food down there, seventeen varieties of potatoes. Got that damn Macho Pico mixed up with Puerto Rico. Easy mistake, anyone coulda made it."

"When you called me," Laura went on in the firm tone of a wife used to her husband's little quirks, "I agreed to forgive you. I let you into this mortuary. To effect a solution, not to start another fight. We can't go on like this. When Daddy dies, I inherit everything anyway. There'll be another fourteen million; maybe there'll even be more."

She cast a hopeful glance at Charles, but he didn't offer any encouragement.

She sucked it up and went on. "So give the money up for now, huh, for me, Ricky? Daddy'll let it all be a bygone, no questions asked. I'm sure he will. We just have to get rid of these two fakers, and we can all go back to the way we were."

Yes, misty water-colored memories. I could almost see Robert Redford and Barbara Streisand all soft and dewy through a Vaseline-smeared camera lens.

Ricky and Charles both looked at each other. Maybe they were sizing each other up; maybe they were considering Laura's idea. Maybe Ricky was wondering what Puerto Rico was like. You could see the wheels turning, but you couldn't tell the direction they were ever so slowly spinning.

Meanwhile, the knee-wounded thug was sliding along the floor toward me even as I inched out from under the table. I inched and I inched until my hand was on Joe's gun and the thug was clawing at me, but I sent the gun flying over to Joe. He dove for it, a neat catch even as Laura screamed.

"Shoot her!"

Charles was aiming for me all right, and the thug on the floor had me pinned, so I couldn't roll back under cover.

I confess I was chicken; I didn't want to see it coming. I closed my eyes. But Joe fired first and fast. When I opened my eyes again, Charles was hit; in fact, he was down and writhing, clutching at his thigh. It didn't matter so much now that the thug on the ground had me by the legs and was pulling me hard enough to rip them out of my hips, or at least, that's what it felt like.

Joe fired at the guy on the floor, getting his other leg, and he loosened his grip on me, and I was free. I rolled up in a little ball again and spun myself backward, another of my Wonder Woman Reunion moves.

I was upside down, and I felt dizzy from the roll and the pain in my arm, but I also felt exhilarated. I was alive. Joe was alive, and he was an excellent shot. All that boyhood target practice had paid off.

Next, Ricky fired, but he wasn't firing at me or

at Joe. He was aiming for Charles; first, he hit the floor, and then he hit the ceiling, and then he got the old man. He got him good, or bad, depending on your point of view.

"Daddy!" Laura wailed and rushed forward.

"Get away from me, you bitch," Charles gasped.

Clearly, there was to be no deathbed father and daughter reconciliation.

Crouched behind the cheap plywood-like coffin, Joe ordered Ricky to "Just drop it," but Ricky didn't. Instead, he made a little speech.

"You're not gonna kill me. Not 'til you find out what I did with that money. Not 'til I give you the names. And you know something, just to see who you really are, I'll give you one and not the other. Your choice. The names or the money. Which one you really want, buddy?"

"Drop it," Joe barked again.

"Or I could just shoot you, see if I get you before you get me. Or shoot your woman. Why don't I start with your woman? I shoot her, you shoot me, oh, well. You'll still be out the broad."

I was crumpled up in the corner I'd rolled into. Before I could get on my feet or do much of anything to keep Ricky's words from coming to pass, Laura was screaming.

"Daddy's gone! He's gone. It's all your fault," and she wasn't shouting at Ricky, she was shouting at me. Then she was on top of me, wrapping her arm against my throat in a tepid imitation of the grip practiced earlier by Ricky. I guess she was trying to beat her ex-husband to the punch, so to speak.

If we all died here in the mortuary, the good news was nobody would have to go far to make burial arrangements.

I struggled with Laura, well aware that if I wrestled her to the ground, I'd just make myself a cleaner target for Ricky.

"Get out of the way," Ricky shouted at Laura, and Joe just blasted him, just took him down, like the money or the names, nothing was important to him now. Except me.

Wow, that was quite an exhilarating realization. On the strength of it, I broke Laura's grip and her nose at the same time. She started rocking herself and weeping again, and I was about to stand up and throw my arms around Joe, but Charles's driver, the third thug, burst into the room way late into the scene we'd played out. He was firing an automatic like the movie he was in was *Scarface*.

"Christy!" Joe shouted.

Pieces of pretty coffins were flying everywhere, satin and brass and wood and velvet. Laura and I were pressed together now in a kind of mad embrace, using each other for cover.

Joe was down low on the floor again and out of bullets.

We were out of tricks.

But suddenly, thug number three went down, tackled by none other than Lt. Handley coming in from behind with a bunch of guys in SWAT uniforms; and the last pieces of the exploding mosaic coffin exploded; and then Joe was backhanding Laura off me, sending her flopping down on the floor next to Ricky.

She started screeching nasty obscenities about how bad Joe was in bed. I knew for certain that she might've wanted to but that she had never slept with him.

Then the paramedics were there and cops not

wearing SWAT gear, and now Handley was brushing me off.

"You okay?" he asked.

"You came faster than I figured," I said to Handley, whose thick face took on a puzzled, even mystified expression, maybe because at the very same moment Joe said "It sure took you long enough."

Chapter Sixteen

"So I didn't even have to pick up a phone?" Louie still sounded a little cranky. "Much less drive all the way down to the police station, and demand to speak to someone in charge, stomp my feet until anyone paid attention to me, and then have cops all over me asking who I was and what I wanted until I end up in a holding cell for disturbing the peace!"

"But," Tad remarked, crunching on mee-krob catered by the hippest Thai restaurant on Highland, "*this* is the true story the v.p. of production was looking for."

Louie's new beau, the executive assistant to the big deal production executive, was looking remarkably sanguine, and his calm seemed to calm Louie down too.

"This is your ticket in, Lou, whereas the weasels, the Christmas tree, and that bald-headed female producer were not quite making it, after all." Tad patted Louie's knee, and Louie nodded, mollified.

We were at the Christmas party to end all Christmas parties, lush with rich food and expensive liquor, and Louie and I were not even contemplating taking the champagne. It felt odd to be at the perfect scene for pulling one of our perfect little crimes, and not pull one. It made me itchy. To settle down, I studied Tad and Louie and what a nice couple they made.

Tad was wearing a stylishly baggy cream-colored three-piece suit with a watch fob on it. His hair, just like the werewolf in the Warren Zevon song, was absolutely perfect. Tad, faintly Asian and slender, had a calm and gentle smile that rather belied his intense agate eyes. Louie was wearing a tailored cowboy shirt with silver braids on the shoulders and his best black leather pants. He'd streaked his hair with seasonal red and white, but just in little artistic stripes on the top so he didn't look too much like a candy cane.

"So you made one phone call this close to Christmas, and the deal to turn our mortuary adventures into a movie is signed?" I asked Tad.

"Don't forget; it's also going to be about my brave efforts to save you," Louie threw in.

"Yes, deal's done. I have the veep's beach house phone," Tad said.

It really wasn't what you knew; it was who you knew and having their phone number.

Tad was very pleased with himself. "Signed, sealed, delivered, and I believe Lou is going to make someone a lot of money. It might as well be me, hence my new position as Lou's manager."

I didn't like that he called Louie Lou, but hey, it was Hollywood, land of men with a thousand names.

Kind of like Joe, who slipped up next to me carrying a plate of glass noodles sprinkled with mint and lime and chilis and put his arm around my shoulders. He stood out in the room, not just because he was good looking, which he sure was, but also because he wasn't wearing an outfit; he just had on clean black jeans and a white shirt, and an admittedly expensive—because I had bought it for him just that afternoon in a last minute holiday shopping spree—modern art-splotched silk tie.

I'd bought Louie his glittery cowboy shirt, a beautiful fruit basket for Joe's parents, and overly large stuffed toys for Joe's niece and nephew that Joe had sarcastically said should be loads of fun to get through security on our last minute Christmas day flight to Houston.

But I was feeling splashy and generous, and I was still high on that glad to be alive feeling that had come over me in the mortuary. Joe was obviously feeling the same way, even as I ran through the last of his money, or at least the money he'd taken from Ricky's Hummer.

I was still dead broke, which a case or two of quietly nabbed champagne from this very party would rectify, except that I wasn't sure Joe would approve. He wasn't a cop, but he was still a pretty righteous dude, all told. And in fact, I wasn't sure I even approved of my petty crimes anymore. Life was too short, or could be, based on the previous evening's gunplay, to spend too much more time on such escapades.

Time was apparently on Joe's mind too. "When can we leave?" he asked, seemingly unimpressed by the thin girls with big, perfect artificial breasts in slithery dresses and the multiethnic buffet feast of Thai and Chinese and Indian, all from the very coolest restaurants and served by guys in satin turbans and women in chain mael sarongs.

"Soon," I whispered.

We had, after all, hit this party not just for sustenance but also to share in Louie's celebration at finally becoming a part of the legitimate Hollywood community, if there is, in fact, such a thing as legitimacy in Hollywood.

Louie was, after all, my best friend, and he had tried, as it turned out unnecessarily, to summon the police and save our lives.

Now that we'd been here a few hours noshing and celebrating, Joe and I were ready to decamp, but Tad, having just recently arrived with the deal memo, was smiling at Joe and pumping his hand.

"When Lou was telling me about you and Christy here, I have to admit I thought about J-Lo's situ in *Maid in Manhattan,* although in your case it would be *Man in Manhattan*—" he pulled a tiny spiral notebook covered in fake fur from the breast-pocket of his unstructured blazer and scribbled something on it.

"A germ of an idea," he resumed. "Anyway, fake identities, manufactured lives, all part of the Hollywood scene."

"Yes, one should get used to it," I said companionably, throwing a dagger look at Louie as he bent over a platter of Pad Thai.

Louie met my look and returned to his recent grievance. "All that trouble I went through. Even though it will make a wonderful addition to this true story, throwing in cops at Christmas time in Tinsel Town. Was it worth the humiliation? The running of prints? The denial of false charges against someone with a similar name in the wine merchant business?"

"Didn't need to deny a thing," Joe said. "Handley took care of it."

"That Handley moves in fast. While I was still in

the hospital, he had you wired," I said. I was more amazed than angry about it, now that I knew the facts.

"Yeah, and he's none too pleased about me trashing his precious equipment along with my baseball hat. But if old Charles frisked me and found it, there would've been trouble."

"There was trouble."

"More trouble."

Handley was mad about the wire; he was also mad that Joe went after Laura on his own.

"You were supposed to wait for my go. For backup. For us to follow!" he'd sputtered.

"Don't you get it? After she almost ran Christy down in that parking lot, I knew positively she was the one who took my brother out. I couldn't wait, knowing that," Joe had insisted.

Handley berated Joe only a little while longer, and then he recovered from his pique pretty fast. He knew a career opportunity when it was handed to him.

As Joe explained to Louie, "When I ran into Handley at Christy's place—"

"Which, of course, you denied doing," I noted. Joe gave a rueful shrug and went on.

"I convinced Handley there was a link inside law enforcement to Ricky and his father-in-law. Hallie had been certain their body business could not operate without the complicity of the police," Joe said. "It's why he asked me to look into Ricky in the first place. Handley gave me forty-eight hours to come up with something concrete, and we came in—pun intended—under the wire on that one."

"Couldn't you have given me the faintest idea we were under surveillance? I'm a good actress. I could've pulled it off and still known," I said.

"I know you're good. It's not a question of good. To get Handley's help, I had to make a few promises, and one of them was that I keep our arrangement private. He thought you'd run at the very idea of him following our every move."

I wouldn't have run. Not anywhere except Joe's arms. But then how could Handley have known that, or even Joe, for sure? I wasn't sure myself at the time.

I sighed. "You've been just about the end of me, Mr. Richter."

"I'm hoping I'm the beginning now," he said.

"You swear to me that there are no more last ditch shoot 'em ups planned? No more hidden microphones or cameras, for that matter?" I'd already asked more or less the same thing twelve times at least. Still, Joe's answer was reassuring.

"I swear. Although we could make a video later, if you like," Joe suggested with a lascivious gleam in his eye. He ran his fingers down my back and just under the spaghetti straps of the little emerald green velvet number he'd bought me as a Christmas present.

He whispered in my ear. "Can we leave *now?*"

"We can get a little air," I whispered back, "and then have dessert and then slip away."

"This is more complicated than leaving the police interrogation room," Joe said.

Outside, the house was strung with thousands of sparkling little white Christmas lights, and there were palm tree-sized silver candy canes along the sidewalk. A snow machine hummed in a courtyard, spewing what looked like a ski slope. It would've been perfect for tobogganing, but there were no little kids around to take advantage. Perhaps later there would be drunken snowball fights.

Yes, it was absolutely exactly the kind of party where Louie would've worked the bar and I would've worked the booze away from the bar, and used my ill-gotten gains to scrape by for another month or two. And all the time act like I was happy enough.

But tonight, I didn't have to act anymore. I really was happy enough. More than enough, maybe. Louie was evidently going to make it in Hollywood at last with Tad to help him, and I was going to make it with Joe somewhere, anywhere, but probably not here.

We were going to make love, make a couple, make a future. We were ready now. Both of us, for different reasons, had put off tomorrow for too many days.

At the edge of the lawn, we stood and admired the electric patchwork quilt of the valley. It looked like the whole world lay glittering at our feet.

If agents and managers and stars and money men and even fat slobs like Ricky spent their time at places like this, no wonder they thought no rules applied to them; you could see how they'd all buy into the illusion that they ruled the world, or Hollywood anyway.

"Can you really give all this up?" Joe asked me.

"Can you?"

"Absolutely. I've got what I want."

Joe was kissing me and holding me and telling me how beautiful I was. That wasn't an illusion; that was very real.

My green velvet was crumpling in his hands, and he pulled a silver clip from my hair and let my curls tumble down around my neck, where he ran his hands through it.

He nibbled on my ear, and I nibbled on his, and

I undid his tie, his expensive silk tie. I started un-buttoning his shirt, kissing his chest.

He slipped a strap off one of my shoulders and then the other, careful still of the bandage on my arm, which was masked under a soft silk shawl.

He was breathing hard, trying to work the velvet down off my shoulders, and I wanted him to. I wanted him to just slip that dress straight off my body and lay me down right there on the grass and take me.

"I don't know why we got all dressed up like this. I just want us to take our clothes off," I noted, my voice a raw, trembling whisper.

"We're not staying for dessert," he said as he pulled me off into the night.

I was letting Joe undress me slowly, tossing off my rhinestone-buckled, wicked-heeled shoes first, then peeling down my black lace stockings.

"You're the most beautiful woman . . ." Joe mur-mured. "And the most understanding . . . I'm sorry things didn't go down more smoothly. But nothing ever goes down smoothly, does it?"

Well, the stockings were coming off pretty neatly.

"I guess not," I said. "For example, we're not rich."

"Maybe there is no fourteen million. Maybe there was once that much money, and Ricky spent it on drugs or parties, and he just said he had it to keep Laura or Nelson around or to keep Charles from killing him. For all I know, he ate it for break-fast or something," Joe said, and he just didn't sound like he cared that much, even if he had, with my help, more or less run through the fifteen grand he'd found in Ricky's glove compartment.

"We'll get by. I cleared my family's name. I put an end to the bad guys. I did that much for my brother and his children at least. And I found you. That's prize enough. You're worth more any day . . . any night . . ."

The kind of body business we were into now, Joe and me, that was really pretty good.

And he had that dress off at last, and the slippery little lace underthings, and then he had me down on the bed; it wasn't Jack Frost nibbling at my toes, even though that's what Nat King Cole was singing on the radio. It was Joe nibbling at my neck, and my shoulders and breasts and arms and fingers, and all the way down to my decidedly unfrosty toes. It was all kisses, all kisses everywhere you can think to kiss until I was damp and squirmy and glowing with kisses.

After we'd progressed from kissing to other forms of intermingling our bodies, still moist and delicious and weak in the knees, we kicked my dress off the bed, and I snuggled down in Joe's arms. Mrs. Marinak's poodle was barking softly, when Joe, who was satiated and yet still wanting, said, "All they had at that fancy party were ninety different ethnic varieties of noodles. I've been wanting a hamburger since we got stuck with biscotti in Pasadena."

"You just had *me*, and you're thinking about hamburger?"

"Only slightly less politically correct than a post-coital cigarette," Joe admitted.

And all of a sudden something struck me, almost like—wow, a psychic flash. I sat up in bed.

"Come on. It's not that un-p.c.," Joe said.

"You want a hamburger. Ricky always wanted pasta with marinara sauce. His favorite dish."

"Yeah," Joe said. "Right. He's a perfect example of why low carb diets are so popular. But I kinda thought we were done talking about Ricky."

"You said maybe he ate the money. Well, maybe he *didn't* eat it," and I was up and out of bed and throwing on a pair of jeans without bothering to explain why.

'Twas the night before the night before Christmas, and nothing was stirring all through Ricky's house except us.

Driving up the coast, through sobriety checkpoints, past cliffside houses winking with holiday lights, the ocean was black velvet, the moon spreading silver tinsel across the water.

Ricky's blank, dark windows reflected shards of moonlight like shattered stars. We crept inside, keeping the lights off, mindful of the neighbors.

I went straight to the kitchen. Yawning, humoring me, Joe held a flashlight, and I ripped into bags of ramen noodles, mostaccioli, and penne. I tore open bag after bag, but there was nothing in them but noodles.

Deeply disappointed, I sank down on a dining room chair much as I had a week before, except this time, I wasn't burning any sage.

"Come on," Joe said. "It was an idea. It didn't pan out. Let's go."

But instead, I went back into the kitchen and lifted one of the heavy vats of marinara sauce from the cabinet. I had to use two hands, it was that big.

I tried to twist the lid, but I couldn't budge it. It had a plastic seal around it, but most plastic seals at least crack when you turn the lid. This one sure was resilient. Of course, maybe it was just my injured arm, weakening my grip.

"Christy, come on," Joe said.

"Get the lid off," I commanded and thrust the jar at him.

Reluctantly, Joe set down the flashlight he was holding and twisted at the lid. It was a struggle, and Joe wasn't getting the upper hand. So it wasn't just me.

"Feels like it's superglued," Joe groaned.

"Maybe it is," I said.

Joe got the idea now, and quiet and neighbors be damned, he threw the jar into the sink hard. The glass shattered, the jar smashed, and thick red sauce poured out.

In the dim light, it looked like blood. I took a step back. "Maybe you're right," I said. "Stupid idea, let's go home—"

But Joe turned to me, laughing because in his marinara-dripping hand was a plastic baggie, inside another plastic baggie, inside another, wrapped up tightly with a rubber band. And inside that baggie was a roll of hundred dollar bills.

I took the roll while Joe washed up, and I counted two hundred hundreds, which meant twenty thousand, which meant in the hundred jars in the cabinets over the stove and beside the stove and under the sink, there might very well be two million dollars. And in the twelve wooden cases in the garage, each, if I remembered correctly, holding fifty mega jars of Prima marinara sauce, there was probably another twelve million.

Joe and I just looked at each other. "Let's get sauced," I suggested.

I thought it was a pretty good line, but Joe didn't laugh. This was serious business now.

Carefully, Joe rinsed off his hands, fished the broken glass out of the sink, and tossed it in the trash. I tucked the twenty thousand in my purse. Joe took the trash bag with the broken glass, the evidence of our discovery, and put it in the back seat of his car. He also took a whole box of empty garbage bags out of a cabinet, and put that in his car, too.

Then we went to the garage, and we backed Joe's car right up to the door before we opened it. It wasn't any different than hoisting those cases of champagne from studio premiere parties, but instead of champagne, we were carting four cases of marinara sauce.

The cases were heavy enough that the tailpipe of Joe's brother's beloved Mustang was almost scraping the ground when we drove out of Malibu Colony and down Pacific Coast Highway.

"Should've taken two cars, I guess," Joe said. "I'm afraid if we make a second trip, somebody's going to notice."

"Four million will be just fine," I said. "Assuming the count is the same in every jar."

Safely inside my place, we took out the box of plastic garbage bags and tripled each bag to make sure they were strong enough to hold all the glass we were about to break. We lined my bathtub with blankets to muffle the noise and more plastic bags to clean up the mess we knew we'd make, and then, using a jack handle from Joe's trunk, we set about smashing all two hundred jars.

It was sort of like opening Christmas presents, messy Christmas presents.

We filled eight triple-layered plastic garbage bags full of glass and goo. Joe got pretty good at breaking the jars—it was kind of like cracking very large, very hard eggs.

The sun was coming up when we finished. We looked like we'd walked into an exploding pizzeria or out of a lousy horror movie. There was sauce in our hair and on our arms and legs and clothes.

"Filthy lucre," I said.

"Very," Joe agreed.

I was glad I had on an old pair of jeans and a baggy tee shirt. We just peeled off our clothes and threw them and the blankets lining the tub in another garbage bag.

We took turns wearing my pair of pink daisy flowered rubber flip-flops in the shower in case there were any shards of glass that we'd missed cleaning up. Joe's feet looked enormous hanging over the backs, and I laughed at him. He laughed too, and then we couldn't stop laughing.

He threw on another pair of jeans and a tee shirt and switched from the flip-flops to his boots, and he carried the plastic bags, rattling and clinking like a demented Santa, back to his car.

He drove the bags to a dumpster two streets away and dumped them.

I counted the cash. Four million, twenty thousand.

"We've only got an hour to get to the airport," Joe said, making coffee. "We'll call Handley from the plane, tell him you had a real psychic perception."

"Will he mind that it's only ten million, eight hundred eighty thousand at Ricky's place?"

"I don't think he'll count too closely. Evidence is evidence."

"Three million to your brother's kids, one million twenty thousand for us to get a place somewhere, not here?" I suggested.

Joe gave me a big smile. "Most people come west to make a new start."

"Maybe we went too far west. We'll just head back east a little bit." I gulped my coffee and scalded my mouth.

"Gulf Coast, I'm thinking," Joe said. "I know a pretty little ranch down there."

"Sounds good to me," I replied, kissing his cheek, "One question though. Now that we've gotten the money out of the sauce, how do we get the money on the plane? Won't it show up on the security monitors and look kind of funny?"

Joe thought for a moment. "We're driving," he said. "Which means we can put those stuffed monstrosities you bought for the kids in the back seat. And if we want to make Christmas dinner, we'd better get going too."

Slurping chocolate date shakes, we called Handley from a phone booth on Interstate 10 just outside Indio Date World. Joe innocently told him to let us know if I had guessed correctly about the money's whereabouts.

"I'm sure you're doing more than guessing," Handley said. "But I'm inclined, as you probably *have* guessed, to look slightly the other way this time. Only this time. Merry Christmas."

Epilogue

"Sorry been so busy. Script development means you develop a chronic headache while you rewrite a million times until you're so sick of yourself and what you said that it doesn't matter how they change it anymore. If you're still thinking of opening a dinner theater in some small town, I'll write the plays. If you're set on using tried and true Neil Simon, I'll just do hair and makeup. You let me know. Have to talk it over with Tad though, who sends hugs, but I send kisses. Miss you. Call you before you get this, I'm sure, but thought you'd like to read the attached."

Louie's scrawled note was paper-clipped to an article about none other than Ricky Littlejohn that he had ripped out of a current issue of the *LA Free Press*.

It was a follow-up to their now months-old exposé on Ricky's death, and it simply reeked of outraged attitude on the part of the reporter, who felt personally insulted by Ricky's feigned demise.

I had to agree with the writer's basic outrage. How dare a guy like Ricky still be alive?

According to the article, alive but not well.

Ricky claimed to be in failing health, weak and forgotten, unjustly lost in the penal system.

He shouldn't even be in prison; he was set up, he
insisted, to take the fall for a scam that was entirely
planned by his former father-in-law, now deceased,
and his ex-wife, who was now facing extradition to
Texas in a hit and run murder case, having failed
to avoid the said extradition despite being institu-
tionalized for acute manic-depression.

A full year after that hit and run, a new investigation was launched, and a witness was found who'd
observed a woman matching Laura's description
driving fast just past the accident scene. A traffic
camera at an intersection nearby showed Laura
herself on tape and that something was wrong with
the front end of the car she was driving. Then, of
course, there was the fact that in the meantime,
Laura had been involved in an attempted homicide while driving the same exact vehicle in a Los
Angeles parking lot.

And to put the final nail in Laura's coffin, a very
appropriate metaphor for her situation, Ricky ratted on Laura for the Texas hit and run first thing,
hoping to get out of jail time as a return favor.
When that didn't work, hardly stopping for breath,
he blurted the names of police and hospital employees who moonlighted on his father-in-law's pay-
roll in LA, Houston, Phoenix, and San Francisco,
assisting in the extremely well-paying disposal of
the vessels of our souls.

Naturally, he hadn't counted on them returning
the favor and fingering him, but they had, certainly encouraged by the fact that none of them
had received the financial payments they'd expected for their efforts.

I read on. "Once a model featured in bathing

suit spreads and razor commercials, strutting the runways and fashion pages of international magazines, his lean, Adonis-like body adorning billboards throughout the Southland, to this reporter, Richard J. Littlejohn now resembles a whale—grotesquely obese, beached in a jail cell for tax fraud, attempted murder, conspiracy to commit murder, and his involvement in a cadaver selling business that violated a number of interstate transportation regulations."

"With bodies and body parts selling for ten to twenty thousand, the dead are a highly profitable product. However, Mr. Littlejohn states that he personally received very little return from his business venture."

" 'Everybody robbed me, and I can't even complain about it,' Mr. Littlejohn said, speaking from his cell on Terminal Island. 'I can't complain 'cause my lawyer says it'll just make things worse, and as it is, if I just keep my mouth shut, I'll be out in under seven, more than likely. I've done time before, and I handled it real fine. I'll handle it again, but I'm not getting any younger.' "

"Nor any thinner. Blaming his weight on the prison diet, Mr. Littlejohn admits to being a 'few pounds' overweight, although a hundred would be closer to the mark."

"Apparently, Mr. Littlejohn is prone to lying about more than his weight. The supersized former supermodel has made a number of outrageous claims, including one against the city of Los Angeles for stealing fourteen million dollars from his Malibu home."

" 'It was fourteen mil, I'm telling you, not the ten and change everybody's saying. And they don't even admit to stealing it. They say it belongs to the city, to the state, for what I didn't pay in taxes. And fines and stuff. And reimbursements to my alleged victims. Dead people are victims now. You believe it? Most unbelievable entirely. They can arrest you for something they say is illegal and then tax you on the illegalities? Now that should be illegal.' "

"While positively vitriolic on the subject of his accused wrongdoing, Mr. Littlejohn waxes sentimental on his fashion industry past."

" 'In spat of everything,' he says, using a favorite colloquialism, 'I look back on those years when I was young, and I was hot, and I was hip, and I was happening, man; the stuff that went on, and the high life I had. New York, Paris, the French Riviera. I always knew exactly how to comb my hair. Didn't need a stylist to tell me a thing. I knew. I was a walking miracle with a jar of hair gel and a comb. Now I know, I know I got lucky with my good life. I had it made, I really had it made for a long time. Now, well. Hey, at least I ain't dead. Don't write me off yet.' "

"Despite his current situation, Mr. Littlejohn reveals a stunning optimism about his future, even as he faces additional charges in other states. He claims confidently that he could still come out 'stinking like a rose. Publicity. There's never a bad thing about publicity. Like what you're giving me here, just writing about me. Could be a positive turn around. There's nothing that says for certain there's not happy never after.' "

"But Mr. Littlejohn is a long way from his days on the French Riviera. He stares out the visiting room window as if he's hoping he'll see bikini-clad women and sparkling white sand or perhaps, an apparition of his former self, sleek in his glory days."

"Instead, Mr. Littlejohn has a view of the San

Pedro shipping channel, its oily water slinking past container ships and cargo bins; chemical drums; and the barbed wire of the Terminal Island prison in which Mr. Littlejohn now dwells. The air is fetid and fishy, just like Mr. Littlejohn's story—"

I threw the paper aside. I already knew as much as I ever wanted to know about Ricky Littlejohn's story, and besides, I found the tone of the article just a bit too condescending and self-righteous.

Sure, Ricky had tried to kill me, and he was the front man for a lot of bad stuff going down, including the death of Joe's brother. I wasn't feeling sorry for him; he was a despicable, corpulent lump with the morals of a sewer rat, which is an insult to sewer rats everywhere. It was nothing like sympathy that I felt. It was the fact that when you come right down to it, isn't everybody's story just a little bit fishy?

I'd be the first to admit that mine was.

Just then, Joe came home from the ride he took late every afternoon around the perimeter of our little ranch. He got us a couple of cold beers out of the fridge and gave me a kiss. His kisses were still long and lingering, and they made me feel like we should be doing a lot more than kissing.

We sat across the kitchen table from each other, holding hands for a while. Yeah, we still like holding hands quite a lot, and we're still communicating pretty well without having to explain ourselves all the time too.

We know things intuitively, like Joe'll probably just scramble up some eggs for dinner, neither one of us wants a big wedding, and the newspaper article lying between us is about somebody we don't need to care about anymore. We're done looking into the dark places and the empty places and trying to fool ourselves into ignoring our own dark and empty spots.

And maybe we're not perfect—we've been cynical and self-involved, and certainly not completely honest—but we're pretty perfect together.

If I were to look into a crystal ball right now, I think I'd actually see the future—I'd see the reflection of both our faces.

As twilight fell, soft and purple as a bruised plum, Joe led me outside. He helped me climb up on the hood of his brother's car, now parked in our backyard between the horse barn and the open range in the middle of nowhere, which is right where I want to be.

Birds sang a night song, and inside the house, through the screen door, I could hear the pages of that newspaper flipping idly forward, scattering across the kitchen table in the summer breeze.

We watch the stars come out just about every night, kissing until the moon rises in the diamond-studded black of the soft, sultry Gulf Coast sky. It's like being at a three hundred and sixty degree giant IMAX screen drive-in, only better, because what I'm seeing, hearing, and feeling is no larger-than-life, projected illusion. It's real.

By Best-selling Author
Fern Michaels

Weekend Warriors	0-8217-7589-8	$6.99US/$9.99CAN
Listen to Your Heart	0-8217-7463-8	$6.99US/$9.99CAN
The Future Scrolls	0-8217-7586-3	$6.99US/$9.99CAN
About Face	0-8217-7020-9	$7.99US/$10.99CAN
Kentucky Sunrise	0-8217-7462-X	$7.99US/$10.99CAN
Kentucky Rich	0-8217-7234-1	$7.99US/$10.99CAN
Kentucky Heat	0-8217-7368-2	$7.99US/$10.99CAN
Plain Jane	0-8217-6927-8	$7.99US/$10.99CAN
Wish List	0-8217-7363-1	$7.50US/$10.50CAN
Yesterday	0-8217-6785-2	$7.50US/$10.50CAN
The Guest List	0-8217-6657-0	$7.50US/$10.50CAN
Finders Keepers	0-8217-7364-X	$7.50US/$10.50CAN
Annie's Rainbow	0-8217-7366-6	$7.50US/$10.50CAN
Dear Emily	0-8217-7316-X	$7.50US/$10.50CAN
Sara's Song	0-8217-7480-8	$7.50US/$10.50CAN
Celebration	0-8217-7434-4	$7.50US/$10.50CAN
Vegas Heat	0-8217-7207-4	$7.50US/$10.50CAN
Vegas Rich	0-8217-7206-6	$7.50US/$10.50CAN
Vegas Sunrise	0-8217-7208-2	$7.50US/$10.50CAN
What You Wish For	0-8217-6828-X	$7.99US/$10.99CAN
Charming Lily	0-8217-7019-5	$7.99US/$10.99CAN

Available Wherever Books Are Sold!